A SPIFFING MURDER

KEITH FINNEY

BOOKS

By Keith Finney

Rex and the Dowager
A Posh Murder
A Spiffing Murder
A Dapper Murder

Norfolk Cozy Mysteries
Dead Man's Trench
Murder by Hanging
The Boathouse Killer
Miller's End
Dead Again
A Yuletide Mystery
Double Cross
The Lavender Killer
Murder RSVP

For Joan

Vinci Books

vinci-books.com

Published by Vinci Books Ltd in 2026

1

Copyright © Keith Finney 2024

The author has asserted their moral right to be identified as the author of this work in accordance with the Copyright, Designs and Patents Act 1988. This work is a work of fiction. Names, characters, places and incidents are the product of the author's imagination or are used fictitiously. Any resemblance to actual persons, living or dead, places and incidents is entirely coincidental.

All rights reserved. No part of this publication may be copied, reproduced, distributed, stored in any retrieval system, or transmitted in any form or by any means, including photocopying, recording, or other electronic or mechanical methods, nor used as a source for any form of machine learning including AI datasets, without the prior written permission of the publisher.

The publisher and the author have made every effort to obtain permissions for any third party material used in this book and to comply with copyright law. Any queries in this respect should be brought to the attention of the publisher and any omissions will be corrected in future editions.

A CIP catalogue record for this book is available from the British Library.

Paperback ISBN: 9781036707866

Chapter One

A ROUGH RIDE

'REVEAL YOURSELF,' demanded my generous benefactor, the Dowager Duchess of Drakeford, following a boisterous "psst...psst" that reverberated through the serene twilight. Our location? - Sir Herbert Cummings' grand reception to celebrate the completion of his newest home, "Hilltop".

As the "psst" faded away into the ether, a suspicious cough exploded from the same direction, instantly grabbing my attention. As I made a sudden turn to the right, I glimpsed a gentleman in his fifties, sporting a chic fedora hat and a well-groomed moustache, coyly peering out from the side of the stunning art deco mansion.

Reveal thyself, Detective Inspector Whipple, Her Grace drawled lazily, with an air of indifference. 'You may be Scotland Yard's finest taker of villains, but a master of concealment you are most certainly not.'

As the detective emerged, I couldn't help but notice the forlorn expression etched on his face, his hands buried deep in his ill-fitting jacket pockets, evoking the image of a wayward schoolboy caught scrumping.

'Come hither, Arthur. What brings you here?'

Whipple sprang to attention and eagerly closed the twenty-foot gap between us, brimming with vital information to share. With a flick of his wrist, the inspector snatched off his fedora and used his jacket cuff to wipe the sweat from his brow, narrowly avoiding a collision with a modernist sculpture that dared to block his path across the lush green lawn.

All appeared lost until the inspector grabbed the chest-high marble edifice and steadying it, before stepping back to view the piece, tilting his head, first to one side, then the other.

'It's got two faces,' said the confused detective.

'Nonsense,' replied HG. 'Do you not recognise cubism when you see it?'

'What "ism?"' replied the befuddled inspector.

HG had finally run out of patience. 'Never mind, one day I shall make it my business to introduce you to the magnificent works of Pablo Picasso and Georges Braque. Now, to return to my original question, why are you here, since it is clearly not to admire Sir Herbert's sculptures, one-thousand pounds' worth of which you almost destroyed?'

Whipple gave a second shake of his head as he left the sculpture in almost the same position he'd found it, before declaring he'd have "knocked it up for fifty quid".

'An answer at once, Arthur, or I'll be done with you and join my host.'

Whipple looked around as if checking for a cell of fifth columnists. 'There's murder afoot', he whispered as if his life depended upon keeping the matter a state secret.

HG's reaction was to offer an exaggerated blink, while maintaining her usual ramrod straight gait, making her slim, tall frame look even more imposing when she wore, as on this occasion, full evening dress and bejewelled regalia. 'What in the world happened?' she demanded.

'Happened? Er...nothing...yet', replied the hapless inspector.

HG shook her head and gave me one of her more intense stares. 'Is it I, Rex, or is Arthur suffering from a deficit of some sort since he speaks in riddles? Come, let us enter the house...perhaps you might wish to remove your chauffeur's cap and gauntlets, lest the butler redirects you to the servant's entrance.'

Wasting no time, my guardian turned on the spot and made off for the striking front entrance to the house, leaving me to follow and Whipple to protest for a second hearing.

'Ah, the thought of being left on your own to mingle in such august company as awaits within these walls brings you to your senses.' HG paused her elegant stride and redirected her focus towards the dejected detective. 'Continue.'

Whipple required no second invitation. With a comical glance over his shoulder like a Keystone Kop, he motioned for us to form a huddle. To my mind, the sight of a bedraggled middle-aged chap, a young man wearing part of a chauffeur's uniform, and a grand lady dressed to the nines could do nothing but attract attention. Thankfully, our clandestine society boasted a safe distance of at least fifteen feet from our nearest neighbours.

Certain we were not to be overheard. Whipple began his exposition. 'I am commanded by no lesser a personage than the Home Secretary, Sir William Bridgeman...vis the 1st Viscount Bridgeman.'

Once again, HG's irritation came to the fore. 'I'm quite aware who the Home Secretary is. In fact, I had tea with the fellow not two weeks ago. Now, conclude your explanation at pace, Arthur. Sir Herbert awaits our arrival, for events will not begin without my presence.' HG wafted a gloved hand towards the impressive cement rendered dwelling, which glistened white as the evening sun gently bathed its pristine walls.

The words tumbled at a ferocious pace from Whipple. 'His Majesty's governments are concerned that certain known troublemakers may attempt to disrupt tonight's proceedings, since they intend serious harm on the owner of this house, Sir Herbert Cummings.'

'Again, you provide information I'm already aware of, Arthur.'

Whipple removed his fedora for a second time before fanning himself with the mis-shaped artifact. 'You already know?' Said the detective as his shoulders dropped and he adopted a forlorn expression.

HG raised her silver chain purse in such a way as I thought she was about to strike the inspector. In the event, she retrieved a small bottle. Delicately unscrewing the lead-crystal container's silver cap, she poured a small quantity of an amber liquid into it, before knocking it back with the dexterity of a personage well below her social standing. 'What ails you, man?'

I ventured two factors that might explain Whipple's low mood. First, That HG had stolen his thunder with news of a potential crime, and two, that inspector's visit came at the cost of missing the opening day's play at Lords Cricket ground.

HG thought upon my words for a few seconds, before advancing her assessment.

'You can surprise me with your insightfulness when the mood takes you, Rex. Now, let us see what Arthur has to say for himself. Well? Out with it, man.'

Whipple slowly reached into an inside pocket of his

oversized jacket, retrieving a slip of paper. 'It took me weeks to get my hands on this.' The inspector held the small strip of stiff paper as if it were a bar of gold bullion. 'I've already missed the opening day of Hampshire's match against Middlesex. All because of a politician's belief that an anarchist called Manny Tufnell stands ready to strike a blow against the ruling class. Added to which, I do not enjoy working on a Saturday. Which I shall now have to do to deal with Tufnell.'

The Dowager offered the sulking detective a comforting smile as she relieved him of his precious ticket. 'If the Secretary of State is mistaken in his belief that the fellow is intent on doing Sir Herbert ill this night, then you have missed only the first day's play. Look on the bright side, Arthur, and consider the outcomes of tonight's proceedings. Either Mr Tufnell will do his worst this day, in which case you will surely apprehend him and complete your investigation in double-quick time over the weekend, or the malcontent's expected visit fails to materialise, and your reassuring presence will have been in vain. In either eventuality, you will be amongst the faithful at Lords to catch the later stages of the cricket match on Monday. Now, shall we enter this splendid abode?'

HG's logic appeared to satisfy the inspector, although he muttered, 'And I definitely don't enjoy working on a Sunday.' All seemed well until a verbal altercation erupted alongside a Daimler motor car that had just come to a halt next to Hilltop's front entrance, whereupon an elderly gentleman dressed in evening attire more suited to the Edwardian era, berated his chauffeur, a small, thin man who looked to be in his late fifties, who's bearing showed the telltale signs of the fellow having endured a hard life.

The Dowager wasted no time in reprimanding the

grand old gentleman. 'My Lord Billington', she began, allowing the regal side of her nature to surface. 'I see you have not changed in the six years since our paths last crossed.'

I noted that although Lord Billington gave Whipple and me the same dismissive glance that he afforded his wretched employee, the fellow's demeanour changed completely with HG as he submitted to her superior rank.

'Your Grace,' he began, 'I apologise for this unseemly display. My new man has —'

'No doubt he fulfilled his duties to the best of his ability,' interrupted the Dowager. 'I suggest your hard-working employee needs refreshments in the servant's hall. Do you not agree?'

Lord Billington appeared stunned at HG's diktat, which we knew to be an order, rather than a friendly suggestion. 'Hmm...yes, a capital idea, Your Grace.' The chauffeur required no second invitation to depart the uncomfortable scene.

HG allowed Lord Billington to evade her clutches with a threat-laced smile as he scuttled past the butler guarding the front entrance to the house.

'A most repugnant individual who displays all that is bad in the landed class. The fellow takes after his late father, second Earl of Cavendale, who was also a bounder of the first order when within ten feet of his female staff,' commented HG contemptuously.

My benefactor took a deep breath as her prey departed the scene with his tale between his bowed legs, shifted her silver chain purse from one hand to the other, and scanned the front elevation of the newly completed edifice.

'I suppose one might understand why the more conservative elements of society remain uncertain about Sir

Herbert's new dwelling,' said HG as she encouraged Whipple and I to survey the brave mix of straight lines and symmetrical curves that characterised the building. I suggested to HG that her rather vague commentary was out of character.

'Excellent, Rex,' she replied. 'You did well to recognise the scepticism in my tone. In short, my peers are less concerned about the house than their disdain for Sir Herbert, since he gained his fortune through "new money", which, as you know, old money abhors.'

I reflected on our journey from the Dowager's home, Drakeford Old Hall, and the time she'd spent briefing me on our host, who, despite hailing from an impoverished background in Norfolk, matured into a talented chemist when aged twenty-five, invented a revolutionary concoction in the back room of his grandfather's cobbler's shop. Namely, a process by which footwear becomes impervious to the ingress of water.

'Do you know,' commented HG, 'The army wears his boots. Also, employers enlightened enough to provide stout footwear when their employees' labours require it. Also, I understand a growing number of people enjoying countryside rambling as a leisure pursuit depends upon his invention to remain dry.'

I knew HG meant no insult to the working classes by referring to an activity unattainable to those toiling in factories or upon the land, but those of the "middling sort" who had time and money for wandering about the countryside and suchlike.

That's another reason the landed gentry can't stand Sir Herbert! His excellent footwear and support for ramblers' conflicts with their avowed desire to keep the land for themselves,' added my mentor.

As I pondered HG's comments and thought it unjust that a little over 600 privileged families controlled access to so much land (though I did not count the Dowager among these, since she has always allowed unencumbered access to her own estate in return for visitors respecting her land and property), a cry pierced the still air, followed by a loud crunching noise.

'Are we condemned never to enter Sir Herbert's new home? What is it now?' HG demanded as she joined us, observing a young gentleman untangling himself from a neatly trimmed hedge just inside the gates to Hilltop. The fellow looked forlornly at a rather splendid, although now mis-shaped, bicycle.

HG's eyes widened in horror as the young man lifted his bedraggled straw boater with one hand and dug into Sir Herbert's hawthorn hedging with the other, searching for the handlebars of his hazardous contraption.

'Queen Victoria was clear on the matter,' opined my guardian as she narrowed her gaze at the unfortunate fellow. 'Her Majesty refused to have anything to do with such dangerous machines and considered the things most unladylike.'

While I understood HG's sentiment, or at least that of the late queen as reported by my guardian, I'd ridden a penny-farthing from time to time and had recently developed a keenness to own one of the new Raleigh Model E Road Racers. At £13, six-shillings and fourpence, it was, for the time being, beyond my means. Instead, I resolved to limit my ambitions by helping the agitated fellow untangle the cycle of my dreams from the hedge.

'Do you know,' began HG, 'that a gentleman by the name of Mathew J. Steffens wrote to the queen in 1898 to inform Her Majesty of his latest patent and requesting an audience to demonstrate the same. That is, an electric bicycle,' continued HG as she bade me onwards. 'Queen Victoria commanded the head of the royal household to send a polite note by return and that was the end of that. I distinctly remember Her Majesty relating the following to me during afternoon tea at Osborne House. "Imagine such electrical contraptions becoming commonplace. Polite society would surely cease to exist, and where might things end when all and sundry ride upon the pavements of London, sending gentle folk scattered to the four winds as uncouth fellows race by at an atrocious speed?"'

I made no comment as HG called me back to take possession of the smelling salts in order to administer the same to the disgraced cyclist who now lay akimbo in the hedge.

'Hurry, urge the gentleman to join us now, for his appearance is making that splendid hedge appear untidy,' commanded the Dowager as I leaned over the bewildered gentleman, who looked to be around my age.

Sensibly, the fellow obeyed HG's order and inhaled a large quantity of the bad-egg-like substance, before repairing into a convulsive bout of coughing, which the Dowager dismissed with a flick of her arm-length gloved hand.

'Cease that nonsense immediately and stand up, young man. Fewer theatrics and more of an apology is, I wager, called for.'

Stirred into action by HG's rebuke, the chap scrambled to his feet, removed his leaf-strewn boater to offer a second acknowledgement of his superior's presence, before replacing the mis-shaped accessory to his head at a jaunty angle.

'Wilberforce Washington at your service, Ma'am,'

croaked the fellow as he discarded an errant twig from one shoulder of his striped jacket. 'Please accept my sincere apology for any distress caused.'

'You may address me as "Your Grace", young man. Why do you ride that strange-looking velocipede in such a manner? Do you have poor eyesight, or some other physical impediment that limits your ability to ride in a straight line?'

I looked longingly at the offending Raleigh Road Racer as it rested upright, wedged in the hawthorn hedge. Oh, how I wished to own such a machine.

Mr Washington adapted immediately to HG's required form of address. 'Of course, Your Grace, I mean, no, I haven't...Oh, dear, what I mean to say is—'

HG cut the fellow off. 'Enough', she said, holding a gloved palm to the unfortunate fellow, not unlike a police officer about their business at a busy road junction. 'Are you capable of mounting that contraption, or do you require transport to your destination?'

The gentleman looked over his shoulder at what remained of his road racer, then inspected a large tear in the right knee of his white flannel trousers. 'Thank you for your kindness, Your Grace. Fortunately, my ultimate destination rests but a matter of yards yonder. That's why I crashed. As I made for the entrance, my left foot slipped from the pedal, and...well, anyway. That is where I'm heading.'

'Hilltop?' exclaimed HG, the surprise, and confusion clear in her tone not escaping my notice. 'You know Sir Herbert?'

'No, not really. I went to school with his youngest son. I'm twelve-months older than he, and sort of fell into being his protector at Rugdean. Older boys can be beastly to the younger ones, you know.'

His words had an immediate effect on HG as she applauded his philosophy of standing up for the underdog.

'I see, Mr Washington, then we shall say no more on the matter and instead, join Sir Herbert to partake in the celebrations, though I should dispense with the haggard boater if I were you, and, perhaps, disguise as best you can the tear in your trouser knee if you are not to be ejected as a ne'er-do-well by the butler.'

As Mr Washington dispensed with his hat by launching it over the hedge, then did his best to pull the ragged edges of his trouser leg together, I noted a wry smile forming across HG's immaculately made-up features and deduced she acknowledged the bedraggled personage before her as a kindred spirit.

'Perhaps we may, at last, make headway in greeting our host,' declared HG.

We had hardly begun retracing our steps to the front entrance when a rough-looking person, who dressed as if about to begin his shift in London Docks, emerged at speed from the front door. The incongruent image of a man in ragged work attire, complete with leather-shorn clogs set against the grandeur of Hilltop, all the while pursued by a livered footman and an athletic-looking gentleman in a tuxedo, made for the strangest of sights.

'What occurs?' shouted Whipple as he bolted towards the escaping felon.

'Murder,' responded the athletic gentleman as he lost ground to the sprightly interloper.

Chapter Two

CAKE, SIR?

THE INSPECTOR LURCHED FORWARD with steely determination. 'Manny Tufnell; stop in the King's name', he shouted, while heading off the fleeing reprobate. A gaggle of bewildered house guests dressed in the latest Paris haute couture watched from the art deco doorway. I sensed the villain spied a means of escape via the Raleigh racing bike, which remained buried in the hedge. The uncouth fellow pulled in vain at the stricken machine. This gave Whipple and the athletic gentleman time to catch up and restrain the ruffian, who put up a commendable struggle for freedom.

While trying to grab his wig, the servant couldn't keep up with the reprobate and his pursuers.

Whipple announced the arrest for breaking and entering, retrieving handcuffs while his deputy held on to the troublemaker for dear life.

'Now, my fellow. What's all this about?' demanded the inspector as he adjusted his hat to an angle more becoming of a police officer and breathed deeply to calm his heaving chest.

'I' am saying nothing', responded the raggedy man in a gravelly voice belaying a life of dusty toil and strong tobacco. I thought his reply ill-advised, given the inspector's disdain for poor manners, and the criminal class.

HG's loud tutting on hearing the arrested man's stilted reply drifted the several yards that separated her from the immediate scene. This added to the general air of displeasure exhibited by house guests, who'd materialised from the interior of the stylish new home.

As I expected, HG's curiosity got the better of her, which exhibited itself in an imperious march to the now securely restrained ruffian. I felt it appropriate to accompany my benefactor, more to observe her approach than any concerns for her physical wellbeing.

'Tell me, my man,' she began as Manny Tufnell eyed up his exquisitely dressed inquisitor. 'Did you mean to kill Sir Herbert?'

Tufnell wore a look of ill-disguised contempt. 'I'm a proud trades-unionist, not an anarchist. My aim is to get back for the working men and women...and child workers, of this country what is rightfully theirs.'

'Sir Herbert's house?' responded HG in a flat tone.

'You don't know the half of it,' replied Tufnell as he wiped the contents of his exhalation on the threadbare upper arm of his grimy coat.

Whipple raised a clenched fist. 'No need for that, Inspector,' said HG as she stepped closer to the prisoner. My mentor retrieved a silk hankie from her silver chain purse; then gathered up the unsightly deposit on the man's ragged clothes and whisper into his ear, 'A hard life for a man of what, sixty years?'

'I'm forty-nine years old,' replied Tufnell.

I was far from the only person to show astonishment among those in hearing range, listening to the outraged voice of Whipple's prisoner. His tired, weather-beaten features made a liar of his actual age, which, by my reckoning, did not bode well for his chances of surviving into his dotage.

His words demonstrably touched HG as she expertly folded her hankie and slipped it into the remnants of Tufnell's left jacket pocket. The man moved not an inch, nor softened his features at HG's tenderness. However, it occurred to me she secretly admired his proud stance.

'When this matter is over and done with, I wish to visit your family. I suppose there is a Mrs Tufnell at home. And perhaps a child or two?'

She spoke so low that I suspect only Whipple, the athletic gentleman, and I heard my mentor's request, which appeared to throw the prisoner off guard.

After taking a few seconds to compose himself and, I surmised, decided not to rebuff HG's proposition, the man spoke. 'I have a wife...not in the legal sense, mind you, we live "over-the-brush", but that makes no difference to us.'

'And children?' enquired HG as she patted the man's torn pocket closed.

For the first time, and despite his hands being bound, Tufnell's features relaxed. There was even a hint of a smile. 'Nine of 'em,' he said. 'Aged twenty-one years to nine-months and every one of them is strong and healthy.'

I could tell that Tufnell took pride that all his children remained alive, which I knew from my experience growing up in dire straits was a spectacular feat. I realised HG admired the fellow's proud boast, given the home for foundlings she'd created and financed. It was from this establishment that she'd plucked me as a young boy and took me as her own.

'Then it's settled. When the inspector has completed his investigations and the magistrate has dealt with your case, we shall meet again.' HG looked at Whipple. He knew of her philanthropy and reputation in fighting for the underdog, nodded his agreement and offered the merest hint of a smile. 'As for you, Inspector Whipple, it is as I predicted. You shall, no doubt, deal with this matter in time to enjoy the second day of the cricket match on Monday. In my case, I shall enjoy a private viewing of Constance Worth's latest silent comedy picture. If memory serves, it is called, *A Bachelor's Baby*, which I'm reliably informed, is presently available to the general populace at picture houses.'

It seemed the thought of watching the cricket hadn't occurred to Whipple until HG mentioned the possibility. A gradual lightning of the inspector's mood signalled his new understanding. 'I shall summon a police motor van to transport our friend to Henley Police Headquarters to await my interrogation.'

The intimate moment passed as our host arrived on the scene. He first gave Manny Tufnell a quizzical glance. Sir Herbert then acknowledged Whipple and me, before turning his attention to HG. 'Your Grace, this is no place for you. Come inside. We really must get the evening underway.'

I observed, as did HG, Tufnell, grimace at the sight of Sir Herbert.

'Why do you look at this noble gentleman in such a manner? Do you not know he is a self-made man? A person who, if I am not mistaken, lived in a single room above his uncle's cobbler's shop.' she looked at Sir Herbert, who offered the faintest of nods.

'That's as maybe, but he's one of yours now, and I don't suppose he told you about the poor devil who perished in his factories, has he?'

For the second time in as many minutes, those in hearing distance took a sharp intake of breath. Others averted their gaze so as not to offend their wealthy host.

'That'll do, Tufnell,' barked Whipple. 'This gentleman has done you no harm, so mind your manners…that's if you have any.'

'Not for the likes of him, I haven't.'

HG had clearly heard enough. 'Well, Inspector Whipple, I think we should leave you to your duty. Sir Herbert, shall we proceed?' As she gestured our host to link arms with her, HG looked back at the prisoner. 'Remember, Mr Tufnell, we shall meet again. You have my word.' Her brief speech appeared to strike a chord with the man, who flicked his head in acknowledgement of a promise made.

With that, Sir Herbert led HG towards the house, causing those around to emulate the parting of the Red Sea so as not to impede their progress. As the pair neared the large entrance door, I overheard HG asking, 'Have there been deaths, Herbert?'

The esteemed gentleman leaned into his companion and whispered, his tone, I thought, a touch emotional. 'My eldest son, Horatio,' Sir Herbert sighed. 'Twenty-seven years of age who thinks he knows it all and can take senseless risks with my workers' lives while chasing excess profits? He understands nothing of the work and appears to care even less for the people. The matter concerned a young man left in charge of a dangerous machine. I was in London for a meeting when it happened. Horatio withdrew the boy's supervisor to start a second machine to increase production. Despite repeated protests from the supervisor, my son persisted in his reckless act. He brings shame to my family, but what am I to do? He is my eldest and will one day run the entire show.'

HG pulled Sir Herbert into her, which appeared to calm our host as he continued, 'Where have his mother and I gone wrong with the boy, Your Grace? He enjoys the best of everything. Yet as he ages, the fellow becomes more contemptuous toward me.' Sir Herbert shrugged his shoulders as the pair disappeared into the cavernous house, while his guests sorted themselves into a pecking order according to social rank before crossing the threshold.

'How...err, striking,' remarked HG as she set her eyes on Sir Herbert's lavish reception hall. Heads, including mine, swivelled to take in every detail of the black and white diamond floor tiles. They were reminiscent of a circus mannequin costume. Also, the ornate cast-iron balustrade that edged the first-floor landing, the two connected by a minimalist spiral staircase. Each wall announced itself with fan-shaped symmetrical plasterwork. To finish, a stylish cornice of interlocking squares tethered wall to ceiling.

'It's not really my thing,' remarked Sir Herbert as he hurried HG across the wide expanse of the hallway. 'However, my wife tells me it's all the rage and insisted we embrace the fashion.' I distinctly heard our host sigh, which I took to represent his bafflement concerning modern architecture. 'Anyway,' continued Sir Herbert, 'We must embrace the new and get "with it", I suppose,' commented Sir Herbert.

HG gave a last look at a large mirror that resembled several shards of ice broken away from a roof soffit and which had embedded themselves in the frozen ground.

The pair processed into a reception room of classical proportions with me close at hand, followed by a phalanx of lords and ladies. The notable feature of the immense room was a raised dais on which stood a small square table covered in exquisite pink silk. Two members of staff fussed over the delicate fabric to make sure each pleat folded neatly into its neighbour.

'It's been the devil's own job to get enough staff to cover this evening,' commented Sir Herbert.

'But you employ so many people,' replied HG.

'Quite simply, it's about money,' said Sir Herbert. 'Wages are much higher in manufacturing, so you might say I've been hoisted by my petard. Working in service isn't the thing these days. So much so, I've had to bring several staff down from my Norfolk home to help this evening. Even then, we've had to top up with several agency staff. Anyway, I'm sure we'll manage.'

Our host's nervous glance around the sumptuous room showed he was unsure all would go according to plan. HG picked up on his pensive tone. 'It all looks splendid, Herbert, and I'm sure your own staff will monitor their agency colleagues. Now, how are Their Majesties? I know your Norfolk residence to be near Sandringham House. Do you see them often?'

Sir Herbert's mood improved immediately. 'Yes, in fact our principal abode is not twenty-minutes from Sandringham. The King and Queen are most gracious and often invite us for an informal meal, or to watch a moving picture in the ballroom. You're aware that my wife helps with the queen's carving school for wounded ex-servicemen?'

HG nodded approvingly. 'I hear wonderful things about the school. I'm sure it is of the greatest help to the brave men who gave so much in the Great War to develop new skills and work opportunities. Queen Mary is to be congratulated on her foresight. Please send my best wishes to Their Majesties when next you meet them,' replied HG.

At that instant, Sir Herbert's butler interrupted their conversation. He sought confirmation of the platform party during the welcoming speeches. A few seconds elapsed as our host checked a penned list held in the butler's gloved hand. 'All is correct, Richardson', said Sir Herbert in a muted tone as he bade the butler to complete relevant preparations.

'A little old-fashioned, don't you think?' said HG once the butler had departed and disappeared into a throng of well-dress guests.

Sir Herbert frowned. 'Oh, you mean addressing the fellow by his surname? I agree and am all for the modern way of calling staff by their first name. However, the man will not hear of it. His father was a butler before him, and his grandfather held a similar position for one of England's oldest families. He insists that the tradition must continue. More than that, if he hears me calling any of his staff by their first name, he gives me one of those looks. You know, the type that makes one wonder who is the employer and whom is the employee.'

'Oh, Herbert, you're such a wag, I—'

The appearance of Lady Eleanor cut HG's light-hearted reply short. 'Ah, there you are. I thought you quite lost. Forgive me, Your Grace, my husband forgets how quickly the evening progresses. Come, dear, we must get on.' Sir Herbert's wife ushered her husband towards the speaker's platform. This left HG's left arm extended in mid-air as our host involuntarily decoupled himself from his guest.

Sir Herbert ascended the steps at one end of the platform. The room quietened from a refined hubbub to silence in anticipation of the host's opening remarks. At his side stood his wife. Her modest, yet modern dress and choice of jewellery showed, I thought, gave a strong sense of her own identity. This, a pleasant digression from the clone-like ladies' present (Her Grace being a notable exception). These souls wore a countenance that belayed the difficult times presently being experienced by the general populace. Behind the pair sat the silk-dressed table, made up with many garlands and floral decoration. In the middle, a rather incongruous space remained. The answer to this puzzle was not long in coming.

A nervous-looking gentleman wearing a tuxedo at least two sizes above his compact frame completed the platform party. From the man's countenance, he appeared to hate every second of his public exposure, which peaked as our host began his address.

'Your Grace, my lords, ladies, and gentlemen. On behalf of my wife and I, welcome to our new home.'

Polite applause and the occasional, "here, here", filled the perfumed air. 'There are, if I may, one or two people I should like, to thank for what is, I'm sure you will agree, a most elegant house.' Sir Herbert awaited an approving response from his guests. Alas, apart from the polite, muffled applause from several gloved ladies, Sir Herbert was to be disappointed.

'Snobs, the lot of them,' whispered HG into my left ear. 'They hate the fact that our host derives his wealth from "trade" and that most of them, for all their aristocratic titles, great houses, and land, cannot afford to construct such a...' HG hesitated, 'An edifice to modernity.' I thought it prudent to nod rather than offer any comment, lest HG thought me to be at odds with her own opinion.

Sir Herbert scanned the room, waiting for the applause

to fade. 'But first, I should like to read you a telegram… more precisely, the words I am commanded by my King to communicate to you all.'

This time our hosts had the august assembly's full attention. Sir Herbert made a particular point of reaching into his breast pocket to retrieve a folded piece of paper. He opened and held out before him with a measure of pomp and circumstance, a telegram. The room fell silent.

"My dear Cummings - STOP -," began Sir Herbert as he held the precious document in his outstretched left hand. "Congratulations on the completion of your new home - STOP -." Sir Herbert gazed around the room. This time, his guests nodded their agreement with the King's sentiments. "Art deco is the thing - STOP - Expect you at Sandringham for church and lunch Sunday - STOP- George Rex - End-"

The room erupted into a cacophony of "here-here" and "God Save the King". I sensed HG leaning into me again as Sir Herbert allowed the scene of royal devotion to continue. 'They'll hate Herbert even more for that telegram,' she whispered.

Eventually, having basked in the reflected glory of royal favour for a full minute, Sir Herbert brought proceeding back to earth. He replaced the precious telegram back into his pocket, then extended both hands, making a sort of downward wave motion. A competition ensued who would be the last to stop clapping and, therefore, seen as most loyal to the Crown.

'As I expected', mused HG as Lord Billington claimed the prize without showing the slightest sign of self-consciousness.

'Thank you, thank you. I'm sure we are all indebted to His Majesty for favouring us with his kind words. However, we must move on. There are several people…two, in fact, that my wife and I wish to thank for our new home. The first is Sir Wilfred Dillon, the esteemed architect of many magnificent creations. We were fortunate indeed to secure his services.'

By now, the gathering was fully engaged in proceedings and offered the absent Sir Wilfred a round of applause, becoming his station in life. Sir Herbert once again quietened proceedings. 'The second person I should like to thank is Mr Earnest Farrier.'

A restrained mutter broke out, stemming from a lack of recognition of the fellow. 'Allow me to introduce my chief accountant.' Sir Herbert turned to his subordinate and offered a warm smile. He extended a hand in the accountant's direction, who bore all the signs of wishing to vanish into thin air.

HG nudged my arm, 'That won't go down well with this shower, he's "staff"', chuckled HG.

Mr Farrier looked at his employer with a pained expression. After all, one imagines a significant trait of his profession to be the invisible hand behind the throne, so to speak. Our host's chief accountant struggled to overcome his aversion to the spotlight and offered Sir Herbert a loyal smile.

'Come, Earnest, the honour must be yours.' Using his first name in public unsettled Mr Farrier. 'Ah, here it is', added Sir Herbert. A ripple of applause ensued as the chef patissier emerged from the kitchen and made his way to the platform through the throng. He bore his elegant creation on a silver serving trolly decked with laurel and rose petals.

Two footmen of considerable stature stood facing one another, immediately below where Sir Herbert held centre stage. At the appointed moment, each took a firm hold on opposite ends of a brightly polished silver serving tray on which the magnificent cake rested. Lifting the white-iced wonderment, which bore a remarkable resemblance to the house we stood in, the two men raised the cake from its carriage. Sir Herbert stood back and applauded, his face beaming. Two staff who'd been waiting, one at each end of the temporary stage, stepped into the limelight to stand immediately above the footmen. Their sole responsibility was to gather the confectionary masterpiece from their colleagues.

'Better them than me', whispered HG as the four men concentrated on their task. Their combined efforts worked a treat in safely delivering Sir Herbert's cake to its allotted place on the highly decorated table before retiring.

The iced imitation of Hilltop drew gasps from the audience. Sir Herbert beckoned his chief accountant. 'Come, dear friend. To you, must go the honour of cutting and tasting the first slice.'

Mr Farrier obeyed his employer and, with a humble bow, hardly discernible unless one paid attention to such things, stepped forward. An obliging lady dressed in a starched white pinafore over a long black dress handed the chief accountant a beautifully engraved silver cake slice. The accountant looked nervous as he held the implement over the cake. Sir Herbert gently encouraged the accountant to pierce the thick icing. This took some effort as the accountant visibly struggled to break the surface. Then success came as the slice did its work and plunged into the depths of the cake's interior.

A round of polite applause met the accountant's determined effort as the crowd waited for Mr Farrier to take a bite into the lightest sponge, I'd ever laid eyes on. Soon, the deed was done. Mr Farrier smiled and held up his reward in one hand, and the silver cake slice in the other.

Suddenly the cheers turned to shrieks of horror as Mr Farrier dropped both cake and silver implement, then grabbed at his throat. Sir Herbert reached out as he watched his employee crumple and land with a thud on the wooden surface of the stage. 'Help, I say, help the poor man,' appealed our host as pandemonium broke out amongst the gentry, who appeared unsure what to do. I reflected that the upper class lived a life in which servants took the burden of decision making from them – and which now left them unable to do anything of practical use.

HG stood out as an exception. 'Come, Rex, we must get to the platform,' announced my benefactor in a determined voice as she made for the staging. I followed in her wake as those nearby stepped aside, relieved that someone else had acted. Whipple closed in on the platform from the far side of the immense room. This resulted in us reaching the collapsed man from different directions within a split second of each other.

Whipple bent over the stricken fellow, while HG issued instructions about what he should check. The inspector knew her well enough, and respected HG as a close friend not to remind her he well understood what he needed to do.

'Is there a pulse?' asked HG in a controlled, muted voice, though many of Sir Herbert's guests will have heard her comment, because of the solemn silence that had descended, which placed the mood at odds with our grand surroundings.

Whipple placed two fingers on the man's jugular vein, then moved closer to check for signs of breath. He held his position for a few seconds before turning to HG. 'Do you have a small mirror I might borrow?' She whipped out a delicate tortoiseshell compact from her purse and handed it urgently to the inspector.

A Spiffing Murder

After a brief interval during which Whipple watched for signs of life manifesting itself on the mirrored surface, the inspector slowly closed Mr Farrier's eyes, then the compact before turning to HG while slowly shaking his head. Everyone waited for the inspector's dread announcement.

He checked for a pulse a second time. 'The man is dead.'

Chapter Three

AN ODD OCCURRENCE

INSPECTOR WHIPPLE LOST little time in ordering the room emptied so that he could begin his investigation. It was at such times that the fellow's presence filled any space he occupied as his professional countenance dominated proceedings.

'No one is to leave this building until I've made sense of this tragedy and given you permission to do so. Is that understood?'

His order settled on the upper-class assembly like a gossamer mist laced with steel. These were people not used to being told what to do by anyone other than their immediate social superior. I observed not one objection, nor a skittish glance, as the inspector swept his attention back and forth across the silent room.

'Sir Herbert, might your staff guide these good people to a room where they may await my further instructions?'

The request plucked our host from his grim stance as he gazed upon his stricken employee. 'Oh, err...yes, of course.'

The shocked fellow looked to his butler, who was already issuing orders to the footmen.

'One more thing,' said Whipple in a professionally calm, yet steely manner. 'No one is to use the telephone or instruct the staff to do so. News of this dreadful matter must not leave the house unless it is by my order. Is that also understood?' Once again, Whipple's words went unchallenged as the glazed entrance doors decorated with stylised roses opened and the staff began their task of leading guests to their new accommodation.

Whipple turned to Sir Herbert. 'On that note, may I ask that your butler rings the local police station and ask they send a couple of bobbies. Tell him to give my name and that I shall appraise them of the situation when they arrive. I presume the butler's discretion is to be relied upon?'

'Assuredly so, Inspector,' responded our host as he glanced at Richardson, who, I had noted previously, rarely took his eyes off his employer. The butler seemed to sense Sir Herbert required his services as if by telepathy. He whispered into the fellow's ear, after which Richardson departed the room without raising so much as a glance from those present.

Two minutes later, the room stood empty apart from the original platform party and a few close family members. Soon Richardson returned, gave a nod to signal he'd made the telephone call to the police station and stood in a dignified silence awaiting further instructions from his employer. Instead, Sir Herbert could not be distracted from his hollow gaze as he alternated his attention between the unmoving shape of his deceased accountant and the splendid, yet understated decoration of the vast room, which seemed, somehow, to sense the sadness its walls envelope.

A shrill cry of a young woman pierced the eerie silence. Primrose Farrier, the only child of the dead man, scurried onto the staging and ran to her father's mortal remains. Immediately, Francis Cummings, our host's youngest son, followed and made a grab for the young woman to stop her from falling upon her deceased father. They exchanged the sort of glance that only two people with a certain understanding of each other display. I sensed more than mere friendship as the newly orphaned young lady fell into Francis' protective embrace.

Such was the attention I gave the couple; I'd missed HG making her way over to the body. She stood within two feet of the afflicted gentleman with Whipple on the opposite side as the two sleuths; one professional to his fingertips, the other, a gifted amateur, devoted their complete attention to the sad scene. They briefly exchanged glances.

HG moved closer to the body before becoming distracted by several people shuffling about her. 'No doubt the inspector wishes nothing to be disturbed. I wonder if we might all remain still?' she said in a muted, dignified yet authoritative tone.

Whipple extended an arm to show that HG should continue her initial investigations. His stern gaze made clear no one else should move.

'I see no sign of choking,' said HG as she concentrated on Mr Farrier's right hand, which remained tightly locked upon his throat. 'Might it have been a devastating seizure? or another physical condition which led to his demise?'

All eyes turned to Primrose, who's gentle sobbing floated in the still air. 'My father is…was… No, this cannot be…'

Sir Herbert's youngest son once more gathered the distraught women into him. 'Hush now, Primrose. We are all here for you. You must be brave for your father's sake and answer the Dowager's question.'

Francis' calm tone gave Primrose the courage she needed to gather her thoughts. 'My father was, to my knowledge, in the best of health. In fact, he had just joined our local bicycle touring club. Not something he'd have done had his health been anything other than perfect for his age.'

A sadness descended upon me as I listened to Primrose's touching eulogy to her father's everyday life amid the tragedy we now witnessed. Looking around, it dawned that I was not the only one to be affected by the poignancy of her simple words. HG continued her relentless search for any clue that might explain the dead man's sudden expiration. Her systematic approach never failed to impress as I observed my benefactor's attention to detail. Working her way down the corpse, touching no part of the gentleman, she lingered at his left hand as it rested upon the bare pinewood of the stage.

'Did your father enjoy fishing, Miss Farrier?' I observed Whipple bend forward to gain a better view of the hand in question.

'Why...yes, my father loved the hobby. Not to catch and keep any living thing, rather to study them. He had a particular fascination with salmon.'

'Ah, the noble salmon,' replied Her Grace. 'So single-minded in its mission to spawn. Well, at least that explains the pinprick on his index finger.'

Intrigue having got the better of me, I asked HG what she meant. The Dowager curled a finger and bade me move closer. 'Observe, if you will, a minuscule entry and exit wound.'

I strained to catch what HG had discovered yet saw only the slightest discolouration of skin almost hidden among the unfortunate fellow's rather rough hands, which I thought odd considering his profession.

'A fishhook, dear Rex. I contend that Mr Farrier suffered a wound often experienced by anglers of all abilities when disgorging a hook from their catch. Then again, he may have injured himself when attaching an artificial lure hook. Do you not agree, Inspector?'

We bent over the poor man's body, observing his hand at close quarters. The inspector straightened himself and rubbed his emerging stubble, which gave the man a slightly rough appearance. 'Your Grace's observational skills continue to astound me.' I noted HG's sardonic glance as she admonished the policeman without uttering a word.

'What?' said Whipple in a confused tone.

HG smiled at the detective. 'Never mind, let us continue. I'm sure the pathologist will confirm my hypothesis.'

This caused Primrose to break into a flood of tears. 'Pathologist? you mean...a...a post-mortem...on my father?'

The Dowager displayed her gentle side as she got to her feet and comforted the young lady. 'Miss Farrier, your father is at peace now. No one can hurt him further. But you must live on. Do you understand what I'm saying?' Primrose sobbed into HG's shoulder while my mentor gently stroked the orphaned woman's hair. Several seconds elapsed until Miss Farrier loosened her hold. 'I...I suppose you're right. At least that way I will know what led to my dear father's death.'

HG beckoned Francis to take her position in comforting his sweetheart. 'That's the ticket, my dear,' said HG. 'It is easier to deal with facts rather than the unknown and I know that together you two young people will gain strength from one another.'

I realised my mentor's words summed up her personal mantra. She had told me little of her own upbringing and early life. However, reliable sources inform me that the wealth and privilege of her family did not shield them from the loss and torment experienced by almost all families, irrespective of rank.

'It seems to me,' remarked HG, 'That a period of rest may be beneficial to you, Miss Farrier. Perhaps Sir Herbert might facilitate the use of a bedroom?'

Our host duly rose to the occasion and bade his butler to guide Primrose to one of the guest rooms. 'No need,' interrupted Lady Cummings. 'I shall guide Miss Farrier personally and offer what company I may provide, my dear.'

Inspector Whipple used the opportunity to command the rest of those present to vacate the room and await his further instructions while he consulted with Her Grace and me. His request met with nothing but polite acquiescence as everyone gave the stricken Mr Farrier a last glance before quietly descending the staging and making their way out of the morose room.

The three of us stood in a huddle over the corpse in an otherwise still space. 'I'm not sure there's anything more we can do here until the fingerprint officers and pathologist complete their work,' said Whipple in a dignified tone. 'I'm satisfied the immediate surroundings are as they were when this poor fellow collapsed. Let's see what the experts come up with, eh?'

HG seemed distracted as Whipple spoke. 'Do you not agree?' asked the inspector.

'What...what did you say?' answered the Dowager in a distracted tone. 'Oh, yes, the experts. Indeed...but what if Mr Farrier died not from natural causes but because of—?'

'Of what?' interrupted the inspector.

The Dowager turned to her right and took half a step towards the remains of the slice of cake Mr Farrier had taken. 'It can only have been natural causes or...poison.' HG's reasoning sent a chill down my spine. I asked the obvious question of who might wish to murder a company accountant in front of his employer and a significant proportion of the Home Counties set. As I gathered my composure, I noticed the inspector also concentrating his attention on the cake remnants, which had spattered as it crashed to the ground.

'Only he ate the cake,' said HG as she pointed to the corpse.

'The same thought had gone through my mind,' said Whipple. 'Except as young Rex rightly points out, who might wish to murder an accountant? How could the braggart know Sir Herbert would give the honour of cutting the cake to Mr Farrier?'

Although miffed at being addressed as a youth by the inspector, I didn't let my irritation show, which I considered the adult and mature thing to do, so undertook to assert myself. 'Perhaps that is the point we are missing in all this. Let us suppose Sir Herbert was the target and through sheer bad luck, the killer murdered Mr Farrier instead.' Pleased with my assessment, I looked at my two companions expectantly. Instead, both wore a curious sort of look and HG scrunched her shoulders up, a sure sign of displeasure.

'I think the "bad luck", as you so clumsily put it, lies with Mr Farrier and not the murderer, if indeed there is one,'

Suitably chastened, I attempted to redeem myself. 'If the chap died from natural causes, well, while unfortunate for him…and of course, his daughter, it means an end to the matter. But what if Sir Herbert was the actual target? Does this not mean danger still exists because the felon may make a second attempt?'

Pressing my case appeared to do the trick as HG's tense expression melted as she and Whipple exchanged a thoughtful look.

'Rex has a point, don't you think?' said the inspector.

After a few seconds spent staring intently at the despoiled confectionary, HG responded. 'He does indeed, Arthur. The question is, what now?'

I glimpsed a twinkle in HG's eyes as she turned to look at me and took comfort from being in her good books again.

'Time to—'

Two fresh-faced police officers cut the inspector's words short, jostling to see who could make it through the entrance doors of the great room first. 'Steady lads,' barked Whipple. 'I know this might be your first body, but remember, you are upholding the King's law.' The tall bobbies stood rooted to the spot. 'Now,' continued Whipple, 'I want one of you at that door. Let no one in without my express permission. The other one I want in front of this staging with your back to the body. Dead the man may be, but he still deserves a measure of privacy. Is that understood?'

The taller of the two policemen gave his companion a nudge, which the fellow tried in vain to resist.

'Get on with it. The man is dead. Have you not seen a corpse before?' Whipple's irritation left nothing to the imagination.

Both young men shook their heads and looked at the

floor before the bolder one spoke. 'Well, only at training school, sir, but it was that old it looked like a wax dummy.'

Whipple turned to HG. 'Would you believe it?'

The Dowager offered the bobbies a welcoming smile. 'Then you should both approach. There is nothing to be afraid of. This gentleman is now at peace and can neither give nor receive harm.'

Her calming words did the trick as the men, who appeared to be no older than myself gingerly approached the stage. After a few seconds, HG once again led the way. 'Mr Farrier still has much of his natural colour and the stiffness of joints has not yet set in. Now, can you remember from your training when physical signs of rigour mortis appear?'

I marvelled at HG's ingenuity at turning the sad scene into a training exercise for the inexperienced constables. The two men looked at the body, then at one another. 'An hour?' said the confident one. 'More like an average of two to four hours I think', offered the quiet one.

Whipple, clearly pleased with their responses, gave a grunt of approval.

'Yes,' replied HG, 'Nearer to two hours in normal circumstances, although the ambient temperature and conditions will affect timings to a considerable extent.'

Now more comfortable in the presence of a corpse, the bobbies debated what might have happened to the fellow.

'Yes, yes, that'll do, you two. Now, one of you back to the door,' said Whipple in a tone notably more relaxed.

This time the problem was getting either of the constables to leave the body's presence.

'I have the answer,' announced HG. 'I see the identity numbers on your collars are sequential. This tells me you qualified together, but, of course, one came before the other when being issued with your service number. I recommend the one with the lower service number guards the body for the first half-hour, then switches position.'

The bobbies looked at each other's service number, before the one with the lower number assumed his position in front of the stage wearing a satisfied smile.

'Of course, that means that to you goes the important role of deciding who does, and who does not enter the room as per the inspector's orders.'

'You are a wily one,' commented Whipple to HG as the other bobby made his way to the door wearing the greater smile of the two constables.

As we followed several steps behind the numerically junior officer, HG offered a general comment on the situation.

'This leaves us with more questions than answers, gentlemen. If Mr Farrier's demise was not because of natural causes, two scenarios present themselves. Either Sir Herbert planned the whole thing, although what motive he might have to murder his accountant eludes me and surely a more private execution might have proved efficacious—for Sir Herbert at any rate. Or, someone planned to kill our host, but it went wrong when Mr Farrier obliged his employer by cutting the first cake slice.

'My concern relates to either outcome. Why poison a cake to kill one person when anyone who imbibed the sponge might be similarly inconvenienced? And let us not forget Rex's most valid point. If the latter is the case, time is not in our favour. By that I mean, to catch the killer before he...or she, makes a second attempt on Sir Herbert's life.'

My mind reeled at HG's assessment. The notion that Sir Herbert might have engineered the demise of his own employee seemed far-fetched, yet the alternative - that someone had targeted our host but inadvertently killed Mr Farrier instead - was equally unsettling. As we exited the grand room, I pondered the Dowager's words. If the killer remained at large, time was indeed of the essence.

Inspector Whipple cleared his throat, drawing my attention back to the present. 'HG, I suggest we question the guests. Perhaps someone noticed something suspicious or out of place.'

HG nodded thoughtfully. 'An excellent suggestion, Arthur. We must leave no stone unturned in our pursuit of the truth.'

As we walked down the opulent corridors of Hilltop, I felt a sense of unease. The grim spectre of death had shattered the previous joyous atmosphere of the evening. As HG's protege, I knew it was my duty to assist in any way I could, but the enormity of the task left me feeling somewhat daunted.

We entered the drawing room to find the guests huddled in small groups, their faces etched with a mixture of shock and confusion. Lady Cummings, having returned from tending to the distraught Primrose, approached us with a worried expression.

'Your Grace, Inspector, what on earth is happening? Poor Miss Farrier is beside herself with grief.'

HG placed a comforting hand on the lady's arm. 'We are doing everything in our power to get to the bottom of this tragic affair, Lady Cummings. In the meantime, we must ask for the cooperation of all those present. Inspector Whipple will conduct interviews to gather any information that may shed light on Mr Farrier's untimely demise.'

As the inspector organised the questioning, I found myself drawn to the far corner of the room, where a small group of gentlemen stood in hushed conversation. Among them, I recognised the architect responsible for the new house, as well as the rude Lord Billington we had encountered earlier. Their furtive glances and lowered voices piqued my curiosity, and I made a mental note to keep a close eye on their movements throughout the evening.

Chapter Four

QUESTIONS, QUESTIONS

AFTER A TIME, Whipple suggested that HG and I interview the family while he continued his work with the guests. 'That way,' he said in a pragmatic tone, 'We can cover more ground…And anyway, the family is more likely to open up to you than me.'

'An excellent idea, Arthur,' ventured HG as she sought Richardson to discover the whereabouts of Sir Herbert, his wife, and two sons. 'We have precisely one hour in which to gather as much information as possible before dinner begins, so let us hop to it, so to speak.'

I noticed Whipple frown as he pondered her words. 'Will dinner still go ahead? Surely not?'

'The conventions must be observed,' replied HG. 'Also, it's been a long time since afternoon tea.'

HG's explanation caused Whipple's frown to deepen. 'At our house, we have dinner at noon, tea at five and supper at nine, ready for bed at ten. Why must toffs always do things differently?' The inspector quickly corrected himself. 'Err… I do not include you, of course.'

A Spiffing Murder

The Dowager offered Whipple a benign smile. 'Dear Arthur, you must indeed include me in your accurate characterisation of the upper class, for I cannot deny the obvious. The simple truth is that the way we talk, the routines we follow, and the unspoken rules of high society exist simply to justify our existence. How else might one come to terms with living the life of leisure when one sees the toil of others all around? It can surely only be the case that the class, to which I belong, manages, with a few honourable exceptions, to convince itself that wealth and entitlement is theirs by dint of historical right. This is, of course, utter nonsense and, as you may have noted, leads to a collection of silly people filling their days entertaining other silly people with not an ounce of common sense betwixt them.'

I ventured the opinion that the Dowager's narration cast the whole of the well-healed in a poor light. HG confirmed she stood by her assessment, adding, 'Almost all will stoop to the lowest form of skulduggery and obsequious behaviour to avoid being cast out from their kind. To prevent this, we must obey one simple rule. That is to do as one wishes, but in no circumstances must one cause a public scandal.'

Before I delved further into the puzzling mechanics of the aristocracy, the inspector broke my train of thought by rummaging noisily in his jacket pocket. His single aim? To retrieve his favourite boiled sweets, affectionately known by one and all as "Everton Mints," named after the famous football club in the north-western part of England—Liverpool, to be exact. It was indeed a sight to behold as Whipple's eyes widened in eager anticipation as he unwrapped his sugar laden treat and popped it into his mouth. He then made a most un-natural sound. A sort of sucking, squelching sound.

'Anyway,' said the inspector in a tone almost drowned

out by the sound of the hard-boiled confection ricocheting from one tooth to another. 'I suggest we each get about our business. To avoid further confusion about what is dinner and what is tea, I further suggest we reconvene after coffee. Although I have to say, my sister always pours me a nice mug of tea, after my tea—if you see what I mean.'

I thought Whipple to be pushing his luck. My assessment proved correct.

'Arthur, are you being deliberately childish, or are you just hungry? I mention the latter, given the urgency with which you set about the confectionary, concerning which, I might point out, you failed to offer either Rex or myself.'

The detective attempted to correct his faux pas by pushing the sweetie to the side of his mouth to avoid further acoustic gymnastics. This gave him the appearance of a squirrel hoarding food for hard times. He next produced a crumpled white paper bag from his jacket pocket and offered the same to HG.

'You know I do not partake in eating such frivolities. My point was merely that you did not invite me to do so. As for Rex, he too shall decline, since he has not long since visited the dentist and I'm sure will wish to do nothing further to endanger his recently filled wisdom tooth.'

Whipple looked flummoxed. I decided not to interject and risk the Dowager moving her fearsome look of displeasure from Whipple to me.

'Now, enough of this silliness,' announced HG as she continued to offer Arthur her special withering look. 'Let us not forget that a man lays deceased, not one-hundred feet from our current position. Let us put into action our agreed plan. Now off with you.'

I distinctly heard Whipple muttering. 'Well, you started

it'. The man was fortunate indeed that HG either did not hear or ignored his rebuttal.

As we continued our progress across the gleaming ceramic floor tiles of the hallway, the butler came into view and responded to the Dowager's clipped question, regarding the whereabouts of the family by silently pointing a gloved hand to an elegant pair of doors on the opposite side of the impressive space.

Losing sight of the inspector as we neared our quarry, I reached out to depress an elegantly slim brass door handle and pulled back the door so that HG might enter.

'Heavens,' said the Dowager in a soft tone as she turned to address me. 'What an extraordinary room.'

The large space looked magnificent. Circular in design, wood panels shrouded the walls utilising various exotic veneers arranged into diamond-shaped pattern so that lighter woods contrasted with much darker specimens. Semi-circular matching wall lights emphasised the curvature of the comfortable room resplendent with a gleaming white painted ceiling of geometrical design and minimalist furniture positioned to stress the modernist look.

It was only now that we notice the family, such was the fine spectacle which until then had occupied our consciousness.

'Ah, there you are, Eleanor'. Sir Herbert's voice rippled around the interior like when one speaks in the Whispering Gallery of St Paul's Cathedral in London. Before us stood our host, his countenance solemn and tone subdued. Lady Eleanor and their two sons, Horatio, and Francis, sat together on a striking sofa, which I thought favoured design over comfort. 'Have the police team arrived yet? I'm sure that Primrose will wish her father's mortal remains to be given a measure of privacy at the earliest opportunity - as, of course, do we all.'

I stood transfixed by the ornate opulence of the circular drawing room, scarcely able to take my eyes from the intricate wood panelling and geometric ceiling design. HG cleared her throat, drawing my wandering attention back to the sombre gathering before us.

'I'm so dreadfully sorry for your loss, Sir Herbert,' the Dowager said, her voice thick with empathy. 'How is Primrose?'

Lady Eleanor rose gracefully from the sofa, a lace handkerchief clutched in her slender fingers. 'The poor girl is bereft. She remains upstairs, trying to compose herself before…' Her voice cracked, and she lifted the handkerchief to dab her eyes.

One of the young men, I presumed Horatio judging by his elder countenance, spoke up gruffly. 'What my mother means to say is that Primrose is being looked after by the staff. This is a deuced difficult time for us all.'

'Of course, of course,' HG soothed. 'We shan't trouble the young lady unnecessarily. Perhaps you could enlighten us as to the dreadful events surrounding Mr Farrier's tragic demise as you witnessed it?'

Sir Herbert sighed heavily, sinking into a plush armchair. 'A senseless death, that's what it was. Poor old Farrier never hurt a fly in his life. Primrose adored him.'

'Farrier had arranged for a cake replicating Hillside to be made, perfectly to scale,' said Francis in a subdued tone. 'He cut into it, then, seconds later…that's when he collapsed.'

A heavy silence fell over the room. HG was the first to speak. Her tone was gentle but firm.

'No one can blame you, Sir Herbert. I promise that the

fiend responsible for this heinous act shall be caught and brought to justice. For now, please try to take some comfort knowing that Mr Farrier passed swiftly, without undue suffering.'

The seriousness of the situation suddenly hit. An innocent man murdered; a young woman's beloved father-figure snatched cruelly away.

HG and I moved slowly forward into the centre point of the great room.

'You will wish to know, I'm sure, that the room is now secured while we await the police pathologist.' She informed Sir Herbert.

Controlling the exchange, HG in typical fashion effortlessly moved from the benign to focused sleuth. 'Forgive me, Sir Herbert, might I ask just one or two questions concerning your accountant's untimely death? It will be of such a help to Inspector Whipple as an adjunct to his own investigations.'

Sir Herbert, his wife, and younger son, Francis, shared a look of concern at the mention of the unfortunate man. Horatio, however, appeared bored and disengaged, his eyes remaining fixed on a glass fronted wall clock on the far side of the spacious room.

The Dowager pressed a case. 'Herbert, Eleanor, you know that I'm not a woman to dance on the head of a pin when something needs saying. In short, can you think of anyone who might wish to injure Mr Farrier?'

Sir Herbert's reaction was immediate, as it was shocking. 'The mere mention of such a thing seems preposterous, yet their Farrier lay in front of me. How can that be? As for anyone wishing him harm, I believed him universally admired for his professionalism and manners.'

As the appalling consequences of HG's question sank

in, Sir Herbert dropped back into his chair and scanned the interlocking-coloured squares of the wool carpet as if seeking to lose himself in the intricate pattern.

HG acted quickly. 'I understand the enormity of what I'm suggesting. However, if his death was not a consequence of malign forces, then we must look to natural causes for the answer. Do you know if he suffered from an illness of any sort while in your employ?'

Our host appeared to gather at least some solace other suggestion of a natural rather than violent death of his loyal employee. 'Nothing serious, at least not to my knowledge,' he responded. 'He complained of heartburn and indigestion from time to time, but on each occasion that I enquired after his health, he dismissed the attacks as inconsequential.'

I ventured to suggest that he might have had a serious heart condition, to which Sir Herbert shook his head, commenting, 'Again, not to my knowledge. Do you think a heart attack took him from us?'

HG moved to Sir Herbert's side, her palm on his shoulder. 'I trust it will be of some comfort to his daughter that Mr Farrier probably had little knowledge of what was happening. If the pathologist does indeed determine your employee's death can be determined as being from natural causes, then that will be an end to the matter, at least for all except Primrose. However, until that time, we must explore the possibility of foul play and be quick about it before your guests leave the premises.'

I observed Sir Herbert exchanging a nervous glance with his wife before turning back to my benefactor. 'Is it true?'

Once again, I took my time in observing how each member of the family reacted to this devastating development. While man and wife were subsumed in shock, the youngest son, Francis, gazed forlornly into space as if his own father had died. Horatio continued to look bored with events and toyed with an expensive-looking cigar lighter. His eyes averted from the rest of the room's occupants. This had not gone unnoticed by HG.

'What a beautiful artifact, my boy.' I sensed that the Dowager's observation contained a barbed edge. 'It seems to occupy your attention to a greater degree than the matter in hand, do you not think, Horatio?'

The fellow continued to rotate the silver item while turning his head away from his interrogator. 'The man is dead. Whether by heart attack or some other means.'

His mother sprang to her feet and berated her eldest for behaving in such an ill-judged manner. 'That is a despicable thing to say, and you shall retract it immediately.'

Sir Herbert reinforced his wife's point. 'Your mother and I did not bring you up to behave in such a way, and stop fidgeting with that lighter, boy.'

The father's stern tone prompted his eldest son to respond with a penetrating stare. 'Huh, you mean packing me off to boarding school from the age of seven and deigning to make your presence known once or twice when I came home for holidays? Or, perhaps, you mean remaining in the business long after you've fulfilled your useful presence. Tell me, father, why are you so resistant in allowing the company to pass into my stewardship?'

The venom with which their eldest son spoke clearly shocked his parents. It was all Lady Eleanor could do to dissuade her husband from manhandling the errant chap. 'Now, at last, we have it, so you wish me dead. Is it true?'

Unseen by Horatio, HG had moved around the room to

approach him from the opposite side. 'Be careful how you respond, Horatio. Detective Inspector Whipple remains nearby and shall hear of this.'

Horatio lazily placed the silver lighter back into his waistcoat pocket and shifted position nonchalantly. 'Stand up at once, young man.'

The fellow made a great mistake of ignoring HG's instruction. 'Stand up, I say. You are in the presence of a Dowager Duchess who most assuredly outranks you. Now, do as I command this second.'

HG's use of power, as expressed by rank, shocked my senses. A startled Horatio rose to his feet yet still averted his eyes.

'You will also look at me when I address you. Is that understood?' barked my benefactor.

Horatio drifted his gaze until HG's eyes locked on to the nervous young man. 'You will apologise to your parents immediately. Is that understood?'

The fellow maintained eye contact with a Dowager awhile, before slowly turned his head towards his father. An awkward silence followed. 'Well, what have you to say for yourself?' HG demanded.

After several seconds elapsed before Horatio mumbled an incoherent sentence, which only increased HG's ire with the chap. 'Speak plainly man, you are not a child. Your father levels a serious charge against you. What have you to say? Do you really wish him dead?'

Horatio shook his head nonchalantly. 'It makes little difference to me. One day I shall run the company. I am the eldest and it will all come to me.'

As Horatio's torrent of venom-laced words continued, I noted the horrified expressions on his parent's faces.

HG smiled, a reflex I at first failed to understand. Then all became clear.

'Not necessarily, young Horatio. A person might change their will, is that not so?' My benefactor glanced at the fellow's father. Horatio's sickly grin subsided.

'Timing is all, isn't it, Your Grace? Anyway, I've had enough of this. One death is enough for today, whether by natural causes or a poisoned cake. If I'm needed, send a servant to fetch me. I shall be in my room.'

The arrogant man placed both hands in his trouser pockets and ambled towards the door without a backward glance, nor giving the impression he had a care in the world. Then I witnessed HG adopt a tactic I'd seen her deploy before. Waiting until her quarry held the door half open, she pounced. 'Who mentioned anyone being poisoned, Horatio?'

The room fell into silence and waited for the eldest son to respond. Instead, he merely gave HG a smirk before exiting the room and quietly pulling the door behind him.

The younger son attempted to console his mother. 'You know what he's like. Horatio doesn't mean a word of it.'

'The boy is a spoilt brat, and we have brought this upon ourselves.'

HG offered a rebuttal to Sir Herbert's assessment. 'He's an adult and must face the consequences of what he says and does. To repeat my earlier comment, I shall have to report matters to the inspector, for it is too serious for Horatio's behaviour to be considered the petulant outburst of a louche and immature gentleman.'

The Dowager's words had the desired effect. A palpable sense of unease enveloped the room, as each member of the Cummings family contemplated the implications of Horatio's behaviour. Lady Eleanor dabbed her eyes with a lace handkerchief, her distress clear.

Sir Herbert rose from his chair and paced the room, his hands clasped behind his back. 'I cannot believe it has come to this,' he muttered, his voice barely audible. 'My son, wishing me dead.'

HG placed a hand on Sir Herbert's shoulder. 'We must not jump to conclusions, Herbert. Horatio's words, while disturbing, may not reflect his true feelings. It is possible he spoke in the heat of the moment, without fully considering the gravity of his statement.'

Sir Herbert shook his head. 'I fear you are too kind, Your Grace. Horatio has always been a troublesome child, but I never imagined he would harbour such resentment towards me.'

The tension in the room was palpable, and I wondered what other secrets the Cummings family might be hiding.

HG turned to me, her expression grave. 'Rex, I believe it is time for us to take our leave. We have much to discuss with Inspector Whipple.'

I agreed, grateful for the opportunity to escape the suffocating atmosphere of the room. As we neared the door, Lady Eleanor called out.

'Please, Your Grace, you must help us. I cannot bear the thought of my family being torn apart by this tragedy.'

HG paused. 'I will do everything in my power to uncover the truth, Eleanor. You have my word.'

With that, we exited the room, leaving the Cummings family to their troubled thoughts. As we walked down the hallway, I felt we had only scratched the surface of the mystery surrounding Mr Farrier's death.

I asked HG what she thought of events.

The Dowager's brow furrowed in concentration. 'There

is more to this than meets the eye, Rex. We must tread carefully and gather all the facts before drawing any conclusions.'

I knew she was right. The investigation had only just begun, and there were still many unanswered questions. But one thing was certain - the death of Mr Farrier had unleashed a storm of pent-up emotions that threatened to engulf the Cummings family.

Chapter Five

ARE YOU SURE?

HILLTOP'S luxurious dining room presented an uncomfortable contrast to recent events. More to the point, that the event continued at all escaped the logical side of my brain.

The soup course was served, a creamy lobster bisque with a hint of sherry. I glanced around the opulent table, trying to gauge the mood. Tension crackled in the air like static electricity, setting my nerves on edge.

Next to HG, Sir Herbert sipped his soup with a pensive expression. 'I apologise for the rather sombre atmosphere,' he murmured to the Dowager. 'But I felt it best to carry on, for appearances' sake. One mustn't let the side down. What?'

HG nodded, though privately I wondered at the wisdom of his choice. Surely cancelling the dinner would have been more appropriate under the circumstances?

Across from us, Horatio Cummings slouched in his chair, toying with his spoon. He caught my eye and smirked, raising one eyebrow as if daring me to comment. I looked away quickly, unnerved by the calculating gleam in his gaze.

Inspector Whipple shifted uncomfortably, tugging at his collar. The poor chap looked distinctly out of his depth amidst all the finery. As the footmen removed the soup plates and bustled in with the fish course - sole meuniere - I studied the other diners surreptitiously. Lady Cummings, regal in midnight blue velvet, presided at the opposite end of the table. Horatio's sibling, Francis, appeared morose. This I thought expected when his sweetheart's father had just perished.

The fish was exquisite, perfectly cooked and seasoned with a delicate touch of lemon and herbs. Yet I could scarcely focus on the flavours, my mind whirling with the events of the evening.

The fish course, once cleared away, allowed for a succulent roast pheasant surrounded by an array of seasonal vegetables to be presented. I eyed the spread, though my appetite remained muted by the undercurrent of tension pervading the dining room.

I again pondered why Sir Herbert had allowed the dinner to go ahead. Conversation remained muted, punctuated by the clink of cutlery and the occasional forced laugh. I observed the furtive glances of Horatio again. His lips twisted in a mocking sneer whenever his father spoke.

HG caught my gaze and arched one imperious eyebrow. A silent reminder to remain focused.

Sir Herbert bravely regaled the table with an anecdote about his recent golfing endeavours. Lady Cummings nodded along dutifully, her expression one of appearing to be interested, but her mind in another place entirely. Francis had abandoned all pretence of enjoying dinner and looked despairingly at his plate.

Horatio, seated opposite me, made no attempt to disguise his boredom. He met my stare with that infuriating smirk, grey eyes glinting with mocking disdain. A muscle twitched in my jaw as I struggled to maintain a neutral facade.

'...And that's how I finally bested Lord Marchbanks on the eighteenth green,' Sir Herbert concluded with a self-satisfied chuckle. 'Though I'm sure the tale has proved dreadfully dull for you all.'

A smattering of half-hearted chuckles greeted his self-deprecation. HG, ever the consummate diplomat, inclined her head graciously.

'Not at all, Sir Herbert. I found it most diverting.' Her tone held just the faintest edge of reproach. 'Although perhaps we might turn our conversation to more...convivial topics?'

An awkward silence descended as the footmen began clearing away the plates. Sir Herbert coughed, suddenly looking rather downhearted.

'Thank you for indulging my attempt to divert myself from the death of poor Farrier.'

The temperature in the room seemed to plummet at the mention of the deceased accountant's name. The Cummings siblings exchanged furtive glances. Horatio's smirk morphing into a contemptuous sneer. As the dessert course arrived - a decadent chocolate mousse - I studied each face around the table, searching for any hint of guilt or unease.

Poor Sir Herbert seemed most affected, his brow furrowed and his eyes distant as he picked at his mousse. My heart went out to the man - to lose a trusted colleague and friend in such a shocking manner, and then to play host mere hours later. It was a testament to his fortitude that he maintained his composure at all.

As the dinner finally drew to a close and the ladies retired to the drawing room for tea and conversation, and men to the billiard room for cigars and claret, I caught HG's eye once more. She gave me a subtle nod, and I knew that our proper work was about to begin.

As I rose to follow HG and Inspector Whipple from the room, I couldn't shake the feeling that we were walking into a wasp nest. Perhaps the sting of truth might prove more painful than any of us could imagine.

Plush leather armchairs met our gaze as we entered the morning room, arranged in a semicircle facing the hearth, their buttery tan upholstery contrasting with the white painted walls, finished with red and blue geometric lines. An impressive oak desk dominated one corner, its polished surface scattered with ledgers and correspondence. On the other side of the room, a drinks bar beckoned invitingly.

'Brandy?' Sir Herbert asked as he moved behind the bar. At our murmured assents, he began preparing our drinks with deft, practiced movements.

Inspector Whipple settled into one armchair with a grateful sigh, extending his long legs towards the fire. 'Much appreciated, Sir Herbert. This old body could use a drop of fortification after this evening's events.'

'Indeed,' our host said, a hint of weariness creeping into his tone as he handed out the snifters. 'I cannot begin to express my regret and dismay over poor Farrier.'

He settled into the remaining armchair, cradling his brandy as if drawing strength from its amber depths. I remained standing, content to let the others take their ease as I observed.

'Perhaps you could enlighten us as to the particulars of

Mr. Farrier's role within your organisation?' HG prompted gently. 'To understand any potential...motives behind this terrible crime.'

Sir Herbert considered her words and remained silent for several seconds. 'Reginald Farrier was, as I mentioned earlier this evening, my chief accountant and trusted advisor for the past twenty years. A brilliant mind for figures and an utterly trustworthy soul. I cannot fathom who could have wished him harm.'

His words rang true - the anguish in his eyes spoke of a man deeply shaken by the loss of a valued colleague and friend. Still, something niggled at the back of my mind, a persistent sense of disquiet I couldn't quite put my finger on.

'I see,' HG said, her sharp gaze missing nothing as it roved between her three companions. 'And what of your family, Sir Herbert? Might any of them have harboured ill-will towards Mr. Farrier?'

The fellow shifted in his seat, suddenly looking distinctly uncomfortable. 'I would hate to think...' He trailed off, shaking his head slowly. 'No, no, I cannot entertain such notions, even hypothetically. My sons and wife are good people, whatever their...' He waved a hand vaguely, 'eccentricities.'

Eccentricities? An interesting choice of words, to be sure. I thought back to the surly indifference of Horatio, the quiet demeanour of Francis. Not your typical eccentric behaviour for the scions of the upper classes. More like deep-seated resentment simmering beneath a veneer of civility.

'With respect, Sir Herbert,' Whipple interjected, 'We must consider all possibilities, however unpalatable. Even those closest to us are not immune to the darker impulses of human nature.'

An uncomfortable silence stretched between us, broken only by the crackle of the fire and the occasional clink of port glasses against wood. Sir Herbert's shoulders slumped, the weight of the inspector's words settling heavily upon him.

'You are correct, of course,' he said at last, his voice tinged with a hint of resignation. 'I shall endeavour to answer your questions as fully as I am able, however unsavoury the implications might be.'

He drained the last of his brandy and met HG's piercing stare levelly. 'Where would you have me begin?'

AS WE LEFT the morning room, and with it, the mournful figure of Sir Herbert, I hurried to catch up with HG and Inspector Whipple. The Dowager's face had that determined expression I knew this meant she had formulated a plan. I detected her eyes narrowing as she strode purposefully towards the library.

'Right then,' she said briskly, once ensconced in the book-lined minimalist room. 'We must question the remaining family members individually. I know well this shall cause further distress. Nevertheless, it must be done. There's something rotten in the state of Denmark.'

Inspector Whipple nodded, pulling out his notebook. 'Denmark? Do the family have connection with that country?'

HG did not take kindly to his remark.

'Arthur,' said HG as she looked down upon the seated detective as if scolding an errant schoolboy. 'Must you forever take me literally? No, the family does not have an interest in foreign parts, to my knowledge. My reference lay in the guise of an idiom—a figurative expression. The reference to that country comes from this nation's most celebrated scribbler. I speak of Shakespeare, no less.'

Whipple did his best to comprehend HG's explanation. She raised an imperious eyebrow at the inspector's blank look. I suppressed a smile; literary references were clearly not Whipple's forte.

She continued, 'No matter. Our first order of business is to speak with Lady Cummings. She may shed light on who would wish her husband harm.'

I cleared my throat and suggested that we ought to question the house staff as well, since they may have overheard or noticed something amiss.

HG turned to me, her eyes sparkling with approval. 'An excellent suggestion, Rex, my boy. One can learn much from observing the machinations of those below stairs.'

She squared her shoulders. 'To work. I shall begin with Lady Cummings. Arthur, I know you will be eager to interview Sir Herbert's guests. However, I suggest you summon the butler first. What was his name again? Ah yes, Richardson. He has been with the family for decades and will know everything there is to know about them. As for you, Rex. Follow your nose with the staff and see what delicacies they may serve you.'

Inspector Whipple looked up from his furious scribbling. 'Should we not make the sons our priority? Especially that Horatio fella. Seems a right dodgy sort, if you ask me.'

'All in good time, Arthur,' HG said. 'I prefer to take a circuitous route through which we may pick up valuable intelligence, before we speak to the sons. Now, let us be about our business. We shall reconvene in this room at the stroke of midnight.'

With that, she swept out of the library, leaving us to follow in her formidable wake. I exchanged a wry glance with Whipple. Another long night lay ahead, but with HG on the case, I had no doubt the truth would out. Even if it took turning the whole house upside down to find it.

BEFORE HEADING TO THE KITCHENS, I took a turn outside, whereupon I found HG on the terrace. Her gaze turned skyward as she studied the twinkling stars. Sir Herbert stood nearby; his shoulders slumped in an understandable show of dejection.

'Ah, Rex,' HG said as I approached. 'Sir Herbert and I were just admiring the celestial wonders above.'

Our host managed a weak smile. 'Though it's difficult to appreciate beauty this evening after such a tragic loss.'

'I know, dear Herbert,' HG said, placing a gentle hand on his arm.

He nodded solemnly. 'A brilliant accountant and an even better man. His passing is a blow to me, both professionally and personally.' He sighed heavily. 'I suppose the aristocracy still looks down on those of us newly elevated to the ranks of the monied class. Old money sneers at the nouveaux riches. But to kill over such petty resentments? It seems inconceivable.'

I could tell that the old versus new money divide weighed heavily on Sir Herbert's mind. As a self-made man who'd clawed his way to fortune through hard graft, he remained an outsider to the aristocratic elite despite his riches.

'The upper crust looks down their noses at folks like me - present company excepted, of course, Your Grace,' he continued, a hard-edge creeping into his tone. 'To them, I'm little more than a lowly tradesman who got lucky.'

HG's eyes remained resolutely on Sir Herbert. 'Is that resentment I detect?'

Sir Herbert waved a dismissive hand. 'Pay it no mind. I've grown accustomed to their sneers over the years. Still stings, though, I'll admit.' He puffed out his chest. 'I built this empire from the ground up with my bare hands. No family connections or inheritance to ease the way, just old-fashioned perseverance. They do not accept me; yet attend this evening. Do you not find that a paradox?'

'Not at all,' HG said. 'Free food and a chance to show off their latest cars and clothes is all it takes to ensure a healthy turn out. Of course, you have the added attraction of being on speaking terms with the King. As for your admirable achievement, take pride in your hard-won success.'

A wry smile tugged at the corner of Sir Herbert's mouth. 'Some don't see it that way, I'm afraid. The old guard views us upstarts as uncouth interlopers overstepping our station.' His gaze drifted across the immaculate grounds. 'Money can buy property and titles, but not the acceptance of the aristocracy, it seems.'

I asked if Sir Herbert might know anyone in his circle who may harbour resentment towards his prosperity to the extent of doing him harm?'

Although I aimed my question squarely at our host, I knew HG held the aristocracy in low regard. I waited with bated breath. As I expected, HG failed to give Sir Herbert time to respond to my enquiry. She was, after all, a member of the landed elite by birth, though her compassion and progressive views set her apart.

'An astute observation, Rex,' she said at last. 'I must confess, the upper classes to which I belong have long turned a blind eye to the plight of the working poor. We live ensconced in our manors and country estates, wanting for nothing as we pursue our leisurely amusements.'

HG's gaze grew distant, her expression troubled. 'We dine on the finest cuisine and adorn ourselves in the latest fashions from Paris and Milan, rarely sparing a thought for the legions of impoverished souls who toil in abject conditions to provide for our extravagances.'

Sir Herbert nodded grimly. Though elevated by his wealth, I suspected that he never forgot his humble origins or the struggles of the working class he once belonged to.

'The aristocracy sees the masses as little more than a faceless, servile underclass,' HG continued, a hard-edge creeping in. 'Out of sight and thus out of mind, they remain oblivious to the suffering endured by families crammed into squalid tenements and children put to work in factories at age six or seven to help make ends meet.'

She shook her head, disgust etched across her regal features. 'While we host lavish soirees and purchase new jewels to adorn our fingers and necks, they subsist on meagre wages, struggling to put bread on the table. The dichotomy between our opulence and their destitution is as stark as it is shameful.'

I experienced a surge of admiration for HG in that moment. Though born to privilege, she refused to ignore the systemic injustices inherent to our class-stratified society. Her determination to lift the downtrodden and fight for a more equitable future burned brightly, as expressed by her charitable deeds and ruffling of politicians' feathers.

'The upper crust would do well to open their eyes and minds,' HG said, her tone hardening further still. 'For how long can such disparities remain before the scales of justice tip irreparably?'

A moment's silence descended on our small gathering.

'I must apologise, Sir Herbert,' HG continued. 'I diverted Rex's true intention with his excellent question. To paraphrase my ward, then. Who of your adopted kind might seek to harm you?'

He frowned as he pondered HG's query. 'Physical harm? No. But there are several who would see me ruined and on the streets.' A derisive snort escaped his person. 'Not to mention the lesser gentry forever clinging to their dwindling fortunes and faded glory.'

'You raise a valid point,' HG said. 'Which is why my colleagues, and I must interview every soul present this evening,' HG said firmly. 'The inspector has the means to detain your guests for a stint. Just long enough for us to probe their knowledge of this horrible crime. We must leave no stone undisturbed,' HG replied steadily. 'Every minute affords the guilty party an opportunity to concoct an alibi or dispose of evidence. Time is of the essence if we are to uncover the truth.'

Chapter Six

A MYSTERIOUS MEETING

AS THE CLOCK tower struck ten, I strode down the ornate corridor of the Cummings' residence, the click of my shoes on marble echoing like a metronome through the silent hall. HG had assigned me to probe the staff, to peel back layers of their loyalty and uncover truths they might otherwise keep hidden. A daunting task, yet exciting; this was a chance to prove my worth beyond merely being a student of amateur sleuthing.

The first door on my left led to the servants' quarters. In this downstairs world, the air hummed with hushed whispers and the scent of beeswax and linen. A young maid, her apron crisp and white, glanced up as I entered. Eyes wide with curiosity, she dipped into a curtsey.

'Evening, Miss,' I said with a nod. 'I apologise for intruding at such a late hour.'

She straightened up, a blush colouring her cheeks. 'Not at all, sir. How may I be of service?'

'I'm looking to have a word with anyone who might've accessed the kitchen during the evening. Particularly those who had dealings with the cake that Mr Farrier bit into before his sad demise.'

Her lips pursed in thought. 'Well, sir, that'd be Mrs Smith, the cook, and Elsie. She's the pantry girl.'

I nodded. 'Might I speak with them?'

The maid bobbed her head and scurried off, leaving me alone amidst the muted clatter of dishes and silverware from an adjoining room. Moments later, she returned with two women in tow: one middle-aged with hands chapped from hard work; the other younger, likely not much older than me.

'Mrs Smith,' I began, 'I understand you prepared tonight's cake.'

'That's right,' Mrs Smith replied, her voice steady despite the gravity of our discussion. 'Buttercream frosting and all. Mr Farrier requested it, special like. You know, as a gift to his employer.'

'And Elsie,' I turned my attention to the pantry maid, whose eyes darted nervously from Mrs Smith to me. 'You helped prepare the creation to be taken upstairs?'

She swallowed hard before nodding.

'Can either of you recount anything unusual about tonight's preparation or service? Any strangers in the kitchen, or anything amiss?'

The cook shook her head vigorously. 'No strangers here, sir. We run a tight ship—no one enters my kitchen without cause, or my permission.'

Elsie fidgeted with her apron; eyes fixed on the floor.

'Elsie?' My tone remained gentle yet insistent.

She looked up at me then, biting her lip before speaking in barely more than a whisper. 'I saw Mr Horatio near the pantry earlier…just before supper, like.' Her voice trailed off as if afraid she'd spoken out of turn.

A Spiffing Murder

'Mr Horatio Cummings?' I pressed for clarification.

'Yes, sir.' She nodded vigorously.

I pondered this new information. Horatio's earlier implication that he wouldn't mourn his father's passing seemed even more sinister now—perhaps his presence near the foodstuffs was no mere coincidence.

'Did he take anything? Speak to anyone?' My questions came quick-fire.

Elsie shook her head, but then hesitated as if recalling something further. 'He...he was holding something. Small-like in his hand when he left,' she said at last.

Mrs Smith interjected. 'Probably nicking sugar again—the man's got a sweet tooth that'll cost him his pegs in the end, I'll wager.' She laughed dryly, but stopped short when she saw neither Elsie nor I shared her mirth. 'He's a rum one, that Horatio. Not beyond a furtive fling in the stables, either.'

Elsie blushed at the mention of Illicit romance. 'You'll find out about it all one day, my girl,' added the cook. 'But for now, you just concentrate on keeping my pantry clean. That way, you'll be safe.'

The young woman wore a confused expression and shrugged her shoulders.

My head raced with possibilities as I excused myself from their company. The implications were too serious to ignore and needed to relay this information to HG post-haste.

I retraced my steps back towards the saloon, where she'd intended to interrogate the lady of the house.

Upon reaching my destination, however, Lady Cummings was not yet present—instead, HG sat alone amidst the greatest finery in furniture and decoration; deep in thought beside an extinguished hearth where only embers glowed dimly.

'Found something interesting?' HG asked without looking up as I approached.

I relayed Elsie's account regarding Horatio Cummings' presence near the pantry before dinner; including his mysterious pocketed item—a detail which seemed to snag HG's interest like a hook in cloth.

Her eyes met mine with an intensity that belied her calm exterior. It was clear we were both considering the same grim possibility—that Horatio could tamper with his father's celebratory confection.

'We need to confront the young pup,' HG stated firmly. After a moment of contemplation, she rose from her chair with a purposeful grace that commanded attention amidst the silence.

I concurred and followed as we made for Horatio's quarters where answers—and perhaps an admission of guilt awaited behind closed doors.

WITH HG'S words still ringing in my ears, we arrived at Horatio's private study. HG paused briefly, straightening her shoulders as if bracing herself, before rapping sharply upon the panelled door.

A muffled voice beckoned entry. I glanced at HG, who gave a curt nod, and turned the handle.

The room beyond was dim, curtains drawn tight against the inky night. A single lamp flickered atop a cluttered desk where Horatio sat, still clad in evening attire, though his jacket and cravat lay discarded.

He looked up as we entered, features twisting in displeasure. 'So nice to see you again...and so soon.' His voice dripped with arrogance befitting the entitled heir.

'We've a matter to discuss, Horatio,' HG replied, unfazed by his arrogance. 'Concerning your whereabouts prior to dinner.'

Horatio sneered. 'Interrogating me in my private chambers like some common criminal? I'll have you know—'

'We're aware you visited the pantry earlier,' I interjected firmly, my patience wearing thin. 'A maid witnessed you there with some unknown item concealed.'

His face paled, mouth opening, then closing like a fish gasping for air. Finally, he seemed to regain his composure, leaning back with feigned nonchalance.

'Merely fetching a treat. Nothing untoward. Not that it is any of your business.'

HG arched an eyebrow. 'Indeed? Then you won't object to allowing us to search your person and these premises.'

For a beat, Horatio looked as though he might protest. But then, with a casual shrug, he pushed away from the desk and spread his arms wide in mock surrender.

'By all means, satisfy your curiosity.'

Wasting no time, I began searching through drawers and cupboards as HG patted down Horatio's jacket. Papers, books, and sundry clutter spilled from sundry spaces. Nothing that raised alarm. Until...

'Here,' HG's voice prompted me to turn. She held up a small vial, half-filled with an innocuous white powder.

Horatio paled again, his earlier bravado crumbling.

'And what might this be?' HG cocked her head quizzically.

He swallowed hard, gaze darting between us and the vial clutched in HG's fingers. At last, with a resigned sigh, he sank back into his chair and buried his face in his hands.

'Very well, you've found me out,' he mumbled, voice muffled. 'It's...oh, what will father say? It's...Epsom salts.' Horatio uncovered his eyes and laughed uncontrollably, pointing at HG and me to mock us. 'Do you really think that if I'd poisoned anyone, I'd still have the stuff on or around me? I required the salts to ease my discomfiture, for I am afflicted by aerophagia this day.' Horatio broke out into a second round of raucous laughter, such that tears flowed from his reddened eyes.

Since I had not come across the condition, I offered my sincere hope for a rapid recovery, only to be cut off by my mentor.

'That will do, dear boy. Nothing more than wind afflicts the reprobate yonder, for that is what his verbal gymnastics signifies.'

HG's clarification made Horatio laugh all the more, while I experienced a sudden flushing of the cheeks. The Dowager refused to be antagonised by the fellow's juvenile jest and made her thoughts known to the gentleman. 'You may laugh, but remember, a man breathed his last tonight, yet your reaction is to act like a King's fool. Be aware that Inspector Whipple shall hear of this. Mark my words, well. His Majesty's constabulary has but begun its initial inquiry into your person. Your behaviour has ensured the closest of attention by Whipple of the Yard. Do not underestimate his deductive powers, or tenacity to uncover the truth.'

As we offered our unwilling host a good evening and turned toward the door, Horatio said something rather odd.

'I look forward to another talk with that Whipple chap,' he said, wearing a smirk. 'Perhaps you might caution him that just as his ill-fitting attire does not bode well in high society, so too might any attempt to implicate me in the events of the day. Oh, and close the door with caution. It has a habit of biting back. A family trait, you might say.'

AS WE STEPPED out of Horatio's room, HG's face was a storm of indignation. She turned to me, her eyes flashing with barely contained fury.

'The audacity of that young man! To speak of Inspector Whipple in such a manner.'

I nodded, my mind racing.

HG's brow furrowed. 'Indeed, Rex. It's as if he's daring us to pursue this investigation further. But why? What could he possibly gain from such bravado?'

I suggested that his intention was to intimidate us, or maybe he held information we were yet to discover.

'Either way, we must tread carefully,' HG mused. 'We need to speak with Arthur immediately. His perspective on Horatio's behaviour could prove invaluable.'

As we made our way down the curved corridor in search of a staff member to help us locate Inspector Whipple, we almost collided with Lady Eleanor. She appeared visibly shaken, though she attempted to mask her distress with a forced smile.

'Oh! I apologise,' she stammered, smoothing her dress nervously.

HG's eyes narrowed, sensing the lady's unease. 'My dear Eleanor, are you quite alright?'

'Yes, yes, of course,' Lady Eleanor replied, her voice wavering. 'Just a touch overwhelmed by the evening's events. I'm sure you understand.'

HG nodded sympathetically. 'Now, my dear, why don't we sit down together and have a chat?'

The pair settled in the cosy sitting room. Pouring her friend a glass of sherry, HG handed it to the melancholy lady. They sat in silence, the room's floral patterns casting a soothing spell.

Gradually, HG coaxed Lady Eleanor into conversation. She confided her worry about the upcoming weekend—the King's invitation weighed heavily on her mind. She cited the death of her husband's accountant, fearing that the family's reputation would suffer irreparably. But HG, ever pragmatic, assured her that the King and Queen would not abandon them. Sandringham awaited, and they should proceed as planned.

The Dowager promised to speak to Whipple, ensuring he remained informed. She suggested accompanying them to Norfolk might be beneficial. After all, she added, it was high time she visited her estate there.

Relief washed over Lady Eleanor. HG's intervention on their behalf was a beacon of hope, and the prospect of her presence nearby during their stay brought comfort.

'Rex, be a dear and find Inspector Whipple for me, will you?'

I understood the unspoken message to leave them to chat alone. As I set off to find Inspector Whipple, I wondered about the conversation unfolding between HG and Lady Eleanor. The tension in our host's demeanour had been palpable, and I knew HG would act as a kind sounding board.

I made my way through the winding corridors, keeping an eye out for the inspector's distinctive silhouette. As I searched, my mind wandered back to the sitting room. I could almost hear the silence that might have fallen between them, heavy with unspoken worries. HG will have waited patiently, allowing Lady Eleanor the time she needed to gather her thoughts.

As I continued my search for Whipple, I theorised what might trouble Lady Eleanor. Was it related to the evening's tragic events? Or perhaps something around harbouring a family secret that now took its toll.

With renewed focus, I quickened my pace, determined to complete my mission and return to unravel the mystery that seemed to grow more complex by the minute.

As I rounded another corner, my eyes glimpsed something out of place. There, tucked behind an ornate folding screen adorned with intricate Japanese garden scenes, was the unmistakable shape of Inspector Whipple. The black lacquer of the screen gleamed in the soft light, creating an almost comical contrast with Whipple's hunched form.

I approached quietly, curious about his odd behaviour. As I drew closer, I realised he was furtively sipping tea from a delicate bone china cup, clearly trying to conceal his actions.

'Inspector Whipple?' I called out, unable to suppress a hint of amusement in my voice.

The effect was instantaneous. Whipple jerked upright, his eyes wide with surprise. He let out a strangled cough and struggled to keep from spitting a mouthful of tea back into the cup. A few drops escaped, splattering onto his already rumpled shirt front.

'Heavens, lad!' he spluttered, hastily setting the cup down on a nearby side table. 'You nearly gave me a heart attack!'

I chuckled at his flustered state. 'Sorry, Inspector. I didn't mean to startle you. HG sent me.'

Whipple straightened his jacket, trying to regain his composure. 'Yes, well, I was just...inspecting this rather interesting screen. Fascinating craftsmanship, don't you think?'

I raised an eyebrow, glancing at the teacup. 'Indeed. And I suppose the tea was part of your investigation as well?'

Whipple's cheeks reddened. 'Ah, yes. Well, you see, I was feeling parched after all the questioning. The maid was kind enough to offer me a cup. Didn't want to refuse and appear rude, you understand?'

I nodded, deciding to spare him further embarrassment. 'Of course. Now, if you're quite finished with your…inspection, HG asked that I update you on our findings so far, and for you to brief me on anything you've discovered.'

We moved to a secluded alcove, away from prying eyes and ears. Whipple straightened his posture, all traces of his earlier embarrassment gone.

'What have you uncovered, lad?' he asked, his voice low.

I quickly recounted our encounter with Horatio, including the discovery of the Epsom salts and his peculiar behaviour. Whipple's brow furrowed as I spoke.

'Interesting,' he mused. 'The young man's arrogance could be a front, or he might genuinely believe he's above suspicion. Either way, we'll need to keep a close eye on him.'

'And what about you, Inspector? Any luck with the staff?'

Whipple sighed, rubbing his chin wearily. 'Not much, I'm afraid. They're a tight-lipped bunch. However, I learned that Sir Herbert had an intense discussion with Mr Farrier just yesterday. Something about discrepancies in the company's accounts.'

My eyes widened at this new information and suggested it might be significant to our investigation and that we should inform HG.'

'Agreed,' Whipple nodded. 'Where is she?'

'She was speaking with Lady Eleanor when I left to find you,' I replied. 'She seemed quite distressed about something. HG wanted to talk to her privately. I imagine they should have finished by now.' I glanced at my pocket watch. 'We should find her and compare notes. I'm sure she'll want to hear about Sir Herbert's discussion with Mr Farrier.'

Whipple nodded. 'Lead the way, young man. The sooner we pool our information, the closer we'll be to unravelling this mystery.'

As we set off to find HG, I experienced a surge of excitement. Despite the gravity of the situation, the thrill of piecing together clues, and uncovering secrets was undeniable. I only hoped that HG's conversation with Lady Eleanor had been equally fruitful.

I ACCOMPANIED HG as we strolled through the expansive grounds of Hilltop. The cool evening air nipped at our cheeks, a stark contrast to the heated discussions we'd been having inside. The lush landscaping, with its manicured hedges and vibrant flowerbeds, seemed almost obscene in its beauty, given the day's grim events.

HG broke the silence first. 'I've had a most illuminating chat with Lady Eleanor,' she said, her voice low. 'It seems Sir Herbert's behaviour has been rather out of character lately.'

Whipple's bushy eyebrows shot up. 'How so, HG?'

'According to Lady Eleanor, her husband had been uncharacteristically short with her yesterday,' the Dowager explained. 'She found it quite distressing, as he's usually a rather doting husband.'

I postulated that there might be a link to the discussion he had with Mr Farrier.

HG's eyes widened. 'Do tell, Rex.'

As I opened my mouth to explain, Whipple suddenly let out a strangled noise. We turned to see him staring aghast at an enormous marble sculpture of a nude figure reclining on a chaise longue.

'Heavens!' he exclaimed. 'That's…that's positively indecent! And in a garden, no less!'

HG chuckled. 'Come now, Arthur. It's a rather fine example of classical sculpture. Though I must admit, the placement is a tad ostentatious.'

Whipple harrumphed, shaking his head. 'If you ask me, it's a waste of expensive stone. Could've made a nice fountain instead.'

'Shall we continue with our discussion, gentlemen?' HG prompted, eager to continue with business.

I nodded, eager to share Sir Herbert and Mr Farrier's exchange the previous day. The housekeeper had overheard them arguing about financial matters, though she couldn't provide specifics.'

HG's eyes narrowed. 'Interesting. A connection to Sir Herbert's recent mood swing, perhaps?'

Whipple scratched his chin. 'It's possible. But why would someone want to poison Sir Herbert over a financial dispute?'

'Perhaps it wasn't about money at all,' HG mused. 'We mustn't jump to conclusions.'

We continued our stroll, discussing various theories. The moonlight cast long shadows across the lawn, giving the entire scene an eerie quality.

After exhausting our theories, HG turned to Whipple.

'Arthur, do you have any reason to hold the house guests any longer?'

Whipple shrugged his shoulders. 'It's unlikely we'll gain anything by prolonging their detention. The staff will probably remain silent while that lot are present, who, are sticking together like my sister's toffee-pudding on the top of my mouth,' Whipple concluded with a grimace.

HG's lips twitched in amusement. 'Arthur, your descriptive prose never ceases to impress.' She then straightened, her expression turning serious. 'Very well. Then we go to Norfolk. Prepare for an early start in the morning, gentlemen.'

Chapter Seven

THE WINDING ROAD

A LATE-NIGHT FLURRY of activity followed HG's announcement that we were to make for Norfolk the following morning. Inspector Whipple advised Sir Herbert's guests they could leave Hilltop, on the strict understanding they remained available for a follow-up interview. Should he determine it necessary?

Later, when relaying his actions to HG, Whipple mentioned that one or two amongst their number complained at the extended time they'd had to remain at Hilltop. It seemed one had a pressing engagement in Paris to attend a Monsieur Paul Poiret for a dress fitting, while another insisted his presence in Monte Carlo required a flight from Croydon Airport.

HG's response was sharp and to the point. 'I know for a fact that Paul Poiret is in London as we speak, so whatever the young lady's need to visit La ville lumiere is, it is not to purchase an oriental-inspired dress. As for Freddy Fenchurch-White, all that awaits him in Monte Carlo is the roulette table, at which he will, as usual, lose heavily.'

A Spiffing Murder

I smiled as Inspector Whipple's brow furrowed at HG's use of French. His mouth opened, ready to ask the inevitable question, but HG, ever perceptive, beat him to it.

'La ville lumiere, Arthur,' she said, her eyes twinkling with amusement, 'is French for "The city of light."'

Whipple's cheeks flushed a shade of crimson that rivalled the plush curtains adorning the library windows. 'Ah, yes, of course,' he mumbled, straightening his tie. 'I knew that. Just...testing you, Your Grace.'

HG's lips curving into a smile. 'Indeed, Inspector. Your dedication to probing our linguistic prowess is commendable.'

I bit my lip to stifle a chuckle. Poor Whipple looked like he wanted the floor to swallow him whole.

'Now,' HG continued, smoothly changing the subject, 'About our trip to Norfolk...'

As HG outlined her plans for our excursion, Inspector Whipple suddenly let out a strangled cough. It wasn't particularly convincing, and HG's eyes narrowed as she turned to face him.

'Are you alright, Arthur?' she asked, her voice dripping with barely concealed irritation. 'Do you require a lubricant for that throat of yours?'

Whipple's cheeks flushed again 'Well, you see, HG, I... er... I'll need to obtain permission from my superiors before I can accompany you to Norfolk. Jurisdiction and all that.'

I held my breath, waiting for HG's response. To my surprise, her expression softened into a matronly smile.

'Oh, Arthur,' she said, her tone reminiscent of a schoolteacher addressing a distracted pupil. 'Do not fret over such trifling details. I will speak to Sir William Horwood, the Commissioner of Police of the Metropolis, by telephone early tomorrow morning. He will give you his blessing for our little jaunt. William is such a charming man, but then he comes from excellent stock.'

My jaw dropped. I knew HG had connections, but direct access to Sir William. I glanced at Whipple, curious to see his reaction.

The poor man looked as if lightning had struck him. His eyes widened. Slowly, almost mechanically, he reached into his jacket pocket and retrieved an Everton Mint. With deliberate movement, he unwrapped the boiled sweet and popped it into his mouth, his gaze fixed straight ahead.

'Do suck, or crunch that thing properly, there's a splendid fellow,' said HG in a muted tone. 'An Englishman always eats with his embouchure closed. And before you ask, loosely translated from the French word of the same spelling, it means "opening," as in one's mouth.'

I contributed my recollection that musicians who play the trumpet, clarinet, and the like used the term.

'Indeed, they do, Rex. I see your language studies are progressing in line with my expectations.'

I caught my detective friend's eyes narrow as he peered at me will ill-disguised disdain, which I pretended not to see. However, HG soon brought our conference back to the business of the day.

'Before we retire for the night, let us review where we are, so that we arrive in Norfolk, fresh, and ready to launch the next phase of our investigation.'

I settled into a comfortable armchair, ready to listen as HG began. Her keen eyes swept over Whipple and me, ensuring we were attentive.

'Let us begin with the obvious,' HG said, her voice crisp. 'Mr Farrier's untimely demise at Sir Herbert's celebration. The poison in the cake, intended for our host, raises several questions. Who had access to the kitchen? And why target Sir Herbert?'

I nodded, recalling the chaos that had ensued after Mr Farrier's collapse.

'Then we have the peculiar behaviour of Horatio Cummings,' HG continued. 'His arrogance and desire for his father's demise are troubling. The substance the fellow contends he procured from the kitchen requires further investigation. Perhaps they're connected to the poisoning?'

Whipple shifted uncomfortably in his seat, still nursing his wounded pride from earlier.

'We mustn't overlook Sir Herbert himself,' HG mused. 'His intense discussion with Mr Farrier the day before his death suggests tension. What was the nature of their disagreement? And Lady Eleanor's observation about her husband's unusual behaviour - that warrants closer examination.'

I leaned forward, intrigued by HG's methodical approach.

'Mrs Smith's passing comment about Horatio's tryst in the stables with a mysterious young lady is another thread we must unravel,' she said, tapping her fingers thoughtfully on the armrest of her chair. 'It may seem unrelated, but in my experience, such secrets often have a way of connecting to larger issues.'

HG paused, her gaze distant. 'What troubles me most is what we might have overlooked. Have we been too focused on the obvious suspects? Is there a detail we've missed, a clue hidden in plain sight?'

She turned to us, her eyes sharp. 'Rex, Arthur, I want you both to consider this carefully. Is there anything, no matter how insignificant it may seem, that struck you as odd or out-of-place today?'

Whipple continued to shuffle in his chair, which prompted my mentor's ire. 'Out with it, Arthur. We have known each other long enough not to dilly-dally when something needs to be said?'

Scotland Yard's finest blinked fast enough to fan the most humid of rooms into a therapeutic spa. 'Not so much have we missed, but may have overlooked in our eagerness to pursue the case.'

As he finished speaking, a telephone rang, which took a measure of locating in the spacious room, filled with books, magazines, and the furnishings associated with fine living.

'Ah,' stated HG. 'That will be for you Arthur, and given your excellent recent oration, I should say, timely.'

On this occasion, both the inspector and I shared a degree of confusion. The telephone continued to ring, waiting patiently to be answered. At last, Arthur overcame his flummoxed gate and put the receiver to his ear, his brow creased in confusion. The voice on the other end was faint, but I could just make out the tinny sound asking, 'Am I speaking to Detective Inspector Whipple of Scotland Yard?'

Whipple's frown deepened. 'Yes, this is he. Who, may I ask, is calling?'

There was a pause, and I saw Whipple's eyes widen.

'Detective Sergeant Albert Muddleford, you say?' Whipple repeated, his voice tinged with surprise. 'Assigned to the case? I…I see.'

I glanced at HG, who was watching the exchange with a knowing smile playing at the corners of her mouth. Whipple listened intently, occasionally nodding despite the caller not being able to see him.

'Yes, yes, I understand,' Whipple said, his voice growing more bewildered by the second. 'We need to meet before we leave for Norfolk. But how did you...I mean, when were you...?'

As the reality of the situation sank in, Whipple's expression transformed. His eyes drifted to HG's position, and a half-smile crept across his face, his mouth hanging open in a mixture of amusement and disbelief.

HG's eyes twinkled with mischief as she watched Whipple's reaction. Feeling a bit lost, I wondered what exactly was transpiring and how HG had orchestrated this turn of events.

The Dowager's smile widened as evidence of her genuine fondness for a man she knew to be of the sharpest intellect on police matters, yet charmingly ill-at-ease when in the company of upper society, even after several years of HG's guidance and protection.

'You see, Arthur. All is well and you can now relax knowing that a fellow officer, working to your orders, will be present at Hilltop while we are in Norfolk.'

Whipple declined to answer. Instead, he stood, made his way to a lead-crystal shaped like a pyramid, cut in a most stylish pattern, and poured three whiskies.

'Ah, Royal Strathythan.' purred HG as she savoured her first sip of the smooth whisky. 'This was a favourite of the late queen from the royal family's visits to Balmoral. Goodness knows how Sir Herbert got his hands on the stuff. Nevertheless, we are the beneficiaries, are we not?'

No answer came forth as we first admired the nectar's fine colour, then smoky aroma, and finally...finally, the heather and butterscotch taste notes of the aged blend.

WERE it not for the unfortunate events of the previous evening, taking an early breakfast with the early morning giving freely of its warming rays, one might describe the scene as idyllic.

That was not the case as a refreshed HG, and grumpy Whipple joined me for kedgeree and kidneys. The detective, more to himself than our party, muttered that he preferred a full fry-up, and anyway, he hated early starts.

I thought for a moment that HG might let the matter rest. That was not to be. 'Arthur,' she began. 'Is it not the early bird that catches the worm?'

From the look Whipple gave the food on offer, one might have thought he took my mentor's use of a metaphor for fact, as he poked around kedgeree with a silver fork as if looking for the wriggling invertebrates.

'No, no. This simply will not do.' HG intoned. 'Sit here, next to me and I shall request the finest pork sausages and scrambled eggs be presented to you. Will that, at least, improve your mood?'

'And tomato ketchup?' Whipple added, pushing his luck.

The Dowager raised her right eyebrow in the manner normally reserved for errant individuals who'd transgressed her sense of civility. On this occasion, the detective found himself lucky to be met only with a deep sigh as HG summoned a footman who still held the silver lid that had previously covered the kedgeree.

Whipple's order placed; we got down to the business of our relocation to Norfolk. 'Remind me again why it's so important we depart for East Anglia?' asked Whipple in a croaky voice that matched his jowly expression.

He'd caught HG mid-point between plate and mouth with a heaped fork of her breakfast, which she proceeded to lower onto her bone china plate with a delicacy that belayed her darkening mood. HG's patience wore thin, her fingers tapping a gentle rhythm on the pristine tablecloth. She fixed Whipple with a look that could have curdled milk.

'My dear Arthur, I fear your faculties are not quite at their sharpest this morning. Did you not pay attention to our discussion last night?'

Whipple let out a strangled cough, his cheeks flushing a deep crimson. 'I...well, you see...'

HG cut him off with a wave of her hand. 'No matter. I shall enlighten you once more. Our journey to Norfolk serves two purposes. First, I am to assist our gracious hosts in their preparations for afternoon tea with Their Majesties at Sandringham House on Sunday.'

Whipple's eyes widened, and I could almost see the cogs turning in his head as he processed this information.

'Second,' HG continued, her voice taking on a more serious tone, 'We shall visit Sir Herbert's factory. I believe it may hold vital clues to Mr Farrier's untimely demise.'

I asked if my mentor suspected someone at the factory might be involved.

She turned to me, a glimmer of approval in her eyes. 'Excellent question, Rex. While I cannot say for certain, it's imperative we leave no stone unturned in our investigation.'

Whipple, now recovered from his earlier embarrassment, chimed in. 'But surely, if there were any suspects at the factory, they would have been present at the party?'

HG smiled enigmatically. 'Not necessarily, Arthur. Remember, we're dealing with a case that may have roots deeper than we initially suspected. The factory might provide the missing piece of this rather perplexing puzzle.'

As I pondered HG's words, a footman appeared with Whipple's requested breakfast. The detective's mood visibly improved as he tucked into his sausages and eggs. I noticed

HG shudder as our mutual friend took a curved silver serving spoon full of tomato ketchup from its ornate boat.

Oblivious to our consternation, Whipple was clearly in a state of near ecstasy, rarely moving his gaze from the plate, nor allowing any morsel of sausage to escape his eagle eye.

A footman entered the cavernous dining room, his polished shoes clicking against the oak floor. He cleared his throat, drawing our attention away from the breakfast table.

'Your Grace,' he announced with a slight bow. 'May I present Detective Sergeant Albert Muddleford?'

A tall, lean man with sharp features and blonde hair stepped into view. A serious expression looked as if it were etched into his face, as if he'd forgotten how to smile years ago.

Whipple scowled, his fork hovering midway between his plate and mouth. The interruption to his beloved breakfast clearly didn't sit well.

HG, ever the gracious host, rose to greet the newcomer. 'Detective Sergeant Muddleford, welcome. I trust your journey wasn't too taxing?'

Muddleford nodded stiffly. 'Thank you, Your Grace. The journey was uneventful.'

'Splendid,' HG replied. 'Have you eaten? We could certainly arrange for some breakfast if you'd like.'

I noticed Muddleford's gaze drift towards Whipple's plate, his eyes lingering on the golden scrambled eggs and plump sausages. A flicker of longing crossed his face, quickly masked by his professional demeanour.

Before Muddleford could respond, Whipple interjected, his voice gruff with irritation. 'Of course, the man has eaten. He's a professional, after all. I'm sure he's ready for his briefing.'

A flash of disappointment spread across Muddleford's

face. His shoulders slumped ever so slightly, and I caught the barest hint of a sigh.

HG gave Arthur a withering glance but knew not to be seen disagreeing with him in front of the subordinate officer.

'Come, Rex,' announced my mentor. 'The forces of law and order must conclude their business, so we shall leave them to it. Perhaps you might prepare the Rolls for our departure, while I thank our hosts for their hospitality and arrange to meet them prior to their audience with Their Majesties.'

Matters settled; HG bade Detective Muddleford a good day as I gave the poor man a last glance to see his eyes fixed on what remained of Whipple's breakfast. Many people underestimated our esteemed Scotland Yard colleague on first meeting the man. However, beneath his somewhat crumpled exterior lay one of the keenest investigative minds in the country, as many a felon had found out to their cost.

In due course, HG, and Arthur appeared from the front door of the impressive home of Sir Herbert. I had previously stowed our belongings in their assigned compartment and run the car up to its optimum running temperature.

'Let us proceed, Rex,' HG proclaimed, holding her arm out in front with a pointed finger in the manner of a scout often featured in American western pictures.

'It is now 8.42am precisely. I have told Graham to expect us at twelve noon, so onward, Rex. We must make haste.'

Graham, the long-standing butler at Thorpe Manor, was a stickler for time. Where I late in delivering his mistress on time, I knew his frosty air awaited. This was not something those of a nervous disposition sought. Although not intimidated by his manner myself, I undertook to meet

HG's deadline. That way I would enjoy a hot evening meal, since the butler took a particular pleasure in sabotaging one's food if crossed.

Our journey from Henley, then onward to Cambridge, and finally Norfolk totalled ninety-three miles, yet held no hardship for the vehicle, nor its passengers, as I guided the almost silent saloon from Hilltop onto the open road and pressed my foot on the accelerator. Thorpe Manor and a new phase of our investigation awaited.

As the towering spire of Ely Cathedral came into view, HG proposed we stop for a light brunch, courtesy of Sir Herbert's cook having furnished us with a wicker basket filled to the brim with edible delights.

Once parked in a delightful spot of open pasture, I set about laying out a large tartan blanket reserved for such occasions, carried the heavy basket over to our chosen spot and liberated its scrumptious contents.

There were dainty cucumber sandwiches with the crusts cut off, slices of cold roast chicken, and wedges of Stilton cheese wrapped in wax paper. A jar of homemade strawberry jam nestled next to freshly baked scones, while a tin of butter biscuits peeked out from beneath a crisp white napkin.

HG took charge, directing me to lay out the food on the blanket with military precision. 'Rex, do place the sandwiches here, and the scones, just so. We mustn't forget the silverware. I believe you'll find it wrapped in the linen at the bottom of the basket.'

I arranged everything to HG's exacting standards, then noticed Whipple eyeing the spread with suspicion. He poked at a neatly wrapped package, his brow deepening.

'I'm afraid you won't find a sausage in there, Arthur,' HG said, with a hint of amusement in her voice. 'You'll have to make do with a smoked salmon sandwich. I assure you, they're quite delicious.'

His expression brightened considerably when I produced a half-bottle of champagne from the depths of the basket. 'Well, well,' he said, rubbing his hands together. 'Perhaps this picnic isn't such a bad idea after all.'

'Indeed,' HG replied, her eyes twinkling. 'Though I'm afraid you'll have to settle for lemonade, Rex. We can't have our driver imbibing, can we?'

I nodded, secretly relieved. The thought of navigating Norfolk's winding roads with even a drop of champagne in my system was less than appealing.

As we finished our repast, the conversation turned to what might await us in Norfolk. HG spoke of her suspicions regarding Sir Herbert's factory, while Whipple pondered aloud about the potential leads, we might uncover.

'What do you think, Rex?' HG asked, turning to me. 'Any theories about what we might find?'

Chapter Eight

A LATE SUPPER

I GUIDED the car up the long, winding driveway of Thorpe Manor, the gravel crunching beneath our tyres. The grand Jacobean facade loomed before us, its weathered stone a testament to centuries of history. As we approached, I glanced at the dashboard clock and winced. Fifteen minutes late, because of an unexpected detour through Swaffham.

HG waved a dismissive hand. 'No matter, Rex. We're here now.'

As I helped HG from the car, a heavy oak door to the noble house swung open. Graham, the butler, stood ramrod straight in the entrance, his face a mask of disapproval. His eyes flicked to his pocket watch, then back to us.

'Your Grace,' he intoned, his voice as crisp as his starched collar. 'You are fifteen minutes behind schedule.'

HG swept past him, unfazed. 'Indeed we are, Graham. How very observant of you.'

I caught Whipple's eye as we followed her into the grand entrance hall. The inspector looked decidedly uncomfortable, tugging at his collar as if it had suddenly grown too tight.

Graham's disapproving gaze swept over us as we entered. 'I'm afraid lunch has been somewhat…compromised by your timekeeping,' he said, each word dripping with barely concealed disdain.

'Oh, come now, Graham,' HG said, removing her gloves. 'Surely a quarter of an hour hasn't rendered the food inedible?'

The butler's lips thinned into a curt line. 'Of course not, Your Grace. However, the souffle has fallen, and the consomme has cooled to a less-than-ideal temperature.'

I felt the chill emanating from Graham as he turned his attention to me. 'I trust you'll be more punctual in the future, Master Rex?'

'Yes, of course,' I mumbled, feeling every bit the chastised schoolboy. 'It won't happen again.'

I followed HG and Inspector Whipple into the Great Hall, my eyes immediately drawn to the magnificent fireplace that dominated the far wall. The room breathed history, its oak-panelled walls adorned with portraits of stern-faced ancestors and intricate tapestries.

'Quite the sight, isn't it?' HG remarked, noticing my wide-eyed gaze.

'It's incredible,' I breathed, taking in the vaulted ceiling with its ornate Tudor plasterwork.

As we approached the fireplace, I spotted an odd protrusion above the mantelpiece. Nestled in the stone, partially obscured by soot and age, was a rusted ball of metal.

'Ah, you've noticed our little souvenir,' HG said, following my gaze. 'A remnant from a rather tumultuous period in Thorpe Manor's history.'

Inspector Whipple squinted at the object. 'Is that what I think it is?'

HG nodded. 'Indeed. During the English Civil War, Thorpe Manor found itself under siege by Thomas Cromwell's forces. That cannonball crashed through the window opposite and embedded itself in the wall. We've kept it there as a reminder of the Manor's resilience, and our loyalty to the Crown.'

I ran my fingers over the rough stone beneath the cannonball. 'It's hard to imagine this place as a battlefield.'

'Oh, but it was,' HG continued. 'The Drakeford's of that time were staunch royalists. They held out for weeks, defending the Manor against Cromwell's men. The siege left its mark in more ways than one. If you look closely at the east wing, you can still see where they hastily repaired the damage after the war.'

As I listened to HG's account, I had a sense of awe at the history surrounding us. Thorpe Manor had stood through centuries of turmoil, witnessing the ebb and flow of England's fortunes. And now, here we were, standing in the same hall where loyalists had once fought to defend their home and beliefs.

As we stood there, marvelling at the history surrounding us, Graham materialised in the doorway. His sudden appearance startled me, and I wondered if he'd been eavesdropping on our conversation.

'Luncheon is served,' he announced, his voice echoing through the cavernous hall. Without waiting for a response, he turned on his heel and strode away, his footsteps fading as he disappeared down the dark panelled corridor.

The three of us exchanged glances with a mixture of amusement and trepidation on our faces. A wry smile played at the corners of HG's mouth.

'We'd better behave ourselves for the remainder of the day,' she said, her voice low, 'Or he'll make all our lives a misery.'

I nodded, suppressing a chuckle. Even Inspector Whipple, who'd been looking increasingly uncomfortable since our arrival, managed a small smile.

'Right then,' HG continued, straightening her already impeccable posture. 'Shall we brave the dining room?'

The space was intimate, almost claustrophobic, with dark wood panelling that absorbed what little light filtered through the heavy curtains. The room felt oddly out of place, as if it belonged to a different era entirely.

A massive Tudor fireplace dominated one wall, its ornate stonework telling tales of centuries past. The flames within cast flickering shadows across the space, lending an eerie atmosphere to our luncheon.

Graham stood at attention near the entrance door, his presence commanding the room without uttering a word. With the slightest inclination of his head, footmen sprang into action, gliding silently around the table. They served and removed dishes from a dark oak buffet table with military precision, their movements choreographed for the task at hand.

I glanced at Inspector Whipple, seated across from me. He eyed each dish with suspicion, pushing the food around his plate more than eating it. I recalled a conversation we'd had earlier, where he'd mentioned his sister, with whom he'd lived since the death of his beloved wife. He revered her skills as a cook - particularly her eel and mashed potato; a dish he looked forward to weekly.

As I watched him pick at his food, I concluded he was wishing for his sister's simpler fare instead of the elaborate spread before us. The Inspector's discomfort became palpable, a stark contrast to HG's ease and Graham's rigid efficiency.

AS THINGS TURNED OUT, we were destined not to complete our meal, which was even more galling since the menu, although written in French, gave a clue to the delight that awaited us; Pots de crème au chocolat. However, a sudden interruption of a maid whispering something into the butler's ear resulted in the delicious creation remaining on the dark mahogany servery.

'What occurs?' inquired HG. 'Is the kitchen on fire again, or had the Mrs Palmer handed in her notice… again?'

I observed Graham dismissing the maid with a curt nod and turned to address us. His face remained as impassive as ever. Not a single muscle twitched as he delivered his news.

'Your Grace, I regret to inform you we've received an urgent call from Roxby Hall.'

HG raised an eyebrow. 'Indeed? And pray tell, what is the nature of this emergency?'

Graham's voice remained as flat as a pancake. 'Your Grace, Lord Billington, has been attacked by persons unknown.'

I noted the slight widening of her eyes. Inspector Whipple, who had been awkwardly fiddling with his napkin, suddenly sat bolt upright.

The butler continued, 'It seems the household knew Detective Inspector Whipple had accompanied you to Norfolk, Your Grace. Lord Billington expressed a preference for Scotland Yard's involvement rather than the local constabulary.'

HG's lips twitched. 'How very like His Lordship.'

Whipple cleared his throat. 'I'm not even supposed to be here officially.'

'Come now, Inspector,' HG said, a glint in her eye. 'Surely you're not one to shy away from a bit of irregular business?'

I grinned. This was turning out to be far more exciting than I'd expected when we set out for East Anglia.

HG's brow furrowed, her mind clearly racing. 'How curious,' she mused, tapping her fingers on the table. 'Billington beating us back to Norfolk from Hilltop? Curious indeed.'

I ventured perhaps it was an urgent matter concerning his estate.

HG snorted. 'Oh, Rex, you sweet summer child. Billington couldn't give a flying fig about his estate, or his staff for that matter.'

Her words caught me off guard. 'Really? But surely as a lord—.'

'As a lord,' she interrupted, 'His only interests are money and his position in society. Just like his father before him.'

Inspector Whipple leaned forward, intrigued. 'You knew his father, Your Grace?'

HG's eyes twinkled with mischief. 'Knew him? Dear Arthur, everyone knew the previous Lord Billington. He was an utter rake in his day.'

'A rake?' I asked, unfamiliar with the term.

'A scoundrel, a cad, a reprobate,' HG clarified, waving her hand dismissively. 'He lived for nothing but pleasure and scandal. That is until gout finally caught up with him.'

Whipple raised an eyebrow. 'Gout?'

'Indeed,' HG nodded. 'Brought on by an insatiable

predilection for expensive port and Camembert. A most undignified end for a man of his standing.'

I chuckled at the image, before suggesting that I'd not thought Gout to be a life-threatening complaint.

'You are correct,' she replied. 'However, when an attack causes one to lose one's balance and poleax oneself on a brass fire-hearth, then it becomes terminal.' HG gave a girlish giggle, which set us all off.

Eventually our juvenile outburst receded, and Whipple reminded us of the serious business at hand. 'And now his son has been attacked? Do you think there's a connection to our investigation?'

WITHIN THIRTY MINUTES of leaving a bright and open landscaped Thorpe Manor, we arrived at to Lord Billington's abode. The Gothic Revivalist structure took on an austere countenance as its harsh red brick facade sat uneasily against a backdrop of tall Cyprus trees and large ferns taking advantage of the dark, dank surroundings.

'Heavens,' HG muttered, her eyes narrowing as she surveyed the building. 'It looks like one of those ghastly churches one sees springing up in urban areas. The Billington's never had a sense of style, only how to spend other people's money on architectural novelties.'

The house was a hodgepodge of styles, with pointed arches, ornate stonework, and grotesque gargoyles peering down from every elevation. It was as if the builder had taken every Gothic trope and thrown them together without rhyme or reason.

As we approached the imposing front door, I noticed the intricate iron knocker fashioned in the shape of a snarling lion's head. The beast's eyes seemed to follow us, sending an involuntary shiver down my spine.

'Well, Rex,' HG said, her voice tinged with amusement, 'Shall we face the lion in his den?'

Before I could respond, the door creaked open, revealing a tall, thin butler; Perkins by name, who looked as if he'd stepped out of a penny dreadful. His gaunt face and sunken eyes gave him an almost cadaverous appearance.

'The Dowager Duchess of Drakeford and party, I presume?' he intoned, his voice as dry as autumn leaves. 'Lord Billington is expecting you.'

As we stepped into the dimly lit entrance hall, we entered a world far removed from the bright interior of Thorpe Manor. The air was heavy with the scent of something I couldn't quite place – a musty, almost medicinal odour that seemed to seep from the very walls.

'Look here,' Whipple intoned to the arcane butler. 'What time did his lordship arrive yesterday evening?'

'Arrive,' replied the testy fellow, which much irritated Arthur.

'Is it not a simple enough question?'

Unphased by Scotland Yard's finest detective's retort, the butler retrieved his fob watch with an exaggerated gesture and flipped open its silver lid to reveal a stylish clock-face.

'Lord Billington returned at 10.17 pm,' came the imperious reply, without the man consulting his timepiece at all.

Whipple's eyes narrowed.

'A somewhat precise recollection?'

'It is my job.'

I noted the butler's calculated disregard of Arthur's official police designation. This caused the inspector's eyes to narrow further, such that I considered he might close them altogether if he persisted. It was at that point HG intervened, her tone one of impatience.

'Be that as it may, Perkins. You will now tell us precisely the events that led up to you calling me at Thorpe Manor.'

This time, Perkins behaved himself and gave HG the respect her position demanded.

'Certainly, Your Grace,' said the butler in a flat tone and precise bow of his head. 'His Lordship, tired from the long journey, retired for the night after a light supper.'

'And his spirits?' Interjected Whipple.

Perkins looked Whipple up and down before responding. 'It is not within my purview to offer an opinion on such matters.'

Arthur rose to the occasion. 'Would you rather we discuss the matter down at the local police station?'

'Bravo,' whispered HG, giving Whipple an affectionate smile.

Perkins' body language revealed his failure to intimidate the indomitable detective. 'Very well,' he said, his tone clipped. 'If you must know, his lordship appeared quite agitated upon his return last night. He paced about the drawing room for some time, muttering to himself.'

I watched HG, who gave a barely perceptible nod for Perkins to continue.

'Eventually, he expressed his dismay over the dreadful matter at Hilltop House. The news of Mr. Farrier's tragic demise upset him deeply.'

Whipple shifted his weight. 'Is that so? Lord Billington was close with the deceased, then?'

Perkins' expression remained impassive. 'No, but his lordship is a man of great compassion and was troubled by such an untimely death.'

'I see,' HG said, her tone neutral. 'Most commendable.

Did his lordship mention anything else regarding the events at Hilltop?'

For a moment, Perkins hesitated, his eyes flickering. 'He remarked on the…unsavoury nature of some guests in attendance. Individuals he felt unworthy of the invitation to attend.'

Whipple growled with disapproval, but HG glanced at him as a signal to stay his hand.

'Thank you, Perkins,' she said. 'Now, will you please escort us to your employer?'

'Momentarily, Your Grace. The doctor is with him at present. He asked that I show you into the drawing room until his consultation has ended. I am assured the delay will be but a few minutes.'

Without waiting for an answer, the immaculately dressed butler strode purposefully toward a pair of impressive mahogany doors, furnished with ornate brass fittings polished to within an inch of their life. The opened doors allowed a peek into a most handsome room, furnished and decorated in the regency style.

As we each selected a comfortable chair, Perkins offered a glass of sherry. HG and I accepted. Arthur sniffed the air in disdain.

'Whisky?'

Perkins twitched his nose as if a bee had inserted itself into his sinus cavity. While giving a pronounced single blink, the butler withdrew a small key from the fob pocket of his waistcoat, then sought out a mahogany framed cradle, which sat upon the drinks table. Carefully inserting the key enabled the man to release a wood frame, granting access to two lead-crystal decanters. Perkins poured a meagre measure into a matching glass and handed it to a smiling Whipple with indifference.

As the minutes tumbled by, my eyes scanned the glorious decoration. One thing caught my attention. In a corner of the wonderfully proportioned room stood an elegant display cabinet in the French style popular in the eighteenth-century.

Inside the expansive cabinet stood an assortment of what I took to be automatons; that is, items to fascinate the observer with their engineering ingenuity for movement. Examples included several birds, a miniature fairground carousel, and a ballet dancer on point.

'Are they not delightful?' advanced HG as she joined me, gazing upon the fine display. 'For all his faults, Lord Billington is a recognised expert in mechanical marvels. Do you know, each summer he puts on a garden party for his tenants? He spares no expense to ensure they enjoy the day and often displays a selection of his gadgetry.'

HG's comments forced me to review the harsh view I took of the fellow after his display of ill-temperedness with his chauffeur at Hilltop.

AS WE ASCENDED the grand staircase, I marvelled at the opulent surroundings. Gilded frames housed stern-faced portraits of Billington ancestors, their eyes seeming to follow our every move. The carpet beneath our feet muffled our footsteps, creating an eerie silence broken only by the occasional creak of ancient floorboards.

Perkins led us down a long corridor with leather wall-covering dominating the space - A richly embossed panorama of hunting scenes. At last, we reached an oak door. The butler rapped his knuckles against it, his voice barely above a whisper.

'My Lord, your guests have arrived.'

A muffled groan emanated from within, followed by a weak, 'Enter.'

As Perkins pushed open the door, the pungent smell of brandy assaulted my nostrils. Lord Billington sat propped up in an enormous four-poster bed, his face ashen and his eyes bloodshot. He looked a far cry from the pompous aristocrat we'd encountered at Sir Herbert's reception.

'Heavens,' he croaked, squinting at us. 'Your Grace, I didn't expect to see you. I apologise for the inconvenience to you all.'

HG stepped forward, her voice gentle. 'My dear Billington, you asked that Detective Inspector Whipple attend you without delay. I thought it ill-mannered not to attend in person. As for my ward, our visit shall act as an instructional event in his pupillage.'

While the exchanges continued, a nurse gestured for her patient to lean forward so that she might fluff up his pillows.

'Doctor Foxton, whom you may have passed on your way up, insisted on round-the-clock nursing supervision. A bit of a to do over nothing, if you ask me. I'm sure it's simply a ruse to inflate his bill.'

I gazed at the nurse, who hesitated for a fraction of a second, but said nothing, before checking her patient's dressing, then leaving the room without engaging in conversation or giving eye contact.

Inspector Whipple cleared his throat. 'I'd like to hear what happened earlier this evening, Lord Billington. Please consider no detail too small. If we are to apprehend the culprit, or culprits responsible for attacking your person, your recollection may prove invaluable to the investigation.'

The patient, it seemed, could not bring himself to look

directly at Arthur, even though it was he who called for my friend's help. Instead, he concentrated his gaze on HG.

'It all happened so quickly. No sooner had I entered my room, than a hard blow to my head felled me.'

'And did you observe your assailant?' asked Arthur as I jotted the exchange down in my notebook, as per HG's instructions.

'I had not yet turned on the bedroom light; so, no. I did not observe the bounder. In fact, I remember nothing else until I heard Perkins' voice urging me to rouse myself. He called the doctor, who attended promptly.'

As I hastily made a note, I witnessed Whipple rubbing his chin, seemingly deep in thought. Eventually, he pressed our host.

'Several questions occur to me, having listened to your distressing account. First, from where did the criminal gain entry to the property? Has the butler mentioned anything to you on the subject?'

Lord Billington's response led to a revelation that puzzled us.

'No…no he hasn't. In fact, I believe the bounder to have climbed through my bedroom window. You see, I always lock the bedroom door when I leave it. Only I and Perkins hold a key.'

We glanced at the partly open sash-window, then at each other.

'And you have complete confidence in your man?' Ventured HG.

The injured party looked aghast. 'Perkins has been in the service of my family since 1878. He is the most trusted among my staff.'

Billington's facial features confirmed he thought the prospect was so fantastic to be unimaginable.

'Then we must consider some other member of staff with knowledge of the comings and goings of the house.'

Whipple strolled over to the window as he spoke. Pushing up the sash to its full extent, he bent forward (holding onto the window board for dear life to prevent him cascading from the opening) and looked down. Satisfied with his observation, Arthur returned his gaze to our host.

'This bedroom is on the second floor. Of necessity, any ladder used to scale the height will have been substantial. Given I see no evidence of such an object, I conclude whoever struck you must have had the means at their disposal to return the ladder whence it came. Pursuing this point further. I doubt the villain wished to hang around once they descended the temporary structure. It can be deduced, therefore, that the person who struck you had in their employ a person to steal the ladder away, or they were the same individual, in which case, they could be none other than a member of the grounds team.'

'Bravo,' responded HG with a brief round of applause, muffled by the silk gloves she always wore when in public. 'You are, indeed, the finest detective England offers, do you not agree, my Lord Billington?'

Our host appeared startled by HG's challenge, although I have to admit, he recovered his composure with aplomb.

'Indeed, Your Grace. Detective Inspector Whipple is first among his peers.'

Whipple, meanwhile, drew attention to his embarrassment by fidgeting in his jacket pocket. HG realised he had rummaged for an Everton mint.

'Not now, Arthur, not now.'

The cautionary direction caused our esteemed investigator to withdraw his hand, and instead fiddle with his collar as if nothing had happened. The humorous element in the brief exchange centred on observing Lord Billington's silent reaction, as though some secret sign had taken place, to which he did not have access.

'Then, there is the thorny question why the braggart entered the room in the first place? As you intimated, My Lord, entry could not have been gained via the door. The alternative? A risky ascent and escape by ladder, and the need to share at least part of their plan with another person in order to procure said ladder. That is, unless, as I ventured earlier, they were the same person. To my mind, such a risk would not be worth taking unless they meant to kill you. More likely, since you were expected to be absent from the house, their secret plan to violate your bedroom focused on retrieving something of great worth to that individual, or a personage they hoped to sell the item to. Is there such an item stored in this room, My Lord?'

Whipple's secret weapon, which I'd seen him to deploy to significant effect previously, was now to cease speaking, forcing his opponent to answer his enquiry.

Several seconds elapsed before our host offered a response, and only then after hesitating while gazing at a small landscape painting on the wall opposite his bed. Whipple picked up on this. He'd tutored me previously that when asking a person in Lord Billington's situation where an item of interest might be, or had been secreted, they inevitably looked toward the secret place.

The inspector turned to view the painting and seemed to discard any thought that it had been the object of the villain's intent. Instead, he gently unhooked the image from the wall to reveal a small enclave unhindered by any form of security.

'There, you have your answer, Inspector, and may I congratulate you on your detective skills?'

As usual, Arthur's nervous cough showed his unease at being complimented.

'Didn't I tell you the Detective Inspector is the best there is, Billington?'

The fellow didn't respond. Instead, his gaze settled on Whipple.

'You've no need to ask, Inspector, since I know what your question entails.'

Whipple moved not a muscle.

'A Chinese vase of immense value. Yuan Dynasty, made by the imperial potteries for an emperor almost 700 years ago.'

Whipple thought for a moment. 'And have you ever shown the item in public?'

'Never,' came Lord Billington's immediate reply.

'Then like it or not, My Lord. A member of your staff now holds that precious object. The question is, why?'

Chapter Nine

NORWICH BECKONS

AS ARRANGED by HG late the previous evening, breakfast appeared mercifully late on Sunday morning. The hurried journey from Hilltop, then startling events at Lord Billington's residence, meant sleep met with little resistance.

Over a delicious selection of delights from the breakfast buffet, HG, Arthur, and I mulled over the curious case of the missing Chinese vase.

I savoured the rich aroma of freshly brewed coffee as I settled into my seat at the breakfast table. HG and Inspector Whipple joined me, both looking rather weary from the previous night's events.

'Well, Rex,' HG began, spreading marmalade on her toast, 'What do you make of this vase business?'

I pondered the question for a moment, before asking why a member of staff might risk their position by pilfering such a valuable item.

Whipple nodded; his brow furrowed. 'A perceptive query. The vase would be nearly impossible to sell without raising suspicion. It's far too rare to turn up on the market without due fanfare.'

It seemed to me that Lord Billington appeared to be a decent employer and recalled Perkins' clear loyalty.

HG tapped her chin thoughtfully. 'Perhaps we're approaching this from the wrong angle. What if the theft wasn't about monetary gain at all?'

This supposed there might be another motive, I suggested.

'Indeed,' she replied. 'We might be overlooking something far more obvious.'

Whipple leaned forward; his interest piqued. 'Such as?'

'Well,' HG mused, 'What if the vase itself isn't important? What if it's what the vase represents, or perhaps what it contains?'

'It's possible,' she said. 'Or perhaps the thief drew the same conclusion.'

We fell silent, each lost in our own thoughts. The possibilities seemed endless. Perhaps we were on the cusp of uncovering something significant?

'The danger is that we allow ourselves to become distracted from our primary task. A task that requires our full attention?' HG espoused solemnly as she spread a dab of marmite on one corner of her marmalade toast (a mix of textures and taste I knew no other to imbibe).

'And there we have a conundrum, HG,' offered Arthur as he bit down on a Cumberland sausage, much to the distress of my mentor, although she refrained from admonishing Whipple for his lack of etiquette.

'If we are to solve the mystery of Lord Billington's vase, it will require at least one further visit, and perhaps, a trawl of local fences known to deal in stolen artifacts. What is your view?'

HG allowed Whipple's question to linger while she savoured her marmite and marmalade toast. At length, she dabbed her mouth with a napkin made of the finest cotton with an embroidered monogram of the Drakeford family crest in one corner.

'I agree, Arthur. Billington's misfortune can wait awhile, which brings me nicely to the order of activities for today. I shall assist Lord and Lady Cummings to prepare for lunch with Their Majesties after church tomorrow. Might I suggest you two visit Sir Herbert's factory to see what intelligences you may gather in connection with the activities and behaviour of the elder son, Horatio?'

I couldn't contain my curiosity any longer. The prospect of HG's intimate knowledge of the royal family was too tantalising to ignore.

I ventured to ask what the King and Queen were like in private.

HG's eyes twinkled with amusement. 'Ah, Rex. Curiosity is a commendable trait, but one must tread carefully when discussing royalty.' She paused, considering her words. 'While Court etiquette must be observed, they are, at their core, human beings like you and me. They share the same anxieties we all do—perhaps even more so, given their position and responsibilities. Consider the aftermath of the war,' HG continued. 'The adoption of their new surname, "The House of Windsor," for political reasons. And then there's the brutal assassination of the Russian Czar and his family, but five years ago…'

I gasped and suggested the situation must have been devastating for them.

HG nodded gravely. 'Indeed. However, what's not widely known is that the King had to make an agonising decision not to send a battleship to get them out of Russia.'

'But why?' I asked, perplexed. 'Surely saving his relatives would have been the right thing to do, if it were possible to do so?'

'Not that simple, Rex,' HG explained. 'He feared the consequences. They couldn't risk appearing to support the old Russian regime too openly when the revolution broke out.'

'You mean they were afraid of a revolution here?' I asked, stunned by the revelation.

'Precisely,' HG confirmed. 'The world order has changed significantly since 1914. Even the monarchy had to adapt to survive.'

This serious turn in the conversation's tone called to mind the many monarchies now gone, as if they'd never existed.

While I found our conversation of the utmost interest, Arthur had spent his time finishing his chops, sausage, and kidneys, as if the next meal might never appear. It was only after polishing off the grease on his plate with a piece of dry bread he noticed the silence.

Inspector Whipple finally looked up from his plate, his eyes raised in surprise. His glance alternated between HG and me, perplexed by the sudden silence that had befallen the breakfast table.

'What?' he asked, a bit of egg still clinging to the corner of his mouth.

HG's eyes twinkled with amusement. A dainty smile played across her lips. I knew she thoroughly enjoyed Whipple's bewilderment.

'You have missed nothing of import, Arthur,' she said, her tone light and teasing. 'How was your breakfast?'

I chuckled at the exchange. It was moments like these that made me appreciate the unique, close relationship between HG and Whipple. Despite their differences in background, there was an undeniable camaraderie between them.

Whipple dabbed at his mouth with a napkin. 'Oh, er, quite satisfactory, thank you,' he replied, still looking baffled. 'I must say, your cook is exceptional. The kidneys were particularly tender; no small feat, as you know.'

HG nodded approvingly. 'I'm glad you enjoyed them, Arthur. A good meal is essential for clear thinking, especially given the tasks ahead of us today.'

WE JOURNEYED to Norwich along the A10 after dropping HG off at Sir Herbert's Norfolk estate. The road trip to the growing city involved driving approximately 79 miles through some excellent countryside, although I found the drive somewhat tiring.

Conversation remained sparse during the three hours it took to complete our journey. Mostly, Whipple snoozed, reawakened intermittently by his own raucous snoring. In a lower calibre vehicle, despite his voluminous exhalations, this might not have presented an issue for other occupants. Unfortunately, the excellent quality of engineering gifted by Messrs Rolls and Royce rendered HG's conveyance almost silent. As a result, I resorted to stuffing my ears with cotton wool retrieved from the car's extensive first aid kit to dampen Whipple's more excitable discharges.

By 2.00 pm, my torture ended as we reached the northern environs of Norwich, once the second city of England grown rich on the wool industry.

I applied the car breaks with, I should admit, an urgency uncalled for by the situation to awaken Whipple from his slumber. My strategy worked, causing him to call out, 'Arrest the braggart'. Realising no danger existed, the detective settled back into his deep leather seat, without offering further comment on the matter.

Not wishing to add further embarrassment to the situation, I instead drew the attention of a still half-asleep Whipple to a large painted sign above a wide opening between brick-faced factory buildings. *The General Vulcanising Company Ltd*.

As I slowed the Rolls to enter the "Goods Inward" yard, an arm appeared from a small, square, sentry-box type of construction. The appendage was connected to a uniformed gentleman who informed me he fulfilled the role of security attendant. He asked if we had an appointment. What to do?

Thankfully, Whipple had now regained his full faculties. He leaned across me to hold up his official police notebook.

'Scotland Yard,' said the elderly uniformed man in an astonished tone. 'Has there been a murder? No one has said anything to me.'

'None of your concern, my man,' Whipple said in a stern, monotone voice. 'Where might we find the factory manager?'

The startled attendant froze for a second (Whipple had that effect on people when he employed his office to its full extent). 'Top floor, you'll see a sign on the door for a Mr Bennet. He's the top man here.' He reinforced the point by pointing to a large window in an otherwise drab row of smaller breaks in the brickwork.

I FOLLOWED Whipple up the stairs to the top floor, our footsteps echoing in the stairwell. We found ourselves before a door with a brass plaque that read "Mr Bennet - Factory Manager". Whipple rapped sharply on a frosted glass pane.

'Come in,' a gruff voice called from within.

We entered a spacious office, austere and practical in its furnishings. Mr Bennet, a portly man with thinning grey hair, rose from behind a large, tidy desk. The only items adorning its polished surface were an ornate ink-pen stand and a nameplate matching the one on the door.

'Gentlemen,' Mr Bennet said, extending his hand. 'How may I assist you?'

Whipple introduced us, flashing his credentials once more. Mr Bennet's eyebrows shot up, but he gestured for us to take a seat at the oblong meeting table dominating the centre of the room.

As we settled into the hard wooden chairs, I gazed around the space. The far wall caught my attention, covered in an array of photographs showcasing the factory and its various products. Rubber tyres, hoses, and other vulcanised goods featured prominently.

Above this display of industrial pride hung a large, ornate picture that seemed at odds with the utilitarian nature of the room. It depicted the King and Queen in their full coronation regalia, their solemn faces gazing down upon the factory's accomplishments.

Mr Bennet cleared his throat, drawing my attention back to the matter at hand. 'Now, what brings Scotland Yard to our humble establishment?'

Whipple leaned forward; his eyes fixed on Mr Bennet. 'I'm sure you've heard of the tragedy at Hilltop on Friday?'

The factory manager nodded solemnly. 'Yes, indeed. A

senior member of Sir Herbert's household staff briefed me. Dreadful business.'

'Quite,' Whipple agreed. 'And your thoughts on the matter?'

'It's awful for the family, of course,' Bennet replied, fidgeting with his silver cufflinks. 'And for the company as well. Mr Farrier will be missed. Hard to replace a man of his calibre.'

I noticed a flicker of something—was it guilt? — cross Bennet's face as he spoke. Whipple must have caught it too, for he pressed on.

'Speaking of tragedies, Mr Bennet, we'd like to discuss the fatal accident that took place here recently.'

The change in Bennet's demeanour was immediate. His shoulders tensed, and a sheen of sweat appeared on his brow. 'Accident? I'm not sure what you mean.'

Whipple's voice hardened. 'Come now, Mr Bennet. We both know what I'm referring to. A worker's death is not something easily forgotten or concealed.'

Bennet's resistance crumbled. He slumped in his chair, suddenly looking much older. 'Yes, yes. It was…unfortunate. A terrible mishap.'

'Who was in charge at the time?' Whipple pressed.

Bennet hesitated, his gaze darting between us. Finally, he sighed. 'Sir Herbert's eldest son, Horatio. He was overseeing operations in his father's absence.'

The pieces fell into place in my mind as I asked if, in his professional opinion, the accident could have been avoided?'

The silence that followed became deafening. Bennet's face paled, and he seemed to shrink into himself. His mouth opened and closed, but no words came out.

'What of the poor young fellow's supervisor? Was he not

on hand to ensure his charges remained safe?' Whipple asked.

Bennet seemed to search for a cogent response. His eyes scanned the image of Their Majesties. Perhaps he thought a royal prerogative might descend and spirit him away to a place of sanctuary. In the event, there was no escape from Whipple's interrogation.

'Mr Bennet?' Arthur pressed.

'Well, er…well, to be truthful, Mr Cummings insisted the production line be sped up. I warned him of the danger, but he would have none of it.'

'And the young man's supervisor. What did he do?'

Bennet's gaze grew hard as he engaged Whipple's eyeline. 'Do? What do you think he did? To have disobeyed the owner's eldest son would have led to his immediate dismissal. The man has a wife and four young children, and jobs are difficult to come by in this city since the war ended.'

I suddenly felt a pang of guilt, which brought on memories of my own unhappy start in life. Looking over to Whipple, I surmised he felt the same as his stern demeanour soften, his shoulders relaxing slightly. He leaned back in his chair, his voice taking on a gentler tone.

'Mr Bennet, I apologise if I came across too forcefully. My only interest here is to gather background information that might aid the investigation into Mr Farrier's death. We're not here to cause trouble for you or the company.'

Bennet's posture eased, the tension in his face melting away. He nodded, a look of cautious relief crossing his features. 'I appreciate your candour, Inspector. It's been a difficult time for all of us here.'

'I can imagine,' Whipple said, his voice filled with genuine empathy. 'Any loss of life is tragic, regardless of the circumstances.'

Bennet's look alternated between us. 'I understand your position, Inspector, but I must ask - what does the unfortunate accident here have to do with Mr Farrier's death? They seem quite unrelated to me.'

The connection wasn't immediately apparent to me either, but I knew HG and Whipple often saw links where others didn't.

'Well, Mr Bennet, in our line of work, we've learned that seemingly unrelated events can often connect in unexpected ways. We're simply trying to build a complete picture of the circumstances of Mr Farrier's death, including any recent events that might have affected the company or its senior staff.'

Bennet nodded slowly, though I could see a hint of scepticism in his eyes. 'I see. And you think this accident might be relevant?'

'It's possible,' Whipple replied. 'We're exploring all avenues. Now, if you don't mind, could you tell us a bit more about the day of the accident? Particularly about Horatio Cummings' involvement?'

Bennet looked at a cufflink while twiddling the silver object. 'I reported a slowdown in production to Horatio. One of the vulcanising presses broke down earlier that week. Because of the time taken to repair it, production suffered. Horatio insisted we had to recoup the losses by the end of that week. I told him it was impossible.'

'And his response?' Whipple asked.

'Speed the production line up. I told him the danger would be extreme.'

'...And?'

'And nothing,' Bennet responded. 'He just repeated his order and bounced out of my office, banging the door so hard that he cracked the glass.' Bennet pointed to a small borrowed-light in the top panel of the door frame, which remained in its damaged state.

The room fell into a reflective silence for a brief time, before Whipple asked a further question. 'Then Horatio has a temper?'

Bennet bristled. 'I should say so. When he doesn't get his way, he can change into a monster.'

I had to intervene. 'But not in front of his father?'

The factory manager gave a strangled laugh. 'When the red mist descends on that young man, it matters not who is in attendance. I swear not even the royal presence could ease his wrath.' Bennet looked at the magisterial portrait on the wall to emphasise the point.

A gentle rap on the office door brought welcome relief from a tense moment.

'Enter,' Bennet said with authority.

A nervous-looking boy in ramshackle work clothes half-opened the door and stood uneasily in the tight opening. His eyes flicked between us as if trying to work out what was going on.

'Yes, out with it, Fleming.' Bennet's tone was sharp to the point of being cruel.

'Mr Brownlow sent me to tell you the…the—'

'Out with it, boy. Tell me what?'

Terrified, the young lad fled, leaving Bennet's door ajar.

The factory manager saw the look on Whipple's face.

'I'm sorry, gentlemen. This is not what it used to be like when Sir Herbert graced us with his presence each day. Now that Horatio runs matters on a day-to-day basis, things are different. Senior staff are expected; I'd suggest encouraged by Mr Cummings to drive all employees hard. His attitude is that there are plenty of unemployed men ready to step in for any employee who cannot pull their weight. It seems I am losing my way. I don't know, perhaps it is time I retired.'

I enquired if matters were really that bad.

Bennet gave me a forlorn look. 'You have just witnessed how awful things are. Believe me, gentlemen, If Sir Herbert really knew the extent of what is happening here, he'd hide his head in shame. The death of the young man we spoke about is but the tip of things when it comes to Horatio Cummings besmirching his father's legacy. He has infected us all.'

For the first time, I felt genuinely sorry for the factory manager and asked why not simply inform Sir Herbert.

Bennet's doleful eyes took several seconds to meet mine. 'Horatio has warned us all. If anyone says anything, we'll be sacked on the spot. We dread the time when he inherits his father's business interests.'

I suggested such a state of affairs was many years away.

'Maybe not,' Whipple muttered in an ominous tone.

Chapter Ten

A RETURN VISIT?

AS WE LEFT Sir Herbert's factory, I sensed Arthur's unease. Mr Bennet's demeanour raised more questions than it answered. All except one, that is. It occurred to me, as it must have to Whipple, that Horatio Cummings intended to take control of his father's business, and who knows what else, at his early convenience - no matter who he needed to displace to achieve his aim.

The drive back to Thorpe Manor remained uneventful as I took in the marvel of the Norfolk countryside, all the time keeping my wits about me as I drove the Rolls along the many narrow lanes. My mind whirled with the new information we'd gleaned. I couldn't shake the feeling that Horatio Cummings was our prime suspect, but I knew I had to be careful not to let my personal distaste for the man cloud my judgement. HG had taught me better than that.

Whipple's snoring began again as he slouched comfortably in the passenger seat. To distract myself from the interminable din, I reviewed our suspects.

Sir Herbert himself seemed unlikely. Why would he

poison a cake meant for his own celebration? Unless it was all an elaborate ruse to throw us off the scent. No, that seemed too far-fetched.

Lady Cummings had been nothing but gracious, but could that be a facade? I recalled her tense expression when Sir Herbert received the telegram from the King. Perhaps she resented her husband's success and connections.

Then there was Horatio. His arrogance and cruel management style certainly painted him as capable of murder. But was that enough to condemn him?

My thoughts drifted to Sir Herbert's youngest son, Francis. He'd been remarkably quiet throughout the entire ordeal, barely saying a word during questioning. At first, I'd attributed his reticence to concern for his sweetheart, Primrose. But now, I wondered if there was more to his silence.

Could Francis' apparent devotion to Primrose be a clever disguise to conceal his own ambitions? We knew precious little about the fellow. While Horatio wore his desires on his sleeve, Francis remained an enigma.

I glanced at Whipple as he made the most peculiar shapes with his quivering lips.

'Inspector Whipple,' I said, forcing the man back to reality with a jolt. 'What do you make of Francis Cummings?'

Whipple grimaced, before I turned my attention towards a Fordson farm tractor as it appeared from around a blind bend. The farmer raised a hand, attached to which was a tightly clenched fist. His sun-haggard face displayed a contempt for strangers using the local roads with the anger I expect Boudicca's warriors battled the Roman Legions. Fortunately, a narrow grass bank to my left allowed me to glide the Rolls out of the farmer's way, for I remained sure he had no intention of stopping.

I should like to report that as our vehicles passed, pleasantries were exchanged. Alas, this was not the case. As the burly built old farmer went by, he growled, 'Is, an' he want a fule ter roid 'im, will yew cum?' This, I took to mean, 'Yes, you want all the road, do you?' in that richest of dialects, the Norfolk twang.

I thanked the gentleman for his understanding and made for a quick getaway, before he took revenge on HG's conveyance with the many sharp accoutrements sticking out from his tractor.

'The younger son, you say?' said Whipple in response to my earlier question, while completely ignoring my run in with the agriculturalist. 'You raise an interesting point. Perhaps I shall instruct Muddleford to look into the man. My motto is to leave nothing to chance.'

This was, indeed, one of several mottos Whipple used to guide his police nose, and startling intuition.

THORPE MANOR PRESENTED a scene of complete calm, in contrast to Sir Herbert's factory. Two gardeners contented themselves trimming the expansive lawn edges. The elder estate hand puffed away on a pipe and worked at a steady pace. Every so often, the man would take in the big skies of Norfolk and tilt his head toward the latest bird to attract his attention. In contrast, his young apprentice set about his task with a fury that foretold of an important evening engagement. A sweetheart, perhaps, or a game of dominos in the village pub.

The Manor ran like a well-oiled machine. As we entered the elegant Tudor hallway, the staff went silently about their duties, with the butler instinctively pointing at the saloon to denote the Dowager's location.

I knocked gently on the saloon door, Whipple hovering at my shoulder. We entered at HG's invitation, and I found myself momentarily stunned by the room's elegance.

The saloon was a testament to centuries of refined taste. Ornate tapestries adorned the walls, their intricate designs telling tales of long-forgotten battles. Sunlight streamed through the leaded glass windows, casting a warm glow on the polished oak panelling. A grand fireplace dominated one wall, its mantelpiece adorned with delicate porcelain figurines and a gleaming carriage clock.

HG sat in the enormous bay window, framed by heavy velvet curtains. She held a leather-bound book in one hand and a fine bone china teacup in the other. The fragrant steam rising from her cup mingled with the scent of old books and beeswax polish that permeated the air.

'Ah, gentlemen,' HG said, setting her book aside. 'I trust your excursion was fruitful?'

We exchanged glances, eager to share our findings from the factory.

'Indeed, HG,' I began. 'We've uncovered some rather disturbing information about Horatio's management style and the recent fatal accident.'

Whipple nodded gravely. 'It seems young Mr Cummings has been pushing production beyond safe limits-just as his father told us.'

HG's eyebrows rose slightly as she took another sip of tea. 'Most interesting. And what of you, Rex? Any thoughts on our prime suspect?'

I hesitated, choosing my words carefully before announcing that I thought Horatio to be the most likely culprit, though I worried we might be overlooking something.'

'How so?' asked my mentor.

I shifted uncomfortably under HG's scrutiny, aware that my reservations might seem foolish in the face of the evidence against Horatio. Still, I felt compelled to postulate that it all seemed a bit too neat. Horatio's the obvious villain, with his harsh management style and disregard for safety. But what if that's exactly what someone wants us to think to throw us off the scent?

HG curled her lips. 'Go on, Rex.'

I suggested we knew Sir Herbert had a robust discussion with Mr Farrier the day before his death. And Lady Cummings…she'd been awfully quiet throughout the whole affair, as had Francis, the younger son.

Whipple frowned. 'But the evidence?'

My repost? That evidence pointed to Horatio. But what if there's a motive we haven't considered?'

HG nodded thoughtfully. 'You raise several valid points, Rex. It's crucial we don't allow our assumptions to blind us to other possibilities.'

Her words gave me the confidence to add a further point that nagged at me. The timing of it all. Why now? What's changed in the Cummings household that prompted such drastic action?'

Whipple's frown deepened. 'You think there might be a catalyst we've overlooked?'

'Possibly,' I replied. 'Or perhaps there's a connection we haven't made yet. Between the factory accident, Mr Farrier's death, and even the attack on Lord Billington. It all seems too coincidental for my liking.'

HG set her teacup down with a soft clink. 'Well, Rex, it

seems you've given us much to consider. What do you propose as our next step?'

I took a deep breath, gathering my thoughts before responding to HG's challenge.

'I believe we should pay another visit to Roxby Hall,' I said, my voice steady despite my nerves. 'This time, however, we ought to focus on speaking with the staff and not Lord Billington. They may have observed or overheard something that might assist our enquiries.'

Whipple's eyebrows shot up. 'And you think Billington will allow that?'

'He might not be thrilled,' I admitted, 'But it's a necessary step. Servants often notice more than their employers realise.'

HG nodded approvingly. 'A sound suggestion, Rex. What else?'

'Well,' I continued, 'I think we should also follow-up on Arthur's idea. We ought to ring Detective Sergeant Muddleford and ask him to interview Primrose and Sir Herbert's younger son, Francis.'

'Ah, yes,' HG murmured. 'The quieter members of the household.'

I nodded. 'Exactly. I know it's a delicate matter, but we must tease out any information they might have. Their silence could be telling in itself.'

Whipple stroked his chin thoughtfully. 'It's true. We've barely scratched the surface with those two. But how do we approach it without arousing suspicion and frightening them off?'

'Perhaps,' I ventured, 'We could frame it as a routine follow-up? After all, it wouldn't be unusual to want to speak with all members of the household.'

HG set her teacup down with a soft clink. 'Well-reasoned, Rex. Your instincts serve you well. I believe these are excellent objectives for our investigation.'

Just then, the butler appeared as if out of fresh air. 'Should the Detective Inspector and Mr Rex like to partake of tea and sandwiches, Your Grace?'

'An excellent idea.'

Graham gave a shallow bow from the neck and disappeared through the wide oak door without making a sound. Five minutes later, he returned with a trolly full of delicate sandwiches and a tempting array of dainty cakes displayed on a silver stand.

'Dig in,' HG said. 'The tea is still fresh and there's plenty to go around.'

Temptation overcame manners as I gently eased Whipple aside to arrive at the trolly first. Graham stood back and, realising his services were no longer required, retired after acknowledging his employer again in the approved manner.

'And now,' HG said once we had filled our plates and seated ourselves, 'I shall tell you how my meeting with Lady Cummings went.'

I chomped on a cucumber sandwich, eager to hear all HG had to say. The Dowager took a delicate sip of tea before beginning her account.

'Eleanor was in quite a state when I arrived,' HG said, her eyes twinkling. 'Fretting about afternoon tea with Their Majesties tomorrow. Can you imagine?'

Whipple frowned. 'Tea with the King and Queen? At a time like this?'

HG waved a hand dismissively. 'It was arranged weeks ago, and if you'd paid attention when Sir Herbert read out the King's telegram, and also to my previous comments on the matter, you should know this already. I assured Eleanor she had nothing to worry about. After all, they'd dined with Their Majesties countless times.'

I nodded, imagining Lady Cummings' nervousness and asked if she was concerned Their Majesties might raise the death of Mr Farrier?

'Precisely, Rex,' HG confirmed. 'She feared Their Majesties might cut them off until the murderer was found, and the scandal subsided. Nonsense, of course. I told her the King and Queen would be far more interested in the grisly details and any gossip she could share about the attendees.'

HG's eyes sparkled with mischief.

Whipple coughed, nearly choking on an iced fancy. 'You didn't!'

HG chuckled. 'Oh, I most certainly did. In fact, I fed Eleanor a couple of tidbits to share.'

My curiosity piqued. 'What sort of tidbits, HG?'

'Well,' she said, lowering her voice conspiratorially, 'I mentioned that Lady Millicent Farthingale was seen sneaking out of young Lord Pembroke's room at dawn at a recent weekend soiree, both looking rather dishevelled.'

I felt my cheeks grow warm at the scandal. HG continued, clearly enjoying herself.

'And I may have let slip that Reverend Smythe was caught behind the greenhouse with a bottle of communion wine and a rather dog-eared copy of James Joyce's salacious book, "Ulysses."'

Whipple spluttered, his face turning an alarming shade of red. 'HG! Surely you jest! That book's banned in England-and quite right, too.'

HG roared with laughter. 'So it is, Arthur...But you can purchase a copy in Paris. Anyhow, how do you know the title is salacious?'

I glimpsed at Whipple as his cheeks flushed. 'I...er, well.' He gave up and tucked in to another iced fancy while looking anywhere but in HG's direction.

'Poor you. I'm sorry to have embarrassed you, but you make it so easy for me. Forgive me, dear Arthur.'

Whipple continued to stare into space, occasionally spitting out cake crumbs in his urgent need to occupy himself on anything but the banned book.

Just then the butler reappeared, sparing Whipple further embarrassment.

'A telephone call for the Inspector, Your Grace.'

Before the Dowager responded, Whipple was up and ushering Graham out of the room in his haste to escape further mention of his reading habits.

In the room's quiet, resplendent in its Middle Ages interior architecture, I noticed HG looking at me with a gentleness I'd come to recognise when she wished to talk privately. As she nursed her drink, I readied myself for the question.

'Dear Rex,' she began. 'Do you remember much about your early life? Forgive me for asking; I have no wish to stir painful memories, but I think it is important we all remember as much as possible to reinforce who one is.'

HG's question took me by surprise. Although it wasn't the first time my mentor had skirted around the question, on this occasion, her enquiry took a directness that stirred my unconscious mind.

I recalled as far back as I could remember. That my mother had died in my infancy. I remembered her kind face as she smiled down at me. Or was it a figment of my imagination-the childhood I should like to have had? What I do have vivid memories of was my poor father struggling to make enough to keep us out of the workhouse, or worse, debtors' prison, whereon I should be separated from him, perhaps never to see him again.

I remember him as a jolly fellow. Short in stature, but with a heart as big as a lion. For employment, he sometimes appeared on stage as an actor; at other times, a magician, for which he gained a measure of fame as an accomplished prestidigitation artist. That is to say, very skilled with his hands to perform magic tricks at close quarters.

HG broke into my response. 'You are correct in one respect. Your father was, indeed, an intelligent man who excelled at illusions. He often gained employment at intimate parties to demonstrate his skills at the dining tables. I saw him once and was astonished not to have been able to detect how he did things. A true magician, indeed. As for your mother, dear boy. She left this mortal coil before you could walk. However, let us hope the memories you have of that saintly woman are real. In that event, they are fact as far as you are concerned. That is all that counts.'

I pondered HG's words for what seemed like an age. She had taken me back to a place I sometimes preferred to forget. Yet, my mentor was surely correct. One must remember the past. Not to dwell, or feel morose, but to understand that no matter what happened, I could have done nothing to change events. HG often said it was how we acted in the present that we could, and should, control. It is a mantra I have tried to live my life by.

'And your father's disappearance? Do you recall the events that led up to that dreadful day?'

My recollection of that painful day was much clearer. As a ten-year-old, I often went with my father when he appeared on stage. This served several purposes. First, that he could be sure I was safe. No money existed to pay a woman to look after me, and the lodging houses he could afford were no place to leave a young child alone. Second, there would often be left-over meals remaining in the changing room of the leading actors after they had left for the night, perhaps to be entertained by their sponsors or the like. Either way, what they left behind, father and I treated as a feast.

Then it all changed. One night, father said he was taking me to a special place where kind people would look after me. There would be a clean bed each night, and three hearty meals a day, every day. At first, I was eager, then I realised father would not be joining me. In fact, he intended to leave me there.

I felt my heart sink as the reality of my father's plan dawned on me. The excitement I'd initially felt at the prospect of a clean bed and regular meals evaporated, replaced by a cold, hollow feeling in my chest.

'But...but why can't you stay with me, Father?' I asked, my voice trembling.

He knelt down, placing his hands on my shoulders. His eyes, usually twinkling with mischief, were filled with a sadness I'd never seen before.

'My boy,' he whispered, 'There are things I must do. Things that are no place for a child. You'll be safe here, and well cared for.'

I wanted to protest, to beg him to take me with him, but the words caught in my throat. I knew, even then, that this was goodbye.

As we approached the imposing gates of the home for destitute children, a sense of dread washed over me. The building loomed before us, a grey, austere structure that seemed to suck the very life from the surrounding air.

Father rang the bell, and we waited in tense silence.

After what felt like an eternity, the door creaked open, revealing a warm, smiling woman in a starched uniform.

'Ah, you must be Rex?' she asked, her voice bright and welcoming.

Father nodded, giving my shoulder a gentle squeeze. 'This is Rex. He's a good lad, clever too.'

The woman's face lit up 'Well then, you must come along, Rex, and tell me all about it.'

I turned to my father, desperate for one last embrace, but he was already backing away, his eyes glistening with unshed tears.

'Be brave, Rex,' he said, his voice barely above a whisper. 'Remember who you are.'

And then he was gone, leaving me alone on the doorstep of my new life.

'And there you remained, Dear Rex, until I noticed you three years later. Do you remember? You stood on a chair in a classroom doing a short routine of your father's magical illusions? Oh, dear boy, you had the other children mesmerised, and your teacher, too. It was then I decided to adopt you as my ward and look where we are today!'

We shared a smile, the deep understanding behind which no observer would detect. Yet one sadness remained. What happened to my father? Why did he have to leave? And was he still alive? One thing I knew was that I'd never give up searching for him, and I knew HG would help when the time came.

Just then the door opened and in stepped Whipple, his cheeks flushed, this time not with embarrassment, but anticipation.

I drew nearer, eager to hear what had Whipple so flustered.

'That was Detective Sergeant Muddleford on the telephone,' Whipple began, his words tumbling out in a rush. 'There's been quite a development at Hilltop.'

HG raised an eyebrow. 'Do tell, Arthur.'

'The butler at Hilltop rang the police station in a right state. An intruder was spotted in the grounds,' Whipple explained, pacing back and forth. 'Muddleford rushed over and apprehended a young man in the kitchen.'

I felt my pulse quicken. 'In the kitchen?'

Whipple nodded vigorously. 'The fellow's been taken to the police station for questioning.'

HG leaned back in her chair, a thoughtful expression on her face. 'Well, well. This certainly adds another layer to our investigation, doesn't it?'

I voiced my concerns, a common thief. Or perhaps one of Manny Tufnell's associates?

'Perhaps,' HG interjected, her voice low and serious, 'Someone directly connected to Mr Farrier's death?'

Whipple's excitement grew as the gravity of the situation sank in. 'That's just it. We don't know yet. Muddleford's about to begin the interview.'

I looked at HG, noting the familiar glint in her eye that signalled her mind was already racing ahead, splicing this new information with what we already knew.

'It seems, gentlemen,' she said, rising from her chair, 'That our trip to Norfolk may need to be cut short. I believe Arthur's presence at that interview might prove most illuminating.'

Chapter Eleven

REGARD AD VICTORIAM

ONCE HG HAD REFLECTED our proposed return to Hilltop, she relented, having been informed by Whipple that he'd asked sergeant Muddleford how he intended to carry out the interview, and was satisfied with his subordinate's approach.

That just left whether we returned to Lord Billington's estate after breakfast or pursue other connections to Sir Herbert's family in the area.

In the event, an invitation for HG delivered by the butler settled the matter.

'"By hand,"' intoned HG as she scrutinised the small white envelope. She pointed to the crest embossed on the face. 'Ah, the Boulton-Hicks family. Do you see, Rex, Lions rampant with the motto, "progredi ad victoriam", meaning, "Advance to Victory"? They always were a competitive lot.'

I moved closer, captivated by HG's words. She had a wealth of knowledge about the aristocracy, and I was eager to learn more.

'The Boulton-Hicks family?' I prompted, hoping she'd elaborate.

HG nodded, a wry smile playing on her lips. 'Indeed. They've quite a colourful history. Their fortune, you see, was gained by backing Charles I against Cromwell in the English Civil War. A risky gambit, that.'

'Did it pay off?' I asked, intrigued.

'Not immediately,' HG replied. 'They lost their family seat for their loyalty to the crown. But fortune favours the patient, Rex. When Charles II ascended the throne, they were handsomely rewarded and regained their ancestral home.'

I whistled softly. 'Talk about playing the long game.'

'Quite,' HG agreed. 'The current Baron, however, seems intent on squandering that hard-won fortune. He's a notorious gambler, always chasing the next big win.'

'And his wife?' I inquired, recalling HG's earlier comment about the invitation.

HG's eyes twinkled. 'Ah, Baroness Boulton-Hicks. They say she could charm the birds off the trees. A formidable woman, to be sure.'

'Any children?' I asked, wondering if there might be a connection to our case.

'Just the one. Percival,' HG said, her tone somewhat dismissive. 'He's recently become engaged to one of those American heiresses, which remains quite the fashion for certain families in need of cash. They marry from across the pond to shore up their dwindling fortunes. In return, the heiress gains an English title.'

As she spoke, HG opened the envelope and unfolded a single sheet of paper.

'Ah, we are invited to call upon the Baron and Baroness

this afternoon at four of the clock. I shall send a note immediately to accept.'

Whipple looked puzzled. 'Is this a good use of our time, what with a follow-up needed with Lord Billington and sergeant Muddleford's report? Anyway, why the short notice? It's odd, isn't it?'

HG took her time to re-fold the note and slip it delicately back into its envelope.

'A valid point, Arthur. However, just as you have your network of narks to feed you interesting snippets regarding the criminal underworld, so too, I have my information sources. In my case, they do not know it, of course. You see, my aristocratic seniority often obliges the marquess', earls, viscounts, and barons of this land to bow to my enquiries, lest they forget their place in polite society. Like you, I do not know what is so urgent. Nevertheless, we shall turn the visit to our advantage.'

'No wonder the Manny Tufnell's of this world get upset…present company excepted, of course,' Whipple offered.

HG smiled. 'I agree. Yet here we are. The aristocracy is fortunate indeed that the populous at large have little appetite for revolution, although change is surely coming. The Great War altered many things. Inevitably, the move away from agricultural work to industry will continue apace. This will bring an end to the current way of things, eventually. And a good thing too.'

The Dowager's endorsement of change surprised me, and I said as much.

'Why are you surprised?' HG responded. 'Most of the aristocracy will have one last hurrah. They will sell up and turn land into money. Land they, including my family, gained centuries ago by guessing correctly which side to back- or jump ship when they realised, they were losing. The time is surely coming when people prosper for what they do, not what their ancestors got up to.'

The room fell into silence as HG sipped her tea contentedly. As I thought about her words, I concluded that although HG may have been correct about the aristocracy; it seemed to me that personal wealth would always allow one person to dominate another.

As I pondered the future, I noticed Whipple look at his watch, then rush over to the radio set which sat in a corner of the large room.

'What is the matter, Arthur?' began HG. 'You appear anxious. Are you quite well?'

Whipple failed to answer HG as he turned on the set, tuned into the BBC Home Service, and waited for the valves to warm up. At one point, he lightly tapped the top of the luxurious mahogany cabinet that contained the electrical contraption.

'Arthur,' HG said in a chastising tone. 'What on earth are you doing? I paid Messrs Prig and Perkins nineteen-pounds, seventeen-shillings and threepence ha-penny to build that, and now you assault it. Have you taken leave of your senses, man?'

Whipple's face suddenly transformed from anxious anticipation to mortified realisation. He stepped back from the radio, his hands raised as if in surrender.

'I...I'm terribly sorry, HG,' he stammered, his face flushing a deep crimson. 'I don't know what came over me. It's just...well, I've been so caught up in this case, and I completely forgot my manners. Please accept my sincerest apologies for my boorish behaviour.'

HG raised an eyebrow, her stern expression softening slightly. 'Well, Arthur, I suppose we can overlook this momentary lapse in judgement. But enlighten us as to what has you in such a tizzy.'

Whipple cleared his throat, straightening his tie nervously. 'You see, the news is about to start. And, well, they'll be announcing the latest cricket test score. It's the match I was forced to miss when my superiors ordered me to Hilltop.'

I had to smile at Whipple's sheepish admission. All knew of his love for cricket. I could see how missing such an important match must have grated on him.

HG's eyes twinkled with amusement. 'Ah, I see. Well, in that case, let us all listen to the news together. Perhaps we can make a small wager on the outcome of the match?'

Whipple's face lit up at the suggestion, and he eagerly turned back to the radio, this time adjusting the volume with utmost care.

As the familiar chimes of Big Ben rang out, signalling the start of the news bulletin, I settled into my chair to receive the cricket scores.

THE JOURNEY TO WINGFORD PRIORY, the family seat of the Boulton-Hicks family, took a little under thirty minutes. A dull early morning had transformed into a bright, warm mid-afternoon as we drew up next to the front entrance of the former prior's house.

As we approached the grand building, I marvelled at the haunting beauty of the ruins that surrounded us. The once-grand priory, a victim of Henry VIII's reformation, lay scattered across the landscape like fallen giants.

Crumbling stone walls, overgrown with ivy and moss, stood as silent sentinels to a bygone era. Arched windows, long since bereft of their stained glass, framed views of the lush countryside beyond. The skeletal remains of flying buttresses reached skyward, as if in a final, desperate prayer.

I imagined the Boulton-Hicks' ancestors, shrewd and opportunistic, acquiring this property from the King for a fraction of its true value. It was a common tale up and down the country – monasteries and priories, once centres of spiritual and economic power, reduced to bargaining chips in the King's grand reshuffling of the realm and pursuing his marriage to Ann Bolyn.

'HG,' I whispered, careful not to disturb the reverent atmosphere, 'Do you reckon the family got this place for a song?'

She nodded, her eyes scanning the ruins with a mixture of admiration and sadness. 'Indeed, Rex. That seen as worthless then became the foundation of their current wealth. Ironic, isn't it? The very act meant to diminish the church's power ended up creating a more powerful aristocracy based on landholdings.'

I pondered this as we reached the Prior's House, now the family's residence. The contrast between the weathered ruins and the well-maintained house was stark, a physical representation of the family's rise to prominence.

I remarked how something considered of little value then gave families like the Boulton-Hicks the basis of their current fortune.

'Quite so,' HG agreed. 'And it's a reminder, Rex, that monetary value often lies where others cannot see it.'

Presently, an elderly butler, dressed in an old-fashioned tailed coat and single-breasted waistcoat, knee-length britches and white silk socks with black patent-leather shoes, opened the great door to the property.

'Oh, I do hate families, the royal family apart, of course,

that insist on their upstairs staff wearing formal wear. I mean, look at that excuse for a wig the poor fellow is wearing. The whole getup is from another age and out of tune with the times.'

Whipple appeared dumbstruck at the sight before him. I mused he might like to dress similarly. His wordless response was to give me a curt side glance and curl the edge of his mouth upward.

'My master and mistress await Your Grace in the orangery. I shall have your chauffeur and the other… gentlemen escorted to the kitchen for refreshments.'

'You will do no such thing, my good fellow,' HG responded in a quiet tone. However, the look said it all, causing the poor chap to shrink into his stiff outfit and his powdered wig to wobble upon his bald head.

'Of course, Your Grace,' the man responded after a moment to collect himself. 'As far as I recall, that was the last time the chap's eyeline met my mentor's as he led the way, opened a pair of gold-gilded white doors and announced our presence.

———

A SCENE of opulence unfolded before us. The orangery was a marvel of glass and ironwork, bathed in the warm afternoon light. My eyes became drawn to the imposing figure of the Baron, standing tall among the grapevines and tropical fruit trees. He cut a commanding figure, his silver hair gleaming in the dappled sunlight, his posture rigid.

To his left, the Baroness sat in a wicker chair. The intricate pattern of the cushion covers seemed to dance in the shifting light, creating an illusion of movement that was almost hypnotic.

HG strode into the room with her characteristic confidence, her presence immediately commanding attention. The Baroness rose to greet her, a warm smile spreading across her face.

'Your Grace, so good of you to accept our invitation at such short notice,' she said, her voice rich with genuine pleasure.

The Baron remained still, his eyes following HG's movement. As her gaze fell upon him, he bowed deeply, a gesture HG acknowledged with a slight nod.

I entered the room next, acutely aware of Whipple's nervous presence behind me. The poor chap seemed to use me as cover, his discomfort palpable in this unfamiliar setting.

The Baroness's eyes widened as she spotted us. 'Oh...I see you have brought your people with you!' she exclaimed, her tone a mixture of surprise and curiosity.

HG swept in to give the Baroness a kiss on each cheek, then offered her hand to the Baron, causing the man to bow once again and make as if to kiss her gloved hand.

'Delighted to accept your kind invitation, Ada, although I must correct you on one point,' HG said in good grace. 'My companions are not, as you suggest, "My people." Young Rex is my Ward, and the refined gentleman, no lesser figure than the famous "Whipple of the Yard". He attends to catch the evil reprobate that murdered Sir Herbert Cummings' chief accountant.'

I observed Whipple straightening his back and puffing his chest out a little. Although his facial features could not hide a measure of discomfiture at HG's fulsome effusion.

'So, you are the famous detective one hears so much about?' said the Baroness in an inquisitive tone.

She then turned to me.

'And Rex. I wasn't aware Her Grace had a Ward. You are most welcome.'

That turned out to be the limit of the Baroness' enquiry into either Whipple's, or my reason for attending. Neither did she offer us a chair, so there we stood like bookends. As for the Baron, he merely stared at us from time to time. On each occasion, scanning his quarry from head to toe without making a comment, save for a low sort of grunt.

HG and Ada settled into their seats, their conversation pivoting to recent events.

'Such dreadful business at Hilltop,' Ada tutted, shaking her head. 'And now poor Billington attacked in his own home. Whatever is the country coming to?'

HG nodded solemnly. 'Indeed, troubling times.'

'England is going to the dogs, I tell you,' Ada continued, her voice rising with indignation. 'It's all these new fads coming over from America. Jazz music and flappers and whatnot. And then, of course, there is the working class!'

I noticed HG's feet shift slightly, a telltale sign of her annoyance.

Ada, oblivious to HG's reaction, ploughed on. 'They're earning far too much in these new factories. It's upsetting the natural order of things. In the old days, people knew their place.'

HG's feet were now tapping a steady rhythm against the floor, her fingers gripping the armrests of her chair.

'It's becoming nigh impossible to recruit reliable staff nowadays,' Ada lamented. 'They all want days off and extravagant wages. Whatever happened to loyalty and knowing one's station?'

I noticed the tightness around HG's eyes and the slight downturn of her mouth. Her feet continued their restless movement, betraying her growing anger at Ada's narrow-minded views.

Whipple caught my eye, raising an eyebrow in silent communication. We both recognised the signs of HG's mounting frustration, knowing full well her passionate beliefs about social equality and the dignity of all work.

'Dearest Ada, what a lovely display of exotica you have in this splendid building! But do you know, I feel a little uncomfortable amid the humidity? Might you perhaps show me around your beautiful gardens?'

It took a measure of self-control for me not to chuckle at HG's subtle put-down for the Baroness, made all the harder as I observed the efforts of the Ada to conceal her anger at being cut off so abruptly. I surmised only HG's superiority in rank stopped the woman from complaining. Instead, she wore a sickly smile of compliance. I had become well used to the social games the upper class played, with competitors vying for attention and shooting barbed comments wrapped in the poisoned wrappings of social grace.

And so, the Baroness rose from her chair and led the way out through an ornate set of wrought iron doors. The Baron, who had spoken not a word, followed several steps behind the ladies, after giving us one last grunt.

So, there we stood, the bookends with nothing to do, other than break out into loud laughter once we were sure the threesome were out of earshot.

Shortly after, the butler entered the splendid space. I assume to offer tea to his superiors. He maintained his cold, formal exterior until he, too, was certain his employers and the Dowager were out of sight. Once content, the most extraordinary thing happened. The fellow slouched into the chair, which until a minute previously, the Baroness had occupied, and pulled off his powdered wig, giving his hairless head a scratch as a cloud of cornflour misted the air.

'Thank the Lord for that,' the man said without a syllable of self-consciousness.

We stood, mouths half open at the spectacle, as the butler unbuttoned his waistcoat. He suddenly realised we were watching him, mouths still gaping.

'What?' he said, while placing a finger between his starched collar and neck to facilitate the circulation of fresh air. 'Them? They won't be back for an hour. She can talk for England about her ruddy roses and suchlike. Anyone daft enough to believe her would think she did all the work herself, instead of the head weed whacker and his team of petal pushers.'

I took the man's colourful description of the outdoor staff in the spirit I think he intended. Whipple occupied himself with picking several grapes from a low-hanging vine branch.

I put it to the now rather unkempt butler that he didn't appear to be a particular fan of the Baroness.

'She's a right madam, that one. No one here likes her. Oh, she's all sweetness and light when they have guests, but as soon as they go, it's back to normal. You know, shouting and having tantrums, nothing gets done properly as far as that one's concerned. She regularly throws stuff at us. Never hit us, mind, we know the score and we're too quick for her. Of course, she always checks to make sure what she chucks about isn't worth much. She's bonkers, but she's no fool.'

As the fellow continued to berate his employer, I gazed around the orangery for Whipple. At length, I observed a starched shirt cuff reaching for a peach among dense foliage on the far side of the glass-walled room.

'...And then there's—'

I felt compelled to interrupt our host to ask why anyone, including himself, remained in the family's employ.

'Like all of us in service,' he began, 'we get bed and board. The wages are rubbish. Do you know she pays the maids and footmen less than £25 a year? The cook only gets about £40, and me not much more. We could all earn more in the factories, but that would mean finding new lodgings and all that. Mind you, some have left for other, better paid positions. One or two have gone to Lord Billington's place. They seem happy enough.'

Before I could ask which staff had left, the sound of the Baroness' high-pitched voice wafted into the room and got louder by the second. The butler reacted in a split second and was up and gone well before the threesome crossed the threshold of the orangery.

'Ah, there you are, you two,' HG said brightly. 'I hope you haven't been up to any mischief?' Her look gave the distinct impression she hoped we had.

'Well, we must be going, Ada, and thank you so much for showing me your wonderful gardens. You must be terribly proud.' HG winked at me as she offered the compliment.

As we prepared to leave, Ada couldn't resist one last opportunity to extol her virtues.

'Oh, you simply must come back in the spring, Your Grace,' she gushed, clasping her hands together. 'That's when the gardens are truly at their finest. You wouldn't believe the effort it takes to maintain such an important estate.'

I caught HG's eye, noting the slight twitch at the corner of her mouth.

'I spend hours every day overseeing the gardeners,' Ada continued, oblivious to our silent exchange. 'It's exhausting work, but someone must ensure everything is perfect. Why, just last week, I directed the replanting of the herbaceous border!'

As Ada droned on about her horticultural expertise, I noticed something quite extraordinary. The Baron, who had remained stoic and rigid throughout our visit, rolled his eyes at his wife's lecture. It was a subtle movement, barely perceptible, but unmistakable.

'And then there is the topiary,' Ada prattled on. 'It requires constant attention. I often find myself out there with the shears, sculpting each bush to perfection.'

I bit my lip to stifle a giggle, picturing the Baroness in her finery, hacking away at the shrubbery. Even Whipple, usually so composed, struggled to maintain a straight face.

HG, ever the diplomat, nodded politely. 'Your dedication is truly admirable, Ada. The results speak for themselves.'

The Baroness beamed at the compliment, completely missing the hint of irony in HG's tone. 'Oh, it's nothing, really. Just a labour of love for one's ancestral home.'

As she continued to expound on her tireless efforts, I caught the Baron's eye. For a moment, his mask of indifference slipped, and I saw a flicker of long-suffering exasperation cross his face. It seemed even he had his limits for his wife's self-aggrandisement.

SAFELY BACK AT THORPE MANOR, we tucked into a light Sunday evening meal while discussing the day's events.

'Now, you too, out with it. What did you get up to while I suffered an entire hour of Ada Boulton-Hicks' boring horticultural monologue?'

I leaned back in my chair, feeling the weight of the day's events settle on my shoulders. 'Well, HG, it was quite the spectacle. After the Baroness dragged you off to admire her prized roses, the butler appeared out of nowhere. He was a sight, I tell you.'

HG raised an eyebrow. 'Go on.'

'Right, so this chap – he sort of slouched into a chair, looking utterly exhausted. But not before he'd checked to make sure the Baroness was well out of earshot.'

'Interesting,' HG mused. 'And what did he have to say for himself?'

I leaned forward, lowering my voice conspiratorially. 'He was quite the chatterbox once he got going. Apparently, the Baroness is a right terror to work for. Simmons said she's driven off several staff in the past year.'

Whipple, who'd been quietly sipping his tea, perked up at this. 'That's right.'

I nodded. 'Oh, it gets better. He mentioned that two staff who'd left ended up in Lord Billington's household. Seems they preferred his lordship's eccentricities to the Baroness' tyranny.'

HG's eyes narrowed. 'Now, that is interesting. Did Simmons mention which staff members made the move to Billington's?'

'That's the problem. Before I could ask, we heard you returning. I tell you, he was up and out of that room faster than that Pietro Bordino chap.'

'Who?' asked Whipple, wearing his customary confused look when anything other than cricket was being discussed.

'The famous Italian racing driver, dear Arthur,' HG replied.

Whipple shrugged his shoulders and ate another forkfull of liver.

I ventured to ask HG if she had learned anything of interest from her hosts.

'What, you mean apart from the fact that the North American, Acer rubrum, more commonly known as Red Maple, is the latest in certain distinguished botanical circles?'

HG, thankfully, did not require a response from me on the subject.

'I teased out one or two interesting facts during the rare occasions Ada paused for breath,' continued my mentor. 'In fact, she, too, mentioned the "bothersome issue", as she put it, of staff leaving her employ. The strange thing was that when I asked her which positions fell into this category, she changed the subject by pointing out yet another "favourite" rose and giving me chapter and verse on its genus.

The exchange appeared to energise Whipple, at least to the extent of forcing him to stop eating.

'Then we have our next objective; To find out who left the Boulton-Hicks household, and where they went.'

Chapter Twelve

SOCIAL GRACES?

THE WEATHER HAD TAKEN a turn for the worst as we set off for our return journey to Lord Billington's residence. The fine, sunny weather of the previous day had been replaced with an overcast, dank morning delivering a drizzle that soaked into one's bones and ponded if this unseasonably cool Monday morning portrayed a portent of what lay ahead.

I turned to HG as we approached Roxby Hall, a question nagging at me.

'Won't Lord Billington find it odd that we're visiting again so soon? And without an invitation?'

HG's lips curled into a smile. 'I shall remain in the Rolls, Rex. You and Arthur will request entry under the pretence of recovering an item I inadvertently left behind.'

I nodded, understanding the ruse. As we pulled up to the grand entrance, I stepped out with Whipple, straightening my jacket against the drizzle.

The butler answered our knock, his eyebrows raised in surprise.

A Spiffing Murder

I wished the fellow a good morning, mustering my most polite tone before explaining that Her Grace believed she left a small item behind during our last visit, and asked if we might enter and look for it.

The butler's scepticism was palpable. 'I'm afraid His Lordship is not at home at present, and—'

His words trailed off as he caught sight of HG in the car, her posture regal and unyielding as she stared straight ahead.

'Well, I suppose…a quick look wouldn't hurt,' he conceded, stepping aside.

As we entered, the butler commented, 'Lord Billington will not be long, and he'll surely wish to receive the Dowager.'

'Oh, Her Grace doesn't wish to impose,' I said hastily. 'We're in quite a hurry to reach another appointment. We only dropped in on the off chance.'

The butler nodded, relieved at the prospect of our swift departure.

After a few seconds of scrutiny, the fellow melted away, saying that he had to attend to a matter with a local tradesperson. and that we had free rein to look for HG's item, save for his master's bedroom. 'If you wish to access His Lordship's private apartment, you must come for me, whereupon I shall unlock the door, but supervise you within.'

As soon as the butler disappeared, I turned to Whipple, keeping my voice low to check our plan.

Whipple nodded, his moustache twitching. 'I'm to find the head gardener and inquire about the ladders, any recent movements, and disturbances beneath Lord Billington's bedroom window.'

Our plan agreed. Whipple left in search of his quarry,

while I planned to speak with any staff I came across to discover if any of them recently left the Boulton-Hicks household.

'Very good, lad,' Whipple said, pulling at the cuffs of his ill-fitting jacket. 'Let's reconvene in the Rolls to compare notes and update HG in, say, twenty minutes?'

I agreed, and we parted ways. Whipple headed towards the back of the house in search of the gardeners' bothy, while I made for the servant's quarters.

As I wandered the corridors, I kept my ears pricked for any signs of life. It wasn't long before I heard the clatter of pots and pans coming from the kitchen.

I poked my head around a painted pine door to an empty kitchen, then a young maid appeared from the scullery. She appeared startled by my appearance.

'Terribly sorry to disturb you,' I said, flashing what I hoped was a disarming smile. 'I wondered if I might ask you a quick question?'

The maid nodded hesitantly, straightening her attire with hands red-raw from hard work at the sink.

'What a well-run household this is,' I began, laying it on thick. 'Have you been with Lord Billington long?'

'Why no, sir,' the girl said. 'Mother only put me into service. Three months passed.'

It was then that I took notice of her fragile frame and tired features and considered that the poor wretch could be little older than fifteen, at best, and possibly a year younger. I noted that she regularly gazed at the kitchen entrance for signs of anyone coming, lest she receive a scolding for not working...and speaking with a stranger, and a man, too.

'I'll keep you but a minute. Have you made any new friends here? Perhaps other recent additions to the household?'

She shook her head, her eyes darting nervously here and there. I waited patiently, sensing there might be more.

After a moment, she spoke in a hushed tone. 'Well...I did hear the others talking at servant's tea the other week. They mentioned an upstairs person and an outside man coming from some other big house.'

My interest piqued. 'Oh? Have you seen them yourself?'

The girl's eyes widened, and she shook her head vigorously. 'Oh no, sir. I'm not allowed upstairs, and I can't go outside without the cook's permission.'

I nodded, understanding the strict hierarchy of the household. 'Thank you. You've been most helpful.'

As I turned to leave, I felt a twinge of sympathy for the young scullery maid, thrust into service at such a tender age. But I had to focus on the task at hand. The new arrivals could be an important step to solve at least one of the two mysteries currently at our feet.

―――

BACK IN THE ROLLS, I sat beside Whipple, who looked rather bedraggled. His already crumpled suit was spattered with mud, and droplets of water clung to his moustache.

I commented he looked as though he'd been through the wars.

Whipple grunted, rolled down a window and wrung out his sodden hat. 'Blasted weather. Traipsing about in the wet and muck is hardly my idea of a pleasant morning.'

HG turned in her seat, eyeing us both with keen interest. 'Well, gentlemen? What have you uncovered?'

I cleared my throat. 'I spoke with a young scullery maid. Poor thing couldn't have been more than fifteen. She mentioned hearing talk of two new staff members - who'd come from another grand house.'

HG's eyebrows rose. 'Interesting. And you, Arthur?'

Whipple shook his head, sending a spray of water across the car's interior. 'Not much to report, I'm afraid. I found the head gardener - surly fellow, built like a brick outhouse. He was adamant his ladders remained securely locked away. Said he'd have noticed any disturbance in the borders beneath Lord Billington's window, and he simply wouldn't allow such a thing.'

'Hmm,' HG mused, tapping her chin thoughtfully. 'It seems our break-in story might be more complicated than we first assumed.'

I nodded and opined that the new staff members might conceivably be connected to the Boulton-Hicks household.

'It's certainly possible,' HG replied. 'We'll need to dig deeper into their backgrounds. Well done, gentlemen, I did not think you'd gain entry so easily.'

I chuckled as I recounted the butler, saying Lord Billington wasn't at home, and gave us free access, other than his master's bedroom without supervision.

'How interesting,' HG replied. 'For a man who gave the appearance, in looks and word, yesterday, of being so ill, he's made a remarkable recovery. I wonder what encouraged him to forego his sickbed. Anyway, that is a matter for later. Now, while we are out and about, there is something else I wish us to investigate. Start up the car, Rex. I shall provide you with directions.'

HG'S ARTICULATED instructions bid me to turn left and head for Kings Lynn. Our destination? A watchmaker somewhere within the medieval streets of the old Hanseatic League port area in Purfleet.

I guided the Rolls Royce through the winding roads towards Kings Lynn, my mind racing with curiosity about our mysterious destination. As we approached the ancient port town, I shared my knowledge with HG and Whipple.

'Did you know Kings Lynn was once a major partner in the Hanseatic League?' I glanced at HG in the rear-view mirror, catching her intrigued expression. 'It was a powerful medieval trade network that stretched across Northern Europe.'

Whipple grunted; his interest piqued. 'Go on, lad.'

'Well, Purfleet, where we're headed, was the heart of it all,' I continued, navigating the car through narrowing streets. 'In the 14th century, Kings Lynn was swimming in wealth thanks to the trade. Ships from all over Europe would dock here, bringing exotic goods and taking English wool in return.'

As we entered the old Hanseatic area, the streets became a maze of history. 'Look at this place,' I marvelled, slowing the car to a crawl. 'It's a higgledy-piggledy collection of warehouses and narrow streets. You can almost smell the centuries of commerce in the air.'

HG leaned forward, her eyes scanning the buildings. 'Fascinating, Rex. And our watchmaker lives in this labyrinth of history.'

I nodded, carefully manoeuvring around a tight corner. 'Somewhere in here, yes. It's like stepping back in time, isn't—'

'Turn left here, Rex,' HG interrupted. 'Yes, that's it. Into the yard.'

The Rolls looked conspicuously out of place and scale in the small space we'd pulled in to.

Ancient brick facades surrounded us, their weathered surfaces telling tales of centuries past. Interspersed among them stood timber-framed buildings, their black beams stark against painted panels, a testament to medieval craftsmanship.

As I turned off the engine, the sudden silence amplified the sense of otherworldliness. Without the modern car lodged at the centre of this secret square, we could have easily been in the thirteen-hundreds. The air hung heavy with history, and I half-expected to see merchants in period dress emerge from the shadowy doorways.

My gaze wandered upward, taking in the intricate details of the buildings. On one side, an external gallery caught my eye, its wooden structure jutting out from the facade. As I studied it, movement drew my attention.

An elderly man appeared, leaning against an old handrail. His wizened face and antiquated attire made me blink in surprise. For a moment, I wondered if I was seeing a ghostly merchant from the past come to life before my eyes.

'HG,' I whispered, not wanting to break the spell of the moment. 'Is that the man you've come to meet?'

She followed my gaze. 'Indeed, it is. Our watchmaker awaits.'

The old man raised a hand in greeting, his movements as precise as the timepieces he crafted. As we stepped out of the car, I couldn't shake the feeling that we'd crossed some invisible threshold into a world where past and present merged.

'Ah, Mr Trimmond. Thank you so much for seeing us at such short notice,' HG intoned.

As HG spoke, the gentleman began his descent from the gallery. I watched, transfixed, as he navigated the rickety wooden steps with a grace that belied his advanced years. His movements were fluid, each step placed with precision and confidence.

The watchmaker's khaki coverall seemed to blend seamlessly with the aged wood of the staircase, as if he were part of the building itself. His white shirt and blue tie peeked out from beneath, a nod to formality in this timeless setting.

As he drew closer, I marvelled at the contrast between his wrinkled face and the sharpness in his eyes. Those eyes, I realised, held a twinkle of mischief and wisdom that spoke of a lifetime of intricate work and patience.

Mr Triamond's hand glided along the banister, barely touching it. This wasn't a man who needed support, but one who moved with the deliberate care of someone accustomed to handling delicate objects.

Halfway down, he paused and smiled at HG. 'Your Grace,' he said, his firm voice carrying the warmth of a well-oiled mechanism. 'It's a pleasure to see you again.'

I observed how his fingers, despite their age, appeared nimble and steady. These were the hands of a master craftsman, I thought, capable of manipulating the tiniest gears and springs with unerring accuracy.

As Mr Trimmond reached the bottom of the stairs, I was struck by how he seemed to exist in two worlds at once. Here was a man firmly rooted in the past, surrounded by centuries of history, yet his eyes sparkled with an intelligence that seemed to peer into the future.

HG stepped forward to greet him, and I hung back, still in awe of this remarkable figure who moved with the precision of the timepieces he created.

A few minutes passed as my mentor and the watchmaker exchanged pleasantries, while he slowly headed back up the stairway and led us into his workshop. This was a place of magic, with timepieces in varying stages of construction, lying on tidy benches. Each watch and clock sat on its own square of black material, with components neatly laid in rows, ready for insertion.

Whipple nudged me. 'What do you reckon we've come here for? It can't have anything to do with our investigations, can it?'

The tonal doubt in Arthur's voice let slip that he'd learned over the years working with HG that she often pulled things out of the hat that he hadn't considered. I was as much in the dark as he was, and before I could enquire into the matter, HG revealed all.

'Arthur, Rex. This gentleman is the premier watchmaker in the land. His family has been making timepieces for the Drakefords' for generations. A mark of the Triamond's masterly craftmanship is that their timepieces rarely need to come back to his workshop for repair. Now, what do you think of that?'

The elderly gentleman blushed and busied himself pushing his hands in the pockets of his coverall, while Whipple and I looked suitably impressed.

The Dowager moved to her next topic without drawing breath.

'Now, Mr Trimmond. I wish to commission a special timepiece for my Norfolk home now that I have made Thorpe Manor my principal residence. Well, I have recently noted that an Adams fireplace in one of the smaller rooms suffers from a lack of embellishment on its over-mantle. Yes, I know, Robert Adam was a matter of symmetry that speaks for itself. However, I wish to move the focal point of the room up a little. Does that make sense to you?'

'It doesn't to me,' whispered Whipple as he leaned into

me. 'What is HG on about? Is she a friend of this Adams gentleman?'

I informed Whipple that it was most unlikely, because the fellow died in the 1790s. Whipple scrunched his face up when I explained that a burst ulcer saw the man off.

HG caught his pained expression. 'What ails you, Arthur?'

Whipple feigned indigestion.

'That does not surprise me. You really ought to give your breakfast sausages more respect. Perhaps, then, they'd refrain from repeating on you, as they appear to be doing now. I must warn you, friend or not, if this episode leads to a preponderance of excess wind, I shall not forgive you if evidence presents itself in my presence. Do we understand each other?'

I stifled a chuckle as Arthur's face turned a deep shade of crimson. The poor man looked as if he wanted the floor to open up and swallow him whole. His eyes darted around the room, desperately avoiding HG's piercing gaze.

'I...I...' Arthur stammered, his hands fidgeting with the brim of his hat. 'My sincerest apologies, Your Grace. I assure you; it won't happen again.'

HG raised an eyebrow, her expression a mixture of amusement and exasperation. 'See that it doesn't, Arthur. We're in the presence of a master craftsman, not a circus side-show for curiosities,'

Arthur nodded vigorously, his embarrassment palpable. 'Of course. I'll keep my, er, eccentric intestines in check, as you say.'

I sympathised with the inspector. He was a brilliant detective, but social graces sometimes eluded him. I offered him a lifeline by suggesting we took some fresh air, intoning that a brisk walk might help settle things.

Arthur shot me a grateful look. 'Capital idea. Yes, that should do nicely.'

A brisk fifteen-minute walk along the waterfront did the trick, and soon we were back in business.

As we turned our attention back to Mr Trimmond and HG's discussion about the commissioned timepiece, I pondered about the peculiar situations we often found ourselves in. Here we were, in a medieval watchmaker's shop, discussing intestinal distress and mantelpiece decorations in the same breath.

Arthur leaned close to me once more, his voice barely above a whisper. 'I owe you one, lad. Never thought I'd be getting a lecture on digestion from a duchess in a place like this.'

I nodded, suppressing another laugh. 'Just part of the job, Inspector. We sleuths must be prepared for anything, mustn't we?'

For the next twenty minutes, HG, and Mr Trimmond became subsumed in a deep conversation about the size, shape, and finish of the mantle clock he was to build. Much conversation, and several sketches followed as the pair exchanged ideas about what special features he might incorporate to entertain and delight visitors.

While their discussions continued, Whipple and I did a circuit of the room, inspecting the many engineering marvels before us. From time to time, I spotted Mr Trimmond allowing himself a side-gaze at what we were up to, presumably checking to see we touched nothing.

It seemed he had reason to observe us as Whipple's eyes lit up at the sight of a solid silver bird perched on one of Mr Drummond's workbenches. The exquisite craftsmanship was clear in every feather and each curve of its delicate form.

'Look,' Whipple exclaimed, his voice filled with childlike wonder. 'It's just like a songbird, down to the very last detail. I wonder if—'

My heart leapt into my throat as I realised what he was about to do. 'Inspector, wait!' I hissed, but it was too late.

Before I could stop him, Whipple's finger had already found a small switch on the side of the automaton. With a soft click, the bird sprang to life.

The transformation was nothing short of miraculous. In an instant, the lifeless silver sculpture became a vibrant, animated creature. Its beak parted, and the workshop filled with the most beautiful birdsong I'd ever heard. The melody was so pure, so crystalline, that for a moment, I forgot to breathe.

As the enchanting chirping continued, I marvelled at the bird's movements. Its wings flapped in perfect unison, each feather catching the light as it moved. The effect was mesmerising, creating the illusion that at any moment, the creature might take flight and soar around the room.

But it was the eyes that truly captivated me. They blinked with such lifelike precision that I wondered if Mr Trimmond had somehow captured the essence of an actual bird within this mechanical marvel. The head swivelled from side to side, taking in its surroundings with an uncanny awareness.

Occasionally, the bird would nod, as if acknowledging an unseen audience. Each movement so fluid, so natural, that it was easy to forget this was a creation of gears and springs rather than flesh and blood.

The inspector need not have worried. HG and Trimmond turned and smiled in amusement.

'Ah, I see you have made friends with the little one?' said the watchmaker in a tone fringed with laughter.

We sighed with relief on realising all was well.

'Might I enquire how much such a creation might cost?' said Arthur in a curious tone.

Mr Trimmond smiled that smile again. 'Inspector, price is not something considered when undertaking a commission. I hope I don't sound evasive or show conceit. It is the case that the price is immaterial. Like many things, that little bird is only worth as much as someone is prepared to pay. You would not, I'm sure, expect me to share further information with you.'

'Quite right,' added HG as she approached and turned the silver bird off. Now it rested, silent and content with the pleasure it had provided.

Whipple still wasn't satisfied. The mechanical marvel had clearly stirred something within. Was it the policeman in him, or the little boy hidden inside every man?

'Is it possible to make such a thing to represent any item?'

Trimmond appeared, unsure of the inspector's question at first.

'You mean specifically, or automatons in general?'

'The latter,' Whipple clarified.

The watchmaker rubbed his chin. 'Well…Yes, I suppose it is. That is, if you mean to cause a created object to have an internal mechanism to cause movement of some sort.'

Whipple gazed around the room, then again at the silent silver bird. 'Thank you, Mr Trimmond. Your response is most informative.'

I looked at HG, who had her gaze firmly fixed on the detective.

'Arthur, what are you up to?'

Chapter Thirteen

A TERRIBLE ACCIDENT

AS WE ARRIVED BACK at HG's Norfolk home, Whipple remained deep in thought. Something we'd seen at Mr Trimmond's workshop had resonated with the detective, yet he refused to be drawn on what that might be.

The situation continued until we sat down for a light lunch in the small dining room of my mentor's exquisite home.

'It is no use, Rex,' HG said as she laid a crisp white linen napkin across her lap. 'Arthur is now ensconced in detective mode. I have observed this look many times and know for certain that he will not speak again until whatever that police brain of his is tumbling around makes sense to him. Instead, let us content ourselves with reviewing our investigations so far.'

I considered this a reasonable approach, given Whipple's silence. Although, I have to say; I found his muted murmurings and hand movements disconcerting. It was as if the man was acting out a scene or testing a scenario.

The arrival of luncheon diluted my unease as I tucked into an excellent plate of mashed potato, chops, and mixed vegetables.

'I'm rather proud that what you see before you emanate from the estate,' HG intoned. 'The sheep are also excellent at keeping the grass down, although my ancestors had to create a ha-ha to keep the beasts off the Tudor knot garden.'

I considered how clever the illusion was at fooling guests of an infinite landscape, yet if caught out, one found oneself at the edge of a vertical drop, hence the name given to the deception.

'Come, come, Rex. Not you, too. I can put up with one of you being present in body only. What is the matter?' HG's reprimand ended my internal wanderings with a start, for which I apologised, cutting into my lamb chop to avoid eye contact with my mentor.

'Very well. Now that you have regained your consciousness, let us review matters to date.'

I nodded, setting down my cutlery. HG was right; we needed to focus on the case at hand.

'So, to an obvious suspect; Horatio Cummings,' HG said, her eyes sharp with concentration. 'His behaviour has been most suspicious, and his motives are clear. What do you make of him, Rex?'

I considered for a moment before responding. Horatio's arrogance and entitled attitude certainly made him a prime candidate, but something didn't quite fit.

His actions seemed too overt, too obvious to someone plotting murder. If he truly wanted to inherit the company, surely, he'd be more discreet in his machinations.

HG listened intently, a smile playing at the corners of her mouth. 'An astute observation, my dear boy. Indeed,

Horatio's behaviour may be a smokescreen for someone else's actions. But we mustn't discount him entirely.'

She paused, taking a sip of her Earl Grey tea. 'What of Lady Cummings? Her position as Sir Herbert's wife puts her in a unique position.'

I hadn't considered Eleanor Cummings as a serious suspect, but HG's mention of her made me reconsider. She had access to Sir Herbert's food and drink, and as his wife, she stood to inherit a substantial fortune if he were to die.

'Precisely,' HG nodded, as if reading my thoughts. 'And let us not forget young Francis. He's been rather quiet throughout this affair, hasn't he?'

I agreed. His silence could signal guilt, or simply a desire to stay out of the spotlight. Either way, it warranted further investigation.

'Now, onto the evidence,' HG continued. 'The cake is our primary lead. We must determine how it was tampered with and by whom. The kitchen staff will need to be questioned.'

I suggested we also look into Sir Herbert's business dealings. Perhaps someone from his past held a grudge, or a rival company sought to eliminate him.

'Excellent thinking, Rex,' HG praised. 'We must not limit our scope to just the family. Sir Herbert's rise to wealth may have left a trail of disgruntled associates in its wake.'

I then turned HG's attention to our second case, the matter of Lord Billington's attacker and the resulting theft of his Chinese vase.

HG fidgeted in her chair; her brow furrowed in contemplation.

It's certainly an intriguing coincidence. The timing is suspicious, to say the least. We must consider the possibility that the two events connect.

I nodded, my mind racing with possibilities.

The vase seems an odd target for a thief. Surely there were other, more accessible valuables in the house.

HG's eyes lit up at my observation.

Precisely, my dear boy. The vase's location in a hidden alcove suggests the thief knew exactly what they were looking for. This wasn't a random burglary.

But how does this tie into Mr Farrier's death? I asked, struggling to see the connection.

HG tapped her fingers on the table, a habit I recognised as a sign of her mind working at full tilt.

'Consider this. What if the vase wasn't the target? What if it was merely a distraction?'

I felt a jolt of excitement as the pieces fell into place.

'You think the attack on Lord Billington was staged?'

HG smiled, clearly pleased with my deduction. 'It's a possibility we must explore. The question is, why? What purpose would such a ruse serve?'

I pondered this for a moment before another thought struck me, and asked HG about the new staff members at Roxby Hall; could they be involved?

'An excellent point, Rex. We must investigate their backgrounds thoroughly. If they came from the Boulton-Hicks household, as we suspect, what motivated their move?'

The complexity of the case was beginning to dawn on me. Two separate incidents, potentially linked by an intricate web of deceit and misdirection. I experienced a mix of excitement and trepidation at the challenge that lay ahead.

Just then, Graham, the butler, barged in. Gone was the calm, measured pace at which he, and indeed men of his station, normally conducted themselves. Instead, we observed before us a fellow in shock.

'I...I apologise for...'

HG's astuteness came to the fore as she sought to calm the man. 'Take your time, Graham. There is no rush.'

Her words had an immediate calming effect on the fellow. His breathing eased, and the handwringing ceased.

'That's the ticket,' continued HG. 'Now, what is it you have to tell me?'

The butler straightened his gate and breathed deeply. 'Your Grace, there has been a most dreadful motorcar accident not one-hundred yards from the estate entrance. I am told the vehicle in question belongs to Lord Billington.'

Mention of Billington shook Whipple from his internal meanderings. 'What's that, you say?'

'A crash, sir. The Bentley belongs to Lord Billington. It is feared the occupants are dead.'

'Dead, you say?' Now HG's calm exterior slipped for a few seconds. 'We must attend and see what sucker we might give to the victims.'

THE SCENE that we came upon was truly shocking. A lone vehicle appeared to be involved.

'He's come around that blind corner too quickly and driven into the ditch,' Whipple exclaimed as he scampered down a steep bank and looked into the rear passenger window. 'No one in the back. That just leaves the driver.'

I watched in horror as the scene unfolded. The car lay at an awkward angle, its front end crumpled against a scarred tree springing from the far side of the ditch. The afternoon sun glinted off the twisted metal, casting eerie shadows across the wreckage.

I joined the inspector, my heart pounding.

'Careful, Rex,' HG called from behind. 'The ground looks treacherous.'

I nodded, picking my way down the slope. Whipple moved along the car's length and pressed his face against the driver's window, hands cupped around his eyes to block out the glare.

'Can't see properly,' he growled, tugging at the door handle.

The door refused to budge. Whipple's face reddened with exertion as he pulled harder, his knuckles white with the effort. With a sudden groan of protesting metal, the door finally gave way.

Whipple stumbled back, nearly losing his footing in the water. He regained his balance and leaned into the car.

'Heavens,' he breathed.

I dreaded what he might say next.

Whipple straightened up, his face grim. 'He's dead. Neck's broken, I'd wager. No other obvious injuries. I assume Lord Billington's chauffeur was on the way to collect his master, which ended in disaster.'

A chill ran down my spine as I gazed at the motionless figure slumped over the steering wheel. The silence that followed was deafening, broken only by the gentle gurgle of water in the ditch meandering around the twisted metal of the Bentley.

'There's nothing to be done for this poor fellow. I suggest we head back and telephone for an ambulance. I'll put a call into the local station to fill them in, and to get a couple of officers to oversee things here.' Whipple's voice tailed off as he stood motionless, eyes firmly fixed on the sad scene before him.

Before scrambling back up the bank, Whipple turned off the ignition and removed the car keys. 'The last thing we want now is for the car to catch fire. Better safe than sorry,' he mumbled in a deflated tone.

It was then that the sound of a vehicle could be heard approaching from around the same blind bend that the Bentley's driver failed to negotiate, with fatal results.

'We don't want another accident,' Whipple shouted as he sprinted to the dangerous curve, seemingly without thought for his own safety. In the event, he just managed to alert the driver of the danger in time. Whatever he said had an immediate effect. The car began the tortuous task of turning around on the narrow road. After several attempts to reposition the car, the driver eased the vehicle forward and out of sight.

It was when Whipple began his slow walk back to our position that matters took a grave turn. Suddenly, he stopped, his eyes fixed on the Bentley.

'What is the matter, Arthur?' HG began. 'Do come away before a car hits you.'

Still, the detective stood rooted to the spot before slowly approaching the Bentley's near-side rear light.

'Is there something wrong? Come, come, Arthur. Speak.'

HG's appeal led to Whipple retracing his steps, then crouching down as if searching for something. After several seconds, he approached our position, a hand stroking his chin. Another sure sign he was on to something.

'I don't think that the chauffeur's death was an accident, or at least the crash wasn't,' commented Whipple.

'What do you mean, Arthur? Surely, the crash explains all the damage we see.'

Whipple shook his head. 'Not quite, HG. Take a closer look at the car. The passenger side rear light is broken, yet the driver miscalculated a left-hand bend and ended up in the ditch. As you would expect, all the damage is to the right side of the Bentley, yet here we have minor damage on the left. How did that happen, I wonder?'

A chill ran down my spine. The detective was right; the damage pattern made little sense. I peered at the crumpled metal, trying to piece together what might have occurred.

HG stepped closer to the wreckage; her eyes narrowed in concentration. 'Are you suggesting that this wasn't an accident?'

Whipple nodded slowly. 'I believe something - or someone - may have struck the car before it careened off the road. The damage to the left rear light couldn't have been caused by the impact with the tree or the ditch. It's inconsistent with the remainder of the crash scene.'

I felt my heart racing as the implications of Whipple's theory sank in. If he was right, we were dealing with something far more sinister than a tragic accident.

'But who would want to harm Lord Billington, assuming they believed him to have been in the car?' I asked, my voice barely above a whisper.

'Let's not get ahead of ourselves,' Whipple began. 'This may be a simple, though unforgivable, case of the other driver leaving the scene of an accident. A not uncommon, panicked response, I'm afraid.'

HG reacted to Whipple's hypothesis. 'Let us attempt to piece together what may have happened. Lord Billington's chauffeur, in a hurry to collect his employer, drives at speed around a blind bend, oblivious to the car behind him.'

'Then the other vehicle gives the Bentley a nudge,' Whipple added, picking up HG's thread. 'A glancing blow is struck, causing damage to the Bentley's left rear light. The chauffeur over-reacts and ends up in the ditch, breaking his neck as the car careers into the tree.'

I felt obliged to add that if the Bentley sustained damage, so too did the other car. I further suggested that since it was likely to be a local driver, it shouldn't be too hard a job to trace it by speaking to car repair garage owners in the surrounding villages.

'You make a valid point,' HG said as she looked at the tarmacadam road surface. 'Notice anything, Arthur?'

Whipple nodded. 'Yes, the skid marks. I noticed them as I walked back from the corner. There's a short trail of tyre rubber that indicates a quick shift to the left. My thinking is that the Bentley's pursuer made contact, then changed direction at speed so it didn't follow its quarry into the ditch. Mission accomplished; the other driver did a runner.'

I listened intently as HG and Whipple discussed the possible motives behind the deliberate collision with the Bentley. Their voices were low, almost conspiratorial, as they pieced together the puzzle.

'I'm content this was no accident,' HG began, her eyes narrowing. 'Why kill by this method? If they were after Billington,' HG mused, 'It could be connected to the attack at his estate. Perhaps someone is determined to silence him, but about what?'

Whipple nodded; his eyes narrowed. 'Billington might have stumbled upon something during his business dealings that made him a target.'

'Or,' HG added, her voice lowering, 'It may be related to his father's past indiscretions. Old vendettas have a way of resurfacing among the landed gentry.'

I interjected, to ask why carry out the mission in such a risky manner?

HG turned to me. 'Perhaps recent events forced someone's hand.'

Whipple suddenly straightened, a new thought clearly

forming. 'What if we're looking at this all wrong? Perhaps the chauffeur was the intended target all along?'

The idea hadn't occurred to me, but it made a certain sense.

HG nodded slowly. 'An interesting theory, Arthur. The chauffeur might have come across information that was a danger to the third party. Or perhaps he was involved in something nefarious himself.'

'Exactly,' Whipple continued, warming to the idea. 'We know little about this man. He could have been blackmailing someone, or maybe he was a loose end that needed tying up.'

My mentor, and Whipple, bounced ideas back and forth, each possibility seeming more plausible than the last. A simple car accident had transformed into a complex web of potential motives and suspects.

'We'll need to dig into the chauffeur's background,' HG declared. 'Find out who he was, where he came from, and who might have wanted him dead.'

Whipple nodded. 'And we mustn't rule out the possibility that both Billington and the chauffeur were targets. Two birds with one stone, as it were.'

Whipple paced back and forth; his brow furrowed. 'Perhaps the chauffeur was on his way to deliver crucial information to someone…Perhaps to you, HG. After all, we are but a few yards from the Estate entrance?'

As we stood in a huddle several yards from the wreckage, the distant wail of mechanical bells grew louder. Within moments, the narrow country lane erupted into a flurry of activity. Two police cars screeched to a halt, followed closely by an ambulance. The scene transformed from eerie quiet to controlled chaos in the blink of an eye.

Two constables leapt from their vehicle, sprinting

towards the blind bend. 'We need to close off this road immediately!'

The ambulance crew approached the mangled Bentley, their faces grim as they assessed the situation. 'What do you reckon, Alf, straight onto the stretcher?' one muttered. 'Yep. He's gone, so it's no use mucking about. We need to get him to the hospital morgue, sharpish.'

As the emergency personnel swarmed around us, HG, Whipple, and I found ourselves pushed to the side-lines. We huddled together, watching the scene unfold.

'Well,' Whipple began, 'it seems our investigation has taken yet another unexpected turn.'

HG nodded, her eyes never leaving the wreckage. 'Indeed. We must tread carefully now, Arthur. This is no longer just about a stolen vase or a poisoning. We're dealing with a dark force here.'

I enquired what our next move might be in a tone barely above a whisper.

Whipple stroked his chin. 'Rex, perhaps you could have a discreet word with some of the local garages, as you suggested. See if anyone's brought in a car with recent damage to the right front corner of the vehicle.'

'Excellent idea,' HG agreed. 'I'll come with you so that we may call on Billington. He may know nothing of this tragedy and will be dumbstruck. On the other hand, if he's involved in this terrible outcome, his best acting skills will be on show, and we must crack the ugly facade.'

'Meanwhile,' Arthur intoned, 'I shall liaise with the local police. They may have information we're not yet privy to, and, perhaps, loan me a patrol car while you two are about your business.'

As we continued to discuss our next moves, the ambulance crew finally extracted the chauffeur's body from the wreckage. They covered him with a sheet and carried him towards the waiting ambulance, a solemn reminder of the gravity of the situation.

HG turned to me, her features unsmiling.

'This whole thing smells like a rotten fish. Care must be our watchword, Rex, or we may be next.'

Chapter Fourteen

THE OTHER LONDON

BY 11PM, all vestiges of the sad scene had vanished, save for the scarred trunk of a substantial oak tree that had taken the life of Lord Billington's chauffeur. The cause of the accident, however, remained a mystery. With this thought hanging over us, we retreated to Thorpe Manor for a late supper.

I slumped into a plush armchair within the library, the events of the day buzzing around my brain. My colleagues joined me at a small reading table, where a steaming pot of tea and a plate of fresh toast awaited us.

Whipple cleared his throat. 'Right, we've been over this case several times in the past few days, but today's tragedy forces us to re-examine everything.'

HG nodded. 'Indeed. The chauffeur's death adds a layer of complexity.'

'Precisely,' Whipple continued, buttering a piece of toast, and causing HG much distress by placing the knife, coated in toasted breadcrumbs, back in the butter. 'We need to determine if we're dealing with separate incidents or if everything leads back to Hilltop.'

'But how can we be sure? It all seems so…disconnected,' HG asked.

She sipped her tea, deep in thought. 'Let's start with what we know. Mr Farrier's death, the break-in at Lord Billington's, and now this fatal accident.'

'But are they truly connected?' began Whipple. 'That's what we need to establish.'

We fell into a contemplative silence, broken only by the gentle clink of teacups against saucers. The weight of the unsolved mysteries hung in the air like a dangerous miasma waiting to strike.

I reminded my compatriots that as we looked upon the sad scene outside, we'd ventured to suggest the chauffeur knew something that made him a target.

HG agreed. 'Yes, that's correct, Rex. But what could that be?'

Whipple shook his head. 'We're speculating wildly now. We need facts, not conjecture.'

I conceded Whipple was correct, but felt we were missing something crucial.

HG set down her cup with a sigh. 'Perhaps we are. But what?'

We continued to discuss the case, going over each detail again and again. But try as we might, we couldn't seem to make the pieces fit together. The more we talked, the more confusing it all became.

As we sat there, mulling over the complexities of our mission, I imagined the gears turning in Whipple's mind. He appeared in a world of his own.

'Right,' the detective declared, suddenly straightening

up. 'I've decided. We're going to treat all the events as one case.'

HG raised an eyebrow. 'Are you certain, Arthur? That's quite a leap.'

Whipple nodded firmly. 'I am. I know it's a risk. If I'm mistaken, we could waste a tremendous amount of time, and it might allow one or more suspects to slip through our fingers.'

HG leaned forward, her eyes narrowing. 'That's precisely my concern. We can't afford to make such a gamble without solid evidence.'

Whipple remained resolute. 'Call it a copper's nose if you like, but I've learned to follow my gut feelings. They're usually correct.'

I watched this exchange with interest. I'd seen Whipple in action before, and I knew that once he set his mind on a course of action, he acted like a terrier sniffing out farm vermin - relentless and single-minded in his pursuit.

HG sighed, recognising the look of determination on Whipple's face. 'Very well. If you're convinced, we'll proceed as if everything is connected. But I hope your instincts are as sharp as you claim.'

Whipple nodded, a glimmer of appreciation in his eyes for HG's trust. 'I assure you I am. I wouldn't suggest such a course of action if I were uncertain.'

As I observed their interaction, I felt a mix of admiration and trepidation. Whipple's conviction was inspiring, but the stakes were incredibly high. If he was mistaken, the consequences could be dire. Yet, I'd seen his instincts pay off before, and I hoped that his copper's nose would lead us to the truth once again.

MONDAY MORNING BROKE with bright sunshine, which rapidly burned off the low mist that smothered the flatlands of Norfolk at this time of year. As I surveyed the lush landscape from a massive bay window in the dining room, the quiet of the morning ended as Whipple crashed through the door, muttering to himself while reading a telegram.

'I am ordered back to London at once,' he announced, showing no interest in the buffet table on which sat several silver heated servers, one of which contained his favourite breakfast sausages.

HG winked at me. 'It must be serious.'

I enquired if Arthur knew why the summons had come at so early an hour. He snorted and continued to pace the cosy room in his baggy suit, made even more wayward by the haste it seemed to have been placed upon his frazzled torso.

Eventually, Whipple slowed his pace and handed the flimsy slip of paper to HG.

'The Home Secretary, no less,' she began. 'This must be about the escalating seriousness of events. I know he will have been briefed about the accident last night. Maybe he has come to the same conclusion as you, Arthur, that events are linked.'

Whipple harrumphed and continued to ignore the buffet table. 'But why today?'

HG dabbed the corners of her mouth with a white linen napkin before placing the item back on her lap. 'You forget the King has an interest in our case. Remember, Their Majesties consider Sir Herbert and Lady Eleanor close friends. I have no doubt the King has made his interest known to the Home Secretary. The pressure is on to get matters brought to a satisfactory conclusion.'

Whipple wandered over to the bay window, although I

doubted he paid much attention to the beauty which stretched out before him. After several seconds, he recovered a watch from the fob pocket of his waistcoat, pressed a small button, and allowed the silver lid to expose the timepiece.

'Ten minutes past nine,' he announced in a rattled tone as he turned to me. 'Do you think you can get me to King's Lynn train station for 10am? I can catch the 10.10am direct train to London Liverpool Street if you can?'

'I'll get the Rolls ready. We've plenty of time.' As I stood at the breakfast table, HG bade me to wait a few seconds. 'We can do better than that. Why don't we all travel to London by car? You remember the promise I gave to Manny Tuffnell? That I would call upon him? It seems too good an opportunity to miss. Also, we can bring you back as soon as the Home Secretary has finished with you. That way we shall minimise the disruption to our investigation.'

The mention of the politician "finishing" with Whipple drained the colour from his cheeks, a point HG picked up on.

'Don't look so worried, Arthur. I know the Home Secretary personally, and I'm no stranger to Their Majesties. All will be well. I assure you.'

Whipple's face contorted into a grimace. 'It's all very well for you to say that, HG, but I've been in a room alone with him before. He doesn't spare the horses, I can tell you.'

I noticed how Whipple's hands trembled as he fiddled with his watch chain. His usual blustering confidence had evaporated, replaced by a nervous energy that seemed to radiate from every pore.

Whipple continued, his voice steadying slightly, 'I appreciate you coming with me, HG. And I must say, it will be interesting to hear how your visit to Tufnell plays out.'

As we prepared to depart, I pondered how HG would be received by Tufnell and his family. She was to keep her word about visiting them, which I knew was important. But would they welcome HG or view her with suspicion? The working-class families I'd known growing up often harboured a deep distrust of the upper classes, regardless of their intentions.

I imagined HG sweeping into their modest home, her aristocratic bearing at odds with the surroundings. Would Tufnell's wife offer her tea in their best china? Would the children stare wide-eyed at this grand lady in their midst? Or would there be tension, resentment at this intrusion into their lives? And would the Rolls survive being left on the street?

As I mulled over these possibilities, I realised how much I admired HG's ability to navigate such delicate social situations. She had a knack for putting people at ease, regardless of their background. Perhaps she would surprise me once again with her tact and diplomacy.

THE THREE-HOUR JOURNEY to London passed without incident. As usual, being a passenger in a car caused Whipple to fall into a sound, noisy slumber. Despite several attempts by HG to rouse the fellow, he refused to comply until my mentor hit him on the shoulder with her parasol.

'What, what…give yourself up at once, do you hear?'

No, the startled cry did not emanate from HG, but from Whipple, as he evidently imagined himself on the trail of a dangerous villain.

'I shall do no such thing, Arthur,' replied a smiling HG. 'However, next time you snore so loudly, you can expect the point of my parasol, and not its silken material. Do we understand each other?'

Despite my first duty to remain focused on the road ahead, I stole several brief glimpses to witness Whipple gradually regaining conciseness.

Presently, we reached Marsham Street in Whitehall, and the location at which Whipple needed to alight.

'Remember, Arthur,' began HG. 'All will be well, and your ordeal will soon be over. I suggest we meet at Fortnum and Mason for a light meal in an hour. I have a table reserved there, so if you arrive first, simply tell them you are with me.'

Whipple alighted the Rolls without saying a word. His eyes locked on the grand entrance to the Home Office's vast edifice. We waited until the austere building swallowed him whole into its vast interior.

'Onwards, Rex. Let us head for Pennington Street in the East End of our magnificent capital city.'

HG settled back into her deep leather seat as I set our course for a particularly poor part of the city, and while I would not contradict HG's view of London. I knew from personal experience that, for many, the riches of the capital failed to penetrate the dank recesses of the working classes' living arrangements.

As we journeyed from the grandeur of Whitehall, a sadness befell me as I observed the stark contrast unfolding before my eyes. The West End, with its glittering theatres and opulent buildings, gradually gave way to a bleaker landscape.

As we entered Wapping, rows upon rows of brick terraced houses, squeezed together, replaced the elegant facades we'd left behind. The streets narrowed, and the air seemed to grow heavier with each turn of the wheel.

Children darted between parked carts and lamp posts, their laughter a stark counterpoint to their ragged appearance. Barefoot and clad in threadbare clothes, they played with whatever came to hand - a stick, a hoop, a battered tin can. Their presence added a touch of life to the otherwise grey surroundings.

As we pulled up to Number 63 Pennington Street, I felt a pang of guilt at the stark difference between our gleaming Rolls-Royce and the paint-peeled door of Manny Tufnell's home.

No sooner had I brought the car to a halt than a swarm of children materialised around us, their eyes wide with wonder at the sight of such a vehicle in their midst.

'Oi, mister! Gis a ride!' came the chorus of tiny voices, hands reaching out to touch the shiny chrome of the radiator grill and immaculate paintwork.

I stepped out, ready to knock on the door, but there was no need. The commotion had brought our quarry to investigate. He stood in the doorway, his face a mask of indifference as I held the rear door of the Rolls open for HG.

In seconds, we were inside Tufnell's tiny home. On the walls, the remains of cheap wallpaper gave the underlying plasterwork a hotch-potch appearance. A small, bare pine table rested against one wall, while opposite an oversized cast-iron hearth with a high mantle dominated the room.

A meagre fire danced lazily in the grate that provided heat to a sizeable iron kettle kept permanently on the boil.

Three young children huddled together near the far corner of the room, their eyes wide as they took in the sight of HG and me in our finery. Despite the squalid surroundings, the children were remarkably clean, in contrast to the urchins we'd seen playing outside.

The oldest child, a boy of perhaps ten or eleven, stood

slightly in front of his siblings. He was the best dressed of the three, wearing a pair of grey shorts and a V-necked long-sleeved jumper without a shirt beneath. The wool looked worn but well cared for, and I admired the pride with which he carried himself.

The two younger children, a boy, and a girl, wore what were clearly hand-me-downs and jumble sale purchases. On the middle child, a boy of about eight, the clothes hung loose, the sleeves of his jumper rolled up to expose his wrists. The youngest, a girl of no more than six, practically swam in an oversized dress, its hem dragging on the floor.

As I took in the scene, my gaze was drawn to the doorway between the living room and what I presumed to be the kitchen. There, leaning against the jamb, stood Tufnell's wife. The years had not been kind to her; she looked older than her age suggested, her face lined and worn. It was clear that the daily grind of keeping the home and taking in washing from anyone prepared to pay a few pennies had taken its toll. Despite her exhaustion, there was a quiet dignity in the way she held herself, watching us with a mixture of curiosity and wariness.

'You came, then,' Tufnell began. 'I didn't think for a second you meant it. Your lot usually don't.'

HG smiled. 'There is a lot to be said for not judging an individual because of the way they live, dress, or speak. Don't you think, Manny...May I call you Manny?'

Tufnell grunted as he took a taper from a narrow earthenware jug on the hearth, lit it in the fire, and used the sliver of wood to light his pipe.

'Try telling the coppers that. To them, were all the same. Thieves and illiterate troublemakers. The only time this country wanted us was during the war. Then we were good enough. And look at us now. We won, yet my union members line up outside the dock gates every morning and wait for a foreman to tap him on the shoulder for a day's work. No tap, no work. "Come back tomorrow", they say, as if the lads have any choice in the matter. The *casual labour system*, they call it. There's nothing casual about needing to feed our families every day, is there?'

His profound discourse brought the conversation to a temporary halt, and I observed that the facts had shocked HG. She gathered herself and continued to probe our host.

'Are you? Illiterate, I mean?'

Tufnell sucked on his pipe to encourage it into life. 'Most of us can read and write. The union sees to that.'

'I'm glad to hear it,' replied HG. 'Is there any way I can help?'

HG's offer brought a look of deep suspicion to Tufnell's eyes.

'You? I suppose you mean money.'

'Husband?' The restraining voice belonged to Mrs Tufnell as she re-emerged from the kitchen carrying a tray, on which stood two mugs and a petite china cup and saucer. 'Mind your manners, husband. The lady said she would visit, and so she has. Don't prove to me you've left your manners at the Dog and Duck.'

The stinging rebuke caused Manny to reconsider his approach.

'I apologise. As my wife says, you've come to visit just like you said. Please, sit at the table and drink.'

As calm settled over the small room, I watched Manny's demeanour soften. He took a long draw from his pipe; the smoke curling lazily around his weathered face.

'The union work, it's difficult,' Manny began, his voice gruff but tinged with pride. 'We're fighting for fair wages, safer working conditions. Every day's a battle against the bosses who'd see us work ourselves to the bone for a pittance.'

HG nodded, encouraging him to continue. I noticed her eyes darting around the room, taking in every detail of the Tufnell's' meagre living conditions.

'That's why I went to Hilltop,' Manny continued, his eyes hardening. 'Sir Herbert, he's one of the worst, or at least his son is. Cutting corners on safety, pushing men and women to work longer hours for less pay. We've tried talking, sent letters, but the company won't budge. I thought if I could just speak to him face-to-face, make him see what he's doing to families like mine…'

Mrs Tufnell, who'd been quietly listening from her spot by the kitchen door, stepped forward. 'The union expects too much of you, Manny,' she said, her voice soft but firm. 'All these meetings, the strikes, the protests. It doesn't put food in our mouths, does it?'

Manny's face fell, and I could see the conflict etched in his features. He looked at his children, huddled together, their eyes wide as they listened to their parents' exchange.

'I know, girl,' he said, his voice barely above a whisper. 'But if we don't fight, who will? Our kids deserve better than this, don't they?'

Mrs Tufnell sighed, a sound filled with both frustration and understanding. 'They do,' she agreed. 'But they also need their father. And a full belly.'

Over the next half-hour, HG and Tufnell engaged in an earnest, sometimes combative, conversation. The toing and froing comprised Manny making a point; HG testing his argument, and so it went on, back and forth like a demented game of ping-pong.

Ultimately, Tufnell and HG came to a point where each appeared to respect the other's view, allowing for a brief, light-hearted conversation about their respective worlds before we took our leave.

It was during this interlude that Tufnell mentioned something that made HG, and I prick up our ears. Retelling the story of his "visit" to Hillside, and the somewhat humorous chase that ensued, Manny said that he hid in the kitchen for several minutes. He admitted that at one point, he'd considered spoiling the cake, especially made for Sir Herbert's celebration. He added that for about a minute, he was alone. Then he heard voices and hid in the scullery. As he peeked around the doorframe, he saw two people. An elderly man dressed in a chauffeur's uniform, and a young man. He couldn't hear what they were saying, but the chauffeur picked up a cake slice next to the cake.

'Then what?' asked HG, her eyes bright with anticipation.

'That's just it. I realised the scullery had a connecting door, so I scarpered without being seen, at least until someone copped me running up some stairs, then all hell broke loose, and you know the rest.'

Our departure from the terraced property saw HG and Manny shake hands and exchange a trusting look. I realised then that each had found an unlikely soulmate.

As we drove across London for our rendezvous with Arthur at Fortnum and Mason, I sensed HG being torn in two directions.

'Your correct, Rex,' said HG in answer to my query to that effect. 'As the Prince of Wales has recently said so eloquently, "Something must be done,"'

I asked HG what she meant.

'The working lives of honest families like the Tufnell's. His Royal Highness made the comment while visiting

Teignmouth in Devon. He is correct. The need is obvious. How to change matters, that is the question?'

As we drove through London's bustling streets, I noticed HG's distracted gaze. She stared out of the car window, her eyes unfocused, lost in thought. The visit to the Tufnell's home had affected her greatly as she contemplated the stark realities we'd witnessed.

'HG?' I ventured, breaking the silence. 'Are you alright?'

She leaned forward from the rear seat, her expression a mix of determination and concern. 'Yes, Rex. Just... processing. There's much to consider after our visit.'

I nodded, understanding the seriousness of our recent experience.

Soon enough, we pulled up outside Fortnum & Mason, where. I helped HG from the car. I marvelled at the opulence surrounding us.

We entered the establishment, and a smartly dressed maitre d' greeted us with a polite bow. 'Ah, Your Grace. Inspector Whipple is already seated. Please, follow me.'

He led us through the bustling dining room, past tables laden with fine china and crystal. The air was thick with the aroma of delicate teas and freshly baked pastries. As we weaved between tables, I caught snippets of conversation - talk of the latest society gossip, political musings, and discussions of upcoming social events.

Finally, we reached our table, where Inspector Whipple sat, looking somewhat out of place amidst the refined atmosphere. His usual confident demeanour seemed shaken, no doubt a result of his meeting at the Home Office.

'There you are,' Arthur, HG said.

Whipple stood as we approached. 'I wondered if you'd got lost in the East End.'

HG smiled wryly. 'Not lost, Arthur. Just…enlightened.'

As we settled into our chairs, HG wasted no time in recounting our visit to Tufnell.

'It was quite astonishing, Arthur,' she began, her eyes gleaming with newfound understanding. 'Manny Tufnell, despite his rough exterior, is a man of principle. He's fighting for better conditions for his fellow workers, often at great personal cost.'

Whipple nodded, seemingly unpersuaded. 'And did you glean anything pertinent to our case?'

'Oh, indeed we did. Manny shared something quite intriguing about his escapade at Hilltop.'

She leaned in, lowering her voice despite the bustling atmosphere around us. 'During his ill-fated visit, Manny hid in the kitchen for several minutes. He admitted to briefly considering sabotaging Sir Herbert's celebratory cake.'

Whipple's eyebrows shot up. 'Did he now?'

'No, no, he didn't go through with it,' HG clarified. 'But here's the fascinating part. While hiding, he overheard voices and peeked from his hiding place. He saw two people near the cake - an elderly man in a chauffeur's uniform and a young man.'

I watched as Whipple's expression shifted from scepticism to keen interest.

'A chauffeur, you say?' he muttered, more to himself than to us.

'Yes, and there's more,' HG continued, her excitement palpable. 'Manny couldn't hear their conversation, but he distinctly remembers seeing the young man pick up a cake slice that was next to the cake.'

Whipple's eyes widened. 'I wonder…?'

HG nodded. 'Precisely. Unfortunately, Manny had to

flee before he could see or hear anything else, but I believe this information may be crucial to our investigation.'

Chapter Fifteen

TO THE BANK

THE DOWAGER TOOK full advantage of the fine weather as we reached her preferred location for our picnic, Holkham. HG's Norfolk Estate had many fine vantage points. However, the lakeside provided a splendid spot from which to view a variety of fields under crop, a thick woodland to our left, and beyond, a tantalising glimpse of the North Sea as it merged with the big skies if Norfolk.

Long gone were the difficulties of the previous day's trip to London. Now, all remained quiet, save for the calming song of the Willow Warbler and occasional choral entrance of the Chiffchaff.

I busied myself unpacking our lunch from the Rolls and set about laying a thick woollen cloth on which to lay the refreshments and provide a comfortable seating position for our intimate gathering.

All the while, Whipple, and HG strode along the reed-edge lake, occasionally pointing to something or other one of the unlikely duo found interesting.

Before I announced lunch, I set out three plates and accompanying cutlery, and a fine cup and saucer beside each place setting. Finally, I double-checked that the most important embellishments were present; Fortnum and Mason Special Relish and sea-salt sent from the Outer Hebrides on annual consignment. That just left me to brew HG's favourite hot beverage, Twining's English Afternoon Tea blend.

As I called my companions and stood back to admire my handy-work, I pondered the previous evening. After such a busy day, there had been much to digest. For once, HG didn't insist on dissecting each element of the new information that came to hand. Instead, she suggested we retire early, so that we may each cogitate upon our own thoughts, and in Whipple's case, make any enquires by telephone that he deemed fit to further our investigation. Over lunch, we were to share our thoughts and plan our next steps.

As HG and Whipple approached, I watched their faces light up at the sight of the picnic spread. HG's eyes sparkled with delight as she surveyed the scene.

'My word, Rex! You've outdone yourself this time. Is that the special relish from Fortnum's, I spy?'

I nodded, pleased with her reaction, and added I'd prepared her favourite tea blend.

'Splendid, simply splendid,' HG beamed, settling herself on the blanket with the grace becoming of a Dowager Duchess.

Whipple, looking slightly out of his element, gingerly lowered himself onto the woollen cloth. 'I must say, this is a far cry from the cheese and pickle sandwiches wrapped in newspaper my sister prepares for me each day.'

HG chuckled, her eyes twinkling with mischief. 'Come now, Arthur, you've had your fair share of al fresco dining during stakeouts?'

'Hardly comparable, HG,' Whipple retorted, a hint of a smile playing at the corners of his mouth.

I grinned at their easy banter. It was a testament to how far we'd come as a team. As I poured the tea, I pondered upon the unlikely friendship that had blossomed between the aristocratic Dowager and the no-nonsense inspector.

HG delicately spread a little relish on a piece of bread. 'Now, gentlemen, shall we discuss our findings over this marvellous repast?'

The conversation flowed as freely as the tea, punctuated by appreciative murmurs over the food and the occasional witty remark. I found myself once again in awe of HG's ability to merge the serious nature of our investigation with the pleasure of a sunny lunchtime picnic.

As we settled into our picturesque luncheon spot, accompanied by the gentle breeze carrying the scent of wildflowers, Whipple made ready to speak.

'I'll start,' he announced, setting down his teacup with a soft clink. 'I believe a brief reminder of what the Home Secretary said is in order.'

HG and I concentrated, eager to hear his report.

'The man was charming, I'll give him that,' Whipple began, his tone measured. 'But he left me in no doubt about the urgency of catching the murderer - or murderers.'

I noticed a slight furrow in HG's brow as she processed this information.

Whipple continued, his voice lowering slightly, 'He also mentioned that persons of the highest station had an interest in the case. I took that to mean Their Majesties.'

'Yes, I did highlight to you that might be the case. Anyway, go on,' HG said.

'He stressed that urgency is of the utmost regard,' Whipple added, his usual gruff demeanour tinged with a hint of concern. 'We're not just solving a murder now; we're potentially averting a scandal that could shake the very foundations of high society.'

I asked Whipple if the Home Secretary had offered any information that might help us expedite the case. His reply provided information that Whipple had not shared the previous day.

'That's a timely question,' he said, his expression one of frustration. 'He briefed me on the outcome of Mr Farrier's post-mortem.'

Whipple sighed as he continued, 'I admit to being irritated at hearing the news second-hand. But then I guess the pathologist's written report will, no doubt, be waiting for me at Scotland Yard.'

HG raised an eyebrow, clearly eager for Whipple to get to the heart of the matter.

'Farrier died from the fast-acting poison, Cyanide,' Whipple revealed, his voice low and grave.

A chill ran down my spine despite the warm summer air. Cyanide was a brutal way to die.

Whipple paused, his eyes darting between HG and me. 'But here's the bombshell, as it were,' he said, leaning in closer. 'The Home Secretary told me the cake itself was an innocent bystander to events.'

HG's eyes widened, and I held my breath.

'Which begs the question,' Whipple continued, his voice barely above a whisper, 'How then was the poison administered?'

A heavy silence followed. Our picturesque luncheon

spot suddenly felt less idyllic as the gravity of this new information sank in.

HG deftly picked up a crustless salmon sandwich with one hand, while slowly stirring her tea with the other.

'This is, indeed, important news,' she began. 'We at last have evidence of what killed poor Farrier, yet it leaves open the means by which the dreadful substance entered the victim's bloodstream.'

I ventured that perhaps the man drank tea, or some other liquid that had been laced with the poison. HG disagreed by reminding me that Sir Herbert was the intended target, and not his chief accountant. A poisoned cake made sense. An opportune decision to imbibe liquid meant for another appeared unlikely, given the public nature of the poor fellow's demise.

I watched Whipple's intense concentration as we spoke. He took a thoughtful sip of tea before speaking.

'You're both right,' he began, his voice low and measured. 'The manner of administration is crucial here. We know it wasn't the cake, which throws our initial assumptions into disarray. Cyanide kills quickly. It would have had to be introduced to Farrier's system just seconds before he collapsed.'

I leaned in, intrigued by the inspector's line of thinking.

'We need to consider every item Farrier came into contact with, in his last moments,' Whipple mused. 'His glass, cutlery, even his napkin. Anything he might have touched or ingested.'

HG interjected, 'And we mustn't forget that Sir Herbert was the intended target. The method of delivery must have been something specific to his place setting or personal effects.'

Whipple nodded gravely. 'Precisely. We're looking for

something that could have easily been mistaken or transferred between Sir Herbert and Farrier. Something innocuous that wouldn't raise suspicion.'

I mentally retraced the events of that fateful evening, trying to recall every detail of the celebration. 'Could it have been something airborne?' I suggested. 'A powder or spray of some sort?'

Whipple shook his head. 'Unlikely. That would have affected others in the vicinity. No, this was a targeted and precise attack.'

The inspector's nostrils flared as he continued. 'We need to revisit the scene. Every inch of that room must be examined. The tiniest detail could be the key to unravelling this mystery.'

A profound silence fell over our gathering. Even the songbirds appeared subdued. I lightened the mood by retracing my steps to the Rolls to unveil a splendid array of iced fancies. On presentation, together with refreshed teacups, my mission succeeded.

'You are a treasure,' extolled HG as she selected a delicacy dressed in her favourite colour. Whipple merely took the two fancies within reach.

'I agree with your assessment, Arthur,' HG said as she delicately peeled the paper casing from her cake selection. 'However, the other vital element to our investigation, now that we know how Farrier died, is to analyse our prime suspects' movements, from the moment the evening began to the second you allowed everyone to leave.'

I watched as my two compatriots mulled over the complexities of the case, their expressions a mixture of concentration and concern. Arthur, having finished his second fancy, gave his further opinions.

'Yet we come back to the question; has the attack on

Lord Bellingham, and the death of his chauffeur have anything to do with the events at Hilltop?' he mused while eyeing up a third iced fancy.

Whipple continued, his voice tinged with frustration, 'For now, it appears an impenetrable question, which we must untangle if we are to avoid an investigative catastrophe, let alone incurring the wrath of the Home Secretary, and the King himself.'

I felt nauseous at the mention of such serious consequences, and Whipple's next words only deepened my unease.

'This is not an outcome I wish to explore from a career perspective,' he said gravely. Then, turning to HG, he added, 'Nor, I imagine, might you wish to suffer the social scandal.'

HG's face remained impassive, but I noticed a slight tightening around her eyes. The gravity of our situation hung heavy in the air, overshadowing the pleasant summer day and our splendid spread.

This time, my re-charging of the teacups failed to lift spirits. Instead, the pair picked up their beverage in unison, both looking into the distance as if waiting for the end of days.

'We must stop this,' HG announced to our consternation.

'Stop what?' the inspector replied.

'The negative air that pervades our soiree. Now is the time for action. Think about it, gentlemen. We now have concrete proof of how Mr Farrier died, and we have made several excellent deductions concerning the who and how of the matter. It is now time for action.'

Whipple made a half-hearted attempt to select yet

another iced fancy but gave up on the idea as he considered HG's challenge.

'We must split our forces. Rex, when we have finished our meal, please take me back to the Manor house so I may speak with certain parties by telephone. You two can then pursue investigations into who jumped ship from the Boulton-Hicks'; who stole the artifact from Lord Billington, and determine if the chauffeur's death was an innocent, if tragic, car accident, or something altogether more sinister.'

Whipple thought for a moment, before agreeing to HG's plan.

'Excellent, so it's settled,' she announced.

I DID NOT INTEND to dwell at Thorpe Manor once we'd dropped HG off. However, as I brought the Rolls to a stop under the carriage portico, Graham, the butler, opened the great door with an urgency one rarely observes in a man of his station.

'Your Grace,' he urged as I opened the rear door and assisted my mentor from the car.

'Yes, Graham. What on earth is the matter?'

'An urgent telegram for the Inspector.'

Whipple seemed as confused as HG and me. 'For me? From whom?' mused the detective.

Graham stepped forward and handed a slip of paper to Scotland Yard's finest.

'It's from Sergeant Muddleford.'

'Do read it aloud, Arthur, or I shall burst in anticipation,' HG said.

Whipple scanned the note a second time: Hilltop

intruder identified. STOP. Bertram Appleyard. STOP. Released on bail. ENDS.

'The name is unknown to me,' HG mused.

I, too, remained a stranger to the name.

Whipple thumbed his chin, deep in thought as he paced back and forth, deep in concentration. The gravel crunched beneath his feet, punctuating the silence that had fallen over us.

'Well,' he began, halting his progress, 'It seems the man has taken quite an interest in Hilltop. I'd wager he didn't stumble in by accident.'

HG nodded; her eyes filled with curiosity. 'Go on, Arthur. What's your theory?'

'News travels fast, and my hypothesis is that the fellow sought to take advantage of what he thought might be an empty Hilltop after the dreadful events of that location. He likely found an open window, or staff entrance through which he gained access to the house.'

HG tapped her chin thoughtfully. 'Might he be working for someone else? A pawn in a greater game?'

'It's certainly possible, HG,' Whipple replied. 'Promises of money or adventure can easily sway young men. Either he works alone and sells his ill-gotten gains to the highest bidder, or he steals to order, a stratagem not unknown among the upper class…isn't that right, HG?'

My mentor sighed. 'Unfortunately, I am saddened to say that is the case in a tiny minority of my contemporaries.'

OUR FIRST STOP of the afternoon involved visiting the local hospital, which took responsibility for the chauffeur's body. Morgues had never been my favourite places to visit, unlike Whipple who, from his body language, appeared quite at home.

Perhaps the smell of formaldehyde, or overbearing white tiles caused my anxiety, or the stark, cold slab upon which post-mortems took place unnerved me. Either way, I knew I'd feel more comfortable when the ordeal ended.

So here I stood, beside Whipple, chatting away to the pathologist about various gruesome cases. I understood gallows humour as necessary in such places. However, the pleasure each took in attempting to out-do the other I found disconcerting.

At last, they got down to the business of the day. The pathologist walked up and down a row of floor to ceiling steel cabinets until he found the correct incumbent. The man called us over as he slowly pulled until the body lay before us on its sliding shelf. I noticed a cardboard label attached to one of the man's big toes. It read, "Albert Fletcher. D.O. B 24/08/1860".

The pathologist reached for a white cloth covering the body, his gloved hands moving with practiced efficiency. As he folded it back to reveal the head and shoulders, I held my breath. The face of Albert Fletcher came into view, his features relaxed, but pale and waxy.

He looked as if he were in a deep sleep. The lines etched around his eyes and mouth, testament to a life lived, seemed softer now. It was difficult to reconcile this peaceful visage with the violent end he'd met.

Whipple broke the solemn silence. 'Any signs of injury, doctor?'

The pathologist's eyes swept over the exposed skin before answering. 'Other than the indentation and bruising to his forehead and neck decolouration consistent with a total fracture of the spinal column, the body is free from injury.'

I winced involuntarily at the clinical description, imagining the force required to cause such damage.

Whipple appeared engrossed, his keen eyes examining every detail.

'So, he had no time to react, meaning he was in control until the car left the road.'

The pathologist nodded. 'Indeed. The impact thrust him forward in his seat, hence the damage to the frontal lobe from coming into contact with the steering wheel, then a sharp recoil, cause the fatal injury to his neck. To be frank, it's a similar injury we find in prisoners who have suffered execution by hanging. At least it was quick. I doubt the man realised what was happening to him.'

I asked if we might see any artifacts found in his uniform pockets. Whipple looked shocked I had blurted out the question, or was it irritation that he had not yet posed the same enquiry?

'Everything is in that envelope.' The pathologist pointed to a desk on the far side of the morgue.

Whipple led the way, looked inside the open container and emptied its contents onto the sterile desk.

'Usual stuff, I suppose. Seven-shilling and threepence in change, an unremarkable handkerchief in need of a good boiling, and a set of house keys.'

He next turned his attention to a leather wallet made pliable through use over a long period. Whipple carefully opened the silk-lined item and searched each compartment.

'An unused stamp costing twopence, three cigarette cards depicting members of the English national football team, and...what's this?' Whipple hesitated for a moment, surprised at his discovery. 'Three ten-pound notes issued by the Gurney & Co. bank of Norwich, each freshly printed and signed. How on earth did the fellow come by such a large amount of money, I wonder?'

I exchanged a baffled look with the inspector. From a personal point of view, I couldn't imagine holding thirty pounds in my hand. Such an amount being beyond my experience.

'No working man collects such riches by virtue of his weekly toil. Other than an inheritance, the cash points to the fellow being paid handsomely by someone to do something nefarious. That is my experience, and I can find no other reason for the presence of such an amount in his personal effects.'

As I stared at the fortune, a thought occurred to me. Each note had a unique serial number embossed on its surface. Might it be possible to ask the bank to trace its issue?

'I'd had that thought myself,' replied Whipple, on hearing my suggestion. 'If we get a move on, we might just make it to Norwich before the bank closes for the day.'

Excited about a dash to the city, I returned the money to Whipple, who diligently placed it back into the wallet. As he closed it, I noticed a run of loose stitching along one edge and drew Whipple's attention to the damage.

'Well, I'll be blown,' the inspector exclaimed. Curious, I watched as he felt for something in his jacket. In seconds, he produced a small set of tweezers and teased out a slip of paper from the wallet's lining.

Eager for more information, I asked Whipple if the meagre scrap had anything written upon it.

'Let me see,' the detective responded as he lay the small strip flat on the desk. From my position I could see several marks, but not clearly enough to make sense of the inscriptions.

'It's a telephone number. The problem is, it doesn't mention the geographic area.'

I knew this to be a major issue, since we might end up calling every main telephone exchange in the country to see if they could match the number to their local subscribers.

'We might make an educated guess that the number relates to a subscriber in either Norfolk, Suffolk, or Cambridge. I think it is unlikely the chauffeur would deal with anyone more distant. At any rate, when we have time later today, I'll give each a ring. For now, we need to get a move on to Messer's Gurney & Co of Norwich.'

WE ARRIVED at the bank with literally minutes to spare. I parked the Rolls on the busy St. Stephen's Street and followed Whipple into the exquisite banking hall.

'May I speak to the manager, please,' Whipple asked as he showed his credentials to a junior clerk who stood behind a richly embellished oak counter. The expensive woodwork extended to a partition around three feet on either side of his position, and repeated between each counter clerk, providing a high degree of protection from unsavoury characters intent on stealing the bank's cash.

A minute later, a tall, immaculately dressed gentleman appeared from an office near where we stood. A pristine handkerchief showed above his suit jacket breast pocket, topped off with a fresh carnation held in place through a lapel buttonhole.

The fellow's highly oiled hair was only marginally less off-putting than his sceptical facial expression.

'You maintain you are an inspector from Scotland Yard. How do I know this to be true?'

Whipple sighed. This was clearly not the first time such a challenge had landed at his feet. He took a notebook, embellished with the insignia of the Metropolitan police, and placed this before the lurking fellow who towered over the inspector.

The man placed a monocle over his left eye and scrutinised the notebook as if it were a bar of gold being presented to the bank for safekeeping.

'Very well. However, I reserve the right to ring Scotland Yard if at any point I doubt your integrity.'

The fellow looked me up and down as if to reinforce his point.

Whipple raised an eyebrow, but chose not to react, instead keeping his focus on the prize of tracing the ten-pound notes.

'Come with me,' the manager commanded. We complied and in seconds, passed from the public domain to the rarefied atmosphere of the bank's inner sanctum.

Whipple extracted the wallet from his inside pocket, opened it and took out three crisp ten-pound notes. He laid them on the highly polished desk of our interrogator.

The fellow picked each note up, recorded the serial number on a piece of paper, and scrutinised the note's signature with a magnifying glass. Finally, he gave the watermark the same care and attention.

'I am satisfied that the promissory notes, as presented, are genuine and that this bank issued them. If you'll wait a short while, I will determine when they were issued. The matter of whom they were provided to is more challenging, and not routinely recorded unless we have reason to suspect fraud.'

As suddenly as the man had appeared in the banking hall, so, too, he vanished from the office, leaving Whipple and I to twiddle our thumbs for several minutes.

At length, he returned, sat in his rich leather chair, and laid the notes out next to one another on the desk.

'Thank you for your patience, gentlemen,' he began. 'All three were issued last Friday at around 2.55 p m. We do not keep a written record of who we issue funds to, but the bank tracks serial numbers.'

We exchanged a thoughtful glance.

'So, a bank teller completed the transaction immediately before you closed for the day?'

The manager sat back in his chair and managed the merest hint of a smile, making this new habit of keen interest to me.

'You are correct, Inspector, and it is for that reason the bank may help you identify the customer.'

Whipple frowned. 'But I thought you said—'

'Forgive me for interrupting, and yes, I said we didn't record who funds are issued to in cash. However, as you mentioned, the person approached the teller late in the day. So late, in fact, that he was the only customer left in the banking hall.'

The inspector immediately jumped on this new information. '"He", you say?'

Our host's smile broadened. 'I did indeed. Also, the teller informs me they remember the fellow distinctly on account of the uniform he wore.'

Now Whipple smiled. 'Let me guess; a chauffeur's uniform?'

'Ah, you have someone in mind?'

'Yes,' Whipple responded in quick time. 'I imagine your staff thought it curious that a working man gained access to such a sum of money. I presume the fellow presented an open cheque?'

'You are ahead of me, inspector. However, yes, you are correct since the chap doesn't bank with us. In fact, I doubt he has a bank account anywhere.'

The rapid-fire toing and froing of the conversation put my mind in a spin attempting to keep up with their exchanges. And so it continued.

'May I anticipate your next question? In fact, the money order belonged to the account of a distinguished Norfolk family. Alas, I'm not permitted to reveal the name of the customer to you.'

Whipple drew a deep breath before responding. 'You should know I have legal remedies at my disposal to force the bank to provide the information.'

The manager's body language stiffened. 'Whatever they are, it will not help you. Of course, the Metropolitan police could mount a court case. Many have tried over the years with this, and other banks. However, the industries' secrecy remains intact, and I see no reason to believe that is about to change.'

'Sir, I'm sorry that our meeting is to end on a matter of disagreement, and I thank you for the information you have willingly provided. As for the matter of secrecy, we shall see,' Whipple intoned.

The combatants exchanged polite nods as the inspector stood up and made for the office door. I followed his example and bade the manager good day as we re-entered the magnificent banking hall and onwards to the entrance doors.

Once on the pavement, we each drew breath as the Rolls beckoned. In the comparative quiet of its calming interior, I heard Whipple let out a great sigh and asked him how he felt about matters.

'Our meeting went far, far better than I expected,' he began. 'How lucky are we that the bank teller remembered the customer because of the uniform the man wore? As for my threat of court proceedings, well, the fellow spoke the truth. Banks will not divulge customer details, and the courts will not force them to do so. However, I thought it useful to apply a measure of pressure. You never know, we may get lucky again and receive further information from the branch manager in due course.'

As we made for Thorpe Manor, we exchanged several theories relating to who the deceased chauffeur's financial patron might be, and for what reason, money changed hands. Whipple summed the matter up with aplomb, bordering on the terrifying.

'We have three questions outstanding as far as the chauffeur is concerned. The first related to why he received the money. Second, if the payment is connected with the death of Mr Farrier, and who knows, the beating Lord Billington took, did the fellow try to reach HG to confess his malevolent involvement out of fear of his erstwhile financial benefactor? If so, then my third question answers itself. Whoever paid him to kill, took revenge for his treachery concerning HG, and arranged for his murder…and, of course, they remain free to kill again. Time is short, Rex; the killer is near at hand. We must stop them before they strike again.'

As a profound silence descended between us, I realised we had forgotten a vital clue. The telephone number Whipple found in the dead man's wallet. I reminded the inspector about the find. His reaction came quickly.

'There, Rex, do you see? Pull over, man. A post office.'

I thought for a moment that Whipple might take the

steering wheel from my control. Such was his determination to discover to whom the telephone number belonged to. As luck had it, I had time to execute an emergency stop, without causing undue alarm to anything behind us. As soon as the car came to a rest, Whipple scurried out and disappeared into the small post office. Minutes later, he returned. I noted the dazed look he wore. His countenance failed to improve once seated in the Rolls. At last, he spoke. His words chilled my spine.

'We have them, Rex. Our killer is unmasked, and we must get them before they silence us.'

Chapter Sixteen

A MASTER ARTISAN

HG'S enthusiastic welcome made clear she awaited a full briefing of our endeavours. As Whipple and I settled once more into the comfort of the Manor's library, she hovered above us, waiting in expectation.

As Whipple provided a fulsome report, I ruminated on the Inspector's warning. The stakes could not be higher. The pieces of the puzzle now lay before us. Yet we were not in control of events, not yet. Rather, a cunning and merciless adversary, with hired killers at hand, knew our whereabouts and may already be moving in on us.

For the first time since joining my mentor and the Inspector on their investigations, genuine fear gripped me. The pieces of the puzzle were at hand, but so too was the realisation of the danger we faced.

I pondered the terrible revenge our unseen enemy might unleash upon us. This mastermind had already showed a willingness to murder, and now, with their back against the wall, what lengths might they go to? The thought of hired killers stalking us made my blood run cold.

We needed to act swiftly to mitigate the danger. Perhaps we could lay a trap, using ourselves as bait to draw out the villain. But the risks were enormous. One false move and we'd find ourselves at the wrong end of a poisoned cup or a fatal 'accident'.

I glanced at my companions; their faces etched with determination. We had to win control of the situation, and fast. The alternative was too ghastly to contemplate. If we failed, not only would justice go unserved, but we might well pay with our lives.

'We need a plan,' I blurted out, interrupting Whipple mid-sentence. 'Something to turn the tables on this fiend before they strike again.'

HG raised an eyebrow, her keen mind no doubt already formulating strategies. Whipple nodded; his usual bravado tempered by the seriousness of our situation.

As we discussed options, I couldn't shake the feeling that time was running out. The mastermind behind these appalling events was surely preparing a foul finale. We had to be ready to avoid becoming their prey.

HG sighed; her usual spark of enthusiasm dimmed. 'I'm afraid my telephone call to Eleanor Cummings, while reassuring her, yielded nothing new for our investigation.'

Whipple spoke next. 'The information about the dead chauffeur and that shocking phone call have narrowed our focus considerably. However, I need to have one or two more conversations before suggesting a plan to ensnare the killer, so I shall remain here and make use of the telephone, if I may?'

HG smiled, then nodded.

He turned to me. 'Rex, I'd like you to spend a couple of hours visiting local car repair garages. We need to follow up on the damage to the car that nudged the Bentley into the tree, killing the chauffeur.'

I readily agreed, eager to contribute.

Whipple then addressed HG. 'Would you mind calling back on the clockmaker in King's Lynn? There's something I want you to check for me.'

'Certainly, she began, 'I'll get the head gardener to drive me over there in his old banger. That should be fun.'

I felt a mix of excitement and trepidation. We were closing in on the truth, but the danger was far from over. As I prepared to leave for my assigned task, I knew we were walking a tightrope with a deadly fall, awaiting one false step.

THE SCENIC LANDSCAPE of North Norfolk stood in stark contrast with the churning of my stomach. Not even the swaying sheaths of wheat, nor the yellow carpet of oilseed rape as far as the eye could see, acted as a tonic. The journey from one garage to another seemed to drag as my mind meandered the complexity of the case.

I drummed my fingers on the steering wheel, my mind a whirlpool of conflicting thoughts. The investigation had split into two distinct spheres, each adding to the tortuous web of clues and dead ends we'd been navigating.

Hilltop had initially commanded all our attention, its opulent halls concealing secrets we'd only begun to unravel. Then Norfolk swept in, somehow placing layer upon layer of confusion on the investigation, culminating in a second death that left us reeling.

As I navigated the winding country roads, I tried to

untangle the twin mysteries. I feared Whipple might set in motion the wrong plan, acting on incomplete information or misinterpreted clues.

I'd had this thought before, but now, everything was coming into sharp contrast. The stakes were higher than ever, and I knew a decision had to be made about where and when we struck. Our task today was crucial: to consolidate as much evidence as possible, ensuring that whatever plan Whipple devised would hit its mark.

The countryside rushed past as I pondered the connections between Hilltop and Norfolk. There had to be a thread linking the two, something we'd overlooked. I replayed conversations in my mind, searching for that elusive detail that might tie it all together.

'We can't afford any missteps now,' I muttered to myself, gripping the wheel tighter. The lives at stake and the complexity of the case demanded nothing short of our absolute best. As I pulled into another garage, I steeled myself for the task ahead, determined to help piece together the puzzle before it was too late.

As I trudged from the Rolls for the umpteenth time in two hours, I held out little hope that the garage owner's response would be any more positive than all the others.

Nevertheless, I pasted a smile across my face and approached a pair of legs sticking out from beneath an Austin 7, or "Baby Austin" to give the vehicle its affectionate nickname.

Keen to avoid startling the fellow and causing him injury, I exhaled two coughs to attract his attention. After several seconds, the legs began to slide toward me, carried on an ingenious trolly to allow effortless movement at a low level.

To my astonishment, the covered appendages belonged to a woman about my age, and whose shoulder-length blond hair carried streaks of oil to match her smudged cheeks.

I wished the mechanic a good afternoon and apologised for the interruption.

'No bother,' replied the woman, her broad Scottish accent carried along on a rhythmic delivery. 'How can I help?' She continued. 'If it's a repair you're after, I'm booked solid for the next week.'

I smiled and explained the reason for my visit.

'The driver's side front headlamp, you say. As a matter of fact, I had a rush job yesterday. It didn't take long. A new headlight and a bit of pushing and pulling on the bodywork. But the damage was to the passenger side, not the driver's side, sorry.'

My heart sank after an initial surge of excitement at news of the repair. So close, I thought, only to be thwarted again. Not in the mood to hang around and driven by the need to visit as many garages as I could, I offered my thanks and turned to leave. As I neared the Rolls, I heard shifting gravel behind me.

'It's just occurred to me,' the mechanic shouted as she approached at lightning speed. 'Although the damage was to the passenger side, that was the right front corner. You see, the car had a left-hand drive. He must have imported the vehicle from France or some such country.'

It felt as if a bolt of electricity had shot from head to toe. At last, a fresh clue. I asked if she could describe the driver.

'Um, well. I'd say mid-twenties. Scruffy for someone driving such a nice car, if you ask me. Oh, and spoke with a Scottish accent and paid cash.'

My mind raced. The transaction probably meant no invoice, so no address to trace the chap. I guessed correctly.

The mechanic gave me a curious look, no doubt wondering why I looked so distracted.

'Are you alright?' she asked, which made me blush with embarrassment.

'Sorry,' I replied, 'I'm a bit of a daydreamer!'

'You can say that again, but you have cute eyes!'

Her reply made me blush more, and incapable of pursuing a sensible conversation, so instead, I held out my right hand, expecting the young lady to reciprocate.

'You are a formal one, aren't you?' she said with a distinct twinkle in her eyes. 'Why don't you come back over at the weekend? The Pig and Whistle is only down the road, and they do a great pickle sandwich and brown ale. Got a dart board, too.'

Her forwardness startled me, and I felt my cheeks beginning to flush.

'You're not used to strong women, are you? Gotta be tough to do what I do, and run the business, too.'

HG came to mind, but I could hardly reveal that side of my life to a stranger. In any event, the mechanic stirred something inside me quite different from my relationship with the Dowager.

I smiled nervously as I climbed into the car and wound the side window down. To my astonishment, she leaned in and gave me a peck on the cheek.

I asked what the kiss was for, trying hard to appear manly, although I think the slight wobble in my voice gave the game away.

'Encouragement. Enough said.'

I concurred with her sentiment and started the car to escape further, embarrassing myself.

'Don't forget. Saturday at six. If you're lucky, I'll be wearing a dress, or do you prefer the overalls?'

Again, her confidence astonished me. It was all I could do to offer a warm smile and nod. As I drove away from the garage, I caught sight of the young lady, hands on hips and wearing the widest smile I'd ever seen. It then dawned that I hadn't even asked her name. Nor had I furnished her with mine.

BY THE TIME I arrived back at Thorpe Manor, HG had already completed her task and sat with Whipple on a swing-seat in the rose garden.

'Ah, there you are, Rex,' said my mentor. 'Do come and join us. There's plenty of lemonade and cake to go around.'

No second invitation was necessary as I made for the refreshments.

I sat opposite the swing-seat, helping myself to a slice of Victoria sponge and a tall glass of lemonade. The sweet aroma of roses mingled with the warm air, created a momentary distraction from the serious matters at hand.

'Well, I've uncovered something rather interesting,' I began, eager to share my findings. 'One garage I visited had recently repaired a left-hand drive car. Unfortunately, the customer paid cash, so no way of tracking him down. All I know is he's Scottish, in his twenties and dresses untidily.

I added that, 'The mechanic was quite helpful. She—'

That was when HG interrupted…

'She?' HG had a mischievous glint in her eye. 'My, my, Rex. It seems you've fallen under the spell of a grease and oil-stained Aphrodite.'

I felt heat rush to my cheeks and glanced away, busying myself with another bite of cake.

'I'm sure I don't know what you mean, HG,' I mumbled, desperate to change the subject. 'How did you fare in King's Lynn?'

HG's lips quirked into a knowing smile, but she mercifully allowed the diversion. 'Ah, yes. I had a most illuminating chat with the watchmaker. He's quite the expert in his field, you know.'

She described her visit in broad strokes, touching on the watchmaker's skill and knowledge, but curiously avoiding any specifics about Whipple's inquiry. I wondered what secrets she was keeping close to her chest.

The detective, who had been uncharacteristically quiet, suddenly straightened up. 'Right then,' he announced, his voice carrying a note of determination. 'My telephone enquiries have also borne fruit. With this new information from both of you, I believe I can finalise our plan. Give me an hour or two to work out the details.'

The inspector stood to equip himself with a clean plate and a fresh slice of Victoria sponge.

'True to form, dear Arthur,' HG said in jest.

'I shall be in my room if I'm needed,' He announced, as he left the rose garden and made his way inside the immense house.

'It really was a favourite of Queen Victoria, you know,' HG began. 'I asked her once who'd first baked it for her. By then, of course, she was an elderly lady and, although as sharp as a pin until the end, sometime trivial details evaded her.'

A vision of a young HG enjoying afternoon tea with the elderly monarch at Buckingham Palace, or Windsor Castle, fascinated me. I asked if the late queen was as sombre as many photographs of her portrayed. The Dowager threw her head back and let out a great laugh.

'Entirely the opposite. Yes, of course, she was a stickler for court etiquette and had a short temper with the many courtiers who refused to leave her be. However, the queen was a delight to be with. Her thirst for gossip was insatiable, and the more risque, the better. No, Rex, her late Majesty, when in the mood, could raise the rafters with her raucous laughter. Of course, Mr John Brown, and later, her munshi - or "teacher," Abdul Karim, brought her immense joy and comfort, much to the disdain, I'm afraid of her children and senior staff, which she found hilarious.'

I could tell HG's recollection of the late queen stirred fond memories as she gently swung back and forth on the swing, while staring around the serene garden, taking in the sweet aroma of old English roses.

Just then, Graham appeared with an ornate trolly to collect the refreshments. 'Might I take the cake and lemonade away, Your Grace?'

'That is so kind. Yes, please do, unless, Rex, you are in need of fresh supplies?'

I shook my head.

'In that case, we shall get out from under your feet and leave things to you. Please thank Mrs Palmer for baking a splendid cake. She has excelled herself this time.'

Graham gave a dutiful nod 'I shall indeed, Your Grace.'

HG eased herself from the swing and bade me link her arm as we traversed the gravel path that lay between each rose bed. 'Time to retire for an afternoon nap, I think,' she began. 'Something tells me we are in for a busy evening preparing to solve this mystery once and for all. By the way, let me tell you what Arthur insisted I ask of our watchmaker, and more importantly, what information he shared with me.'

I listened with interest to HG's discourse as we strolled together before entering the Manor and retiring.

I SETTLED into the plush armchair, sinking into its soft embrace as the warm glow of the saloon enveloped us. My colleagues lounged nearby, their faces relaxed and jovial as we bantered about cricket.

'I must say, the terminology is quite baffling,' HG mused, her eyes twinkling with amusement. '"Silly mid-on"? It sounds more like a dance move than a fielding position.'

Whipple chuckled, shaking his head. 'And don't forget "the slips". One might think we're discussing ladies' undergarments rather than a game.'

I grinned in support of their playful exchange. 'Perhaps that's why it's called a gentleman's game – only they can decipher such cryptic language,' HG added.

Whipple's laughter faded into a wistful sigh. 'I regret missing that test match, though. Had a ticket and everything.'

Before his disappointment could take root, Graham appeared with a trolley ladened with steaming dishes. The aroma of roasted meats and savoury sides filled the air, instantly lifting our spirits.

'Your Grace has opted for an informal buffet this evening,' the butler announced, unveiling the spread with a flourish.

Whipple's face lit up like a child on Christmas morning. 'Splendid! No need for starched collars and stuffy dinner jackets, then?'

HG smiled indulgently. 'Indeed, not, Arthur. I thought we could all do with a bit of comfort and relaxation this evening.'

We filled our plates generously and settled back into our seats. As we devoured the delicious fare, the conversation meandered comfortably until Whipple felt ready. A gleam of anticipation in his eyes.

'Now then,' he began, setting his plate aside. 'I believe it's time I shared my plan with you both.'

Chapter Seventeen

A GARDEN PARTY

THE GENTLE CLINKING of ice in crystal tumblers and the soft rustle of cards being shuffled filled the air in Thorpe Manor's elegant saloon. HG, Whipple, and I had settled into a game of Gin Rummy, a welcome respite from the weight of our investigation.

I watched as HG's nimble fingers deftly arranged her cards, her eyes twinkling with mischief. She laid down a perfect set, earning an appreciative nod from me.

Leaning back in my chair, I savoured the moment. The warm mid-morning sun streamed through the tall windows, casting a golden glow across the polished mahogany table. It felt surreal to be engrossed in such a trivial activity amidst the gravity of recent events.

Whipple looked utterly bewildered, occasionally mumbling under his breath.

'Is it my turn again?' he asked, for the umpteenth time.

HG smiled like a mother putting up with her irritated child. 'Yes, Arthur, and remember, you're trying to create sets or runs.'

'Sets or runs,' he echoed, nodding vigorously. 'Right, right?'

We both chuckled as Whipple hesitantly placed a single card on the table, looking rather pleased with himself.

'I'm afraid that's not quite how it works,' HG gently explained.

Whipple's shoulders slumped. 'Blast it all. I never could get the hang of these confounded games.'

HG collected the cards, reshuffling with practiced ease. 'Perhaps we should try something simpler. How about Go Fish?'

Whipple's eyes lit up momentarily, then clouded with confusion once more. 'Is that the one with the little pegs?'

'No, that's cribbage,' the Dowager corrected, trying to stifle a laugh.

Whipple huffed, pushing his chair back from the table. 'Might I be excused? I'm afraid I'm rather useless at this sort of thing.'

HG's lips curved into a kind smile. 'Of course, Arthur. We all need an hour's relaxation, and there will be time to complete our plans after Graham brings our late morning tea and biscuits at half-past eleven.'

Whipple nodded gratefully, muttering something about 'actual police work' as he lumbered out of the room.

As soon as the door closed, HG and I dissolved into fits of giggles.

'Poor Whipple,' my mentor managed between laughs. 'I've seen no one so utterly confounded by a simple card game.'

HG wiped a tear from her eye. 'Though I must admit, his determination is rather endearing.'

We played our game happily for the next forty-five

minutes. First HG would gain the upper hand, then me, and so it continued throughout the play.

Just before 11.30, Graham entered the room with his usual silent efficiency. HG's eyes twinkled as she glanced at her watch.

'Time passes so quickly, Rex. I think we deserve our snack. Shall we call it quits?'

I suppressed a smile, knowing full well that HG favoured this outcome when she found herself on the losing end of our card games. Still, I agreed without complaint, happy to be in her company.

As the butler began arranging the tea and biscuits, Whipple's heavy footsteps announced his return. He appeared in the doorway, nostrils flaring as if sniffing the air.

HG's lips curved into a mischievous grin. 'I'm sure you can smell fresh tea leaves from a mile away, Arthur.'

Whipple's chest puffed out with mock pride. 'A policeman's nose comes in handy sometimes. It's led me to many a criminal…and many a fine cup of tea.'

We shared a hearty chuckle as Graham finished laying out our refreshments, before leaving us to it.

The aroma of Earl Grey mingled with the sweet scent of freshly baked biscuits filled the room with a comforting warmth. HG poured the tea with practiced grace, while I helped myself to a generous serving of Mrs Burges's lemon shortbread.

For a few moments, we savoured our treats in companionable silence. The tension of our investigation seemed to melt away, if only briefly. I watched as Whipple waited for HG to avert her gaze, then dunked his biscuit into the tea, looking for all the world like a contented schoolboy.

As we finished the last crumbs, HG set down her cup

with a decisive clink. Her expression had shifted, the playful gleam in her eyes replaced by a more serious look.

'Well, gentlemen,' she declared, 'to work.'

Whipple cheered up at the mention of work, his posture straightening as if someone had yanked an invisible string. 'HG, have you had any further thoughts on the garden party I mentioned last evening?'

'I completed the arrangements while you two busied yourselves in the billiards room earlier this morning. Invitations have been sent to the list you gave me to catch the first post. All should receive them by late afternoon.'

I felt a twinge of concern. Surely some people might decline because of other engagements. It being short notice for such an event.

As if reading my thoughts, HG straightened up, her chin lifting. 'No person declines an invitation from me, save the royal family, and then only on good grounds.'

The conviction in her voice left no room for argument. I marvelled at her unwavering confidence, a trait that had served her well throughout our investigations.

Whipple's face lit up with excitement. He rubbed his hands together, a spark of triumph in his eyes.

'Then the trap is sprung,' he declared, his voice brimming with satisfaction.

HG leaned forward, her elbows resting on the arms of her chair. 'Arthur, would you mind going over your plan one more time? I'd like us all to be clear about the timings and the part each of us is to play.'

Whipple swapped an earnest look with each of us as he explained his strategy. He pulled out a small notebook from his jacket pocket and flipped it open.

'Right, then. The garden party will begin tomorrow afternoon at 2.00 pm sharp. HG, you'll be hosting, of course. Rex and I will mingle with the guests as if we're simply there to enjoy the social gathering.'

HG nodded. 'And our suspects?'

'They'll all be in attendance,' Whipple continued. 'Lord Billington, the Cummings family, including Horatio, and a few other key players. We'll observe their interactions, looking for any suspicious behaviour or conversations.'

I asked about the evidence we'd gathered.

Whipple's moustache twitched. 'Patience, Rex. We'll let them stew for a bit, get comfortable. Then, at precisely 2.30 pm, I'll make my move. HG, you will call for everyone's attention and offer a few words of condolence to Mr Farrier's daughter.'

'Yes. that's an excellent idea,' HG said.

Whipple took up the discourse. 'The gathering will think this entirely appropriate and applaud your comments. Just as you are telling your guests to continue enjoying the hospitality, I will interrupt you and say that new evidence has come to light, and that, if I may, I should like to tell everyone about the death of the chauffeur, to stop the nasty rumours that are going about. Of course, I do not know of any rumours, they will not know that either.

'Some may feign they know nothing of the latter event. However, HG has frequently reminded me that little escapes the attention of the upper classes when events impinge on their lives or reputation.'

HG nodded. 'And this, together with our joint prodding at pre-determined junctures, will prompt our culprit to reveal themselves.'

'Indeed,' Whipple nodded confidently. 'We'll be watching closely for any reaction. I've arranged for four constables from the local station to provide close cover.'

As if predicting the intensity with which we now

worked, Graham silently entered the room carrying a large silver tray, on which rested a crystal glass jug filled with iced lemonade and three matching tumblers. Without saying a word, the butler placed the tray on the side table, collected up our tea things and retreated from the room.

'Such a splendid fellow,' HG commented. 'Do you know his family has ensured the smooth running of the Estate since my great grandfather's day? Quite remarkable when one thinks about it.'

For my part, I could understand the loyalty Graham's family showed to the Drakeford dynasty, if HG's ancestors were as kind as she.

'Should I serve?' asked the inspector.

The shocked expression appeared to amuse Whipple.

'I can pour a glass of lemonade, you know.'

HG frowned. 'Thank you for your generous offer, Arthur, but I think one ruined Persian carpet is enough for any friendship, don't you?'

'That was not my fault HG. Rex bumped into me.'

Astounded at the inspector's accusation, I looked at my mentor for protection. Instead, she winked at me.

'If you say so, Arthur. At any rate, allow me to serve. That way, if there is an incident, however caused, the blame will be upon my shoulders.'

Whipple sniffed the air but had the grace to smile.

'So, all is in place,' the inspector intoned. 'I suggest we spend the next twenty-four hours preparing for our little surprise, tomorrow. We must be prepared, be ready for the unexpected, and above all sure of our facts if we are to deliver justice to Mr Farrier, the chauffeur, and all those affected by the tragic events of the last seven days.'

A Spiffing Murder

I AWOKE EARLY on Saturday morning with the anticipation of our plan coursing through my veins. As I stepped out onto the terrace of Thorpe Manor, the warm sun caressed my face, and a gentle breeze carried the sweet scent of roses.

The grounds were a hive of activity. Two gardeners trimmed hedges and tided borders with meticulous precision, while others arranged vibrant flower displays in striking urns. The groundskeeper, a stocky man with weathered hands, directed a team of outside staff, setting up tables and chairs on the immaculate lawn.

I took a deep breath, savouring the clean Norfolk air. The roses were in full bloom, their colours a dazzling array against the backdrop of the Tudor mansion. Crimson, pink, and yellow petals danced in unison, their fragrance intoxicating.

Near the kitchen entrance, I spotted Mrs Palmer, the cook, conferring with her staff.

Graham, HG's butler, emerged from the house, his posture impeccable as always. He surveyed the preparations with a critical eye, occasionally offering quiet instructions to the staff. His presence seemed to lend an air of calm efficiency to the proceedings.

Descending from the terrace via a set of wide stone steps, I wandered along the gravel paths, and marvelled at the contrast between the lush, informal English garden and the structured grandeur of Thorpe Manor. The intricate patterns and tall chimneys of the Tudor brickwork stood in stark contrast to the riot of colours and textures in the flowerbeds.

A group of staff emerged from a side entrance, their arms laden with crisp white tablecloths and gleaming silverware. They laughed and chatted as they worked, their excitement for the upcoming event clear in their voices.

I paused by a stunning rose bush, its deep red blooms reminding me of the gravity of our mission. Despite the beauty surrounding us, we were here to uncover a killer. The tranquillity of the morning belied the tension that would soon descend upon this idyllic scene.

As I made my way back indoors, HG, and Inspector Whipple emerged from the east wing of the noble house, and nearest the stables.

Knowing the inspector's aversion to equine pursuits, I doubted their visit had anything to do with riding. More likely, they'd sought a moment of privacy to discuss our plans for the day.

The memory of Whipple's last attempt at horsemanship flooded back to me. It had been a sight to behold, truly. The poor inspector had clung to the reins like a drowning man, his face a mask of sheer terror. The horse, a placid old mare named Buttercup, had looked equally perturbed by her rider's lack of finesse.

As they drew closer, I noticed HG's eyes twinkling with amusement. Whatever they'd discussed in the stables had clearly lightened her mood.

'Ah, Rex,' HG called out. 'Enjoying the morning air?'

I nodded and gave way for HG to enter her home first.

THE SCENT of old books and polished wood enveloped me in a warm embrace as I perused shelf after shelf of valuable titles.

HG perched elegantly on the edge of a settee, her posture a testament to her upbringing in the ways of the upper class, while Whipple leaned against the mantelpiece, deep in his own thoughts.

Arthur retrieved his fob watch, flipping open the silver cover with a deft motion. 'One-forty-five,' he declared, the metallic click echoing in the stillness. 'We'd better take up our positions in the garden. Guests will begin arriving soon.'

HG nodded, her eyes sharp and alert. 'Remember, we must give the appearance of looking calm. It's vital that we circulate and engage in polite conversation.'

Whipple's expression shifted, a hint of mischief flickering in his eyes. 'We must give nothing of our intentions away. I suggest that if anyone brings up the subject of our investigations, we say it's slow going and nothing of real importance has yet emerged. That way, we put everyone at their ease, including our quarry. Of course, Mr Farrier's daughter will be disappointed. She will have hoped to hear better news from us. If we do our job well today, that is a situation we will rectify.'

I glanced at HG, who seemed lost in thought for a moment. The weight of our task hung heavily, yet her resolve remained unbroken.

'Indeed,' HG replied. 'It's a delicate balance, isn't it? We must navigate our small talk with finesse, while keeping our eyes peeled for anything amiss among the guests.'

'Precisely,' Whipple affirmed, unsuccessfully attempting to straighten his waistcoat. 'The slightest hint of suspicion could lead to certain persons attempting to flee.'

As the clock ticked on, I felt apprehensive. The garden would soon transform into a stage where our investigation would take on an extra dimension among the gathered guests. Each smile, each word exchanged, could unveil hidden truths or deepen the enigma surrounding the case.

HG smoothed her dress, her presence commanding yet graceful. 'Let us prepare ourselves. The game is afoot.'

I nodded, a thrill coursing through my veins. With a shared understanding, we made our way to the door, ready to face the impending onslaught of guests, our minds sharp, and our wits at the ready.

Whipple pulled open the ornate front door, the intricate carving catching the sunlight, casting playful shadows on the stone steps. As we stepped onto the lawn, a sense of anticipation filled the air. Everything had been prepared to perfection.

House staff stood at their designated stations, ready to serve the incoming guests with a range of impeccably prepared fare. The sweet scent of freshly baked pastries mingled with the crisp aroma of herbs from the kitchen garden. I spotted Mrs Palmer adjusting a delicate arrangement of cucumber sandwiches on a tray, her hands moving with precision, ensuring each piece was just so. Nearby, Graham patrolled the scene like a hawk, straightening cutlery sets and ensuring net covers protected the food, his sharp eyes scanning for anything that might disrupt the day's festivities.

In the distance, the first car approached, its shiny exterior gleaming in the afternoon sun. I felt my pulse quicken, a mix of excitement and trepidation swelling within me. The arrival of guests meant the beginning of our pursuit. I glanced at HG, then Whipple. All our work had led to this moment. Now it was time to test our theories.

It occurred to me that our plan might make for a gripping theatre play; the relentless investigator chasing down dangerous killers, all wrapped around the veneer of upper-class respectability. I even thought of a title. "A Spiffing

Murder," since much of life's tragedies seemed to entertain the leisured classes (HG excepted, of course).

My mentor brought an end to my mental wanderings.

'It is time, gentlemen,' she announced, her voice firm and clear.

The words settled in my mind like a call to arms. I straightened my posture. This was our moment to blend in, to gather insights and observe behaviours that would lead to the truth. We knew who we were after; failure was not an option.

First to arrive was a sleek Rolls Royce, its polished black surface reflecting the sunlight like a mirror. The chauffeur stepped out, adjusting his cap with a flourish before opening the rear door. Lord and Lady Cummings emerged. They surveyed the scene with a pained smile, their eyes darting about as if searching for something hidden.

Next, a Renault came into the turning circle, its engine almost silent as the car came to a halt. The driver, less refined than the former, clambered out and hurriedly opened the door for a pair of middle-aged gentlemen. They exited with hearty laughter, oblivious to the undercurrents of tension that hung thick in the air. As they ambled towards the food, their joviality felt like an unwelcome distraction.

Chauffeurs, clad in their neat uniforms, emerged from their vehicles, each one methodically making their way to the front of the house, the crunching gravel marking their passage. I watched as they disgorged their charges—ladies in the latest fashion for a daytime function; gentlemen in white flannel trousers, striped jackets and straw boater—each one an actor in this elaborate play of social graces.

The chatter among the arriving guests rose and fell like a tide, punctuated by the crisp sound of fabric brushing against itself and the occasional burst of laughter. Yet, amidst the gaiety, I felt a creeping sense of unease.

As per our plan, I mingled with the guests, engaging in polite conversation. The chatter was light, a stark contrast to the seriousness of our true purpose.

Lady Ashworth regaled me with tales of her prize-winning chihuahuas. Her enthusiasm infectious, though my mind wandered to more pressing matters.

Across the lawn, I caught sight of HG. She moved with effortless grace, her refined laughter tinkling like fine crystal as she conversed with a small group of gentlemen.

Whipple looked less at ease. His attempts at small talk were stilted. His posture was rigid as he navigated the unfamiliar terrain of upper-class social niceties. I suppressed a smile as I watched him fumble with an asparagus tip as he attempted to plunge it into a delicate dip of hollandaise sauce, clearly more comfortable with his usual fare; pie and mash (by his own admission).

My eyes were drawn to the grand clock above the front entrance of the magnificent house. Its ornate hands had marked the passage of time for over three centuries, bearing silent witness to countless gatherings like this one. But never, I wagered to one quite so fraught with hidden tension.

I swallowed hard, my throat suddenly dry. Two minutes to go. The moment of truth is almost upon us.

Glancing to my left, I noticed HG also checking the time. With practiced nonchalance, she made her way towards the stone steps leading up to the Manor's entrance. Her movements were unhurried yet purposeful. She positioned herself where she could be seen by everyone, her presence commanding attention without seeming to demand it.

The time? 2.29 pm.

Chapter Eighteen

A RECKONING

WHIPPLE'S EYES darted across the gathering, taking in the scene before him. He muttered to himself, narrating the unfolding events.

The chatter amongst the guests faded to a hush as HG tapped a silver fruit knife against her champagne flute. The gentle ring cut through the air, drawing all eyes towards her. Not a soul seemed to find this action unusual; they expected the Dowager's formal welcome, as was customary at such gatherings.

HG's voice, clear and commanding, carried across the lawn. She thanked the guests for their attendance, especially given the short notice. Then, her tone softened as she dedicated the gathering to the memory of Mr Farrier, Lord Cummings' most devoted accountant.

A chorus of "hear, hear's" rippled through the crowd. I noticed a few guests nodding solemnly, while others raised their glasses in silent tribute.

HG continued, her words painting a picture of Farrier's dedication and loyalty. She spoke of his tireless work ethic and his unwavering commitment to Sir Herbert's business. As she praised his character, I saw a flicker of emotion cross Sir Herbert's face - was it guilt, or sorrow?

Then, HG's voice took on a gentler tone as she commended the brave fortitude of Farrier's daughter, Primrose. At the mention of her name, the guests turned in unison, searching for the young woman.

I followed their gaze, my eyes landing on a petite figure standing near the edge of the gathering. Primrose stood with her eyes burning into the ground, her hand clasped tightly in that of Sir Herbert's youngest son, Francis. As the attention of the crowd settled on her, she slowly raised her head. Her eyes, filled with unshed tears, met HG's gaze across the lawn. She offered a silent, demure "thank you" with an almost imperceptible nod of her head.

The moment hung in the air, heavy with unspoken emotions and hidden truths. I glanced at Whipple, noting the narrowing of his eyes as he observed the scene.

As HG finished her speech, I watched her carefully. She was about to invite everyone to enjoy the afternoon when Whipple stepped forward, interrupting her. This was the moment we'd planned for.

'Begging your pardon, Your Grace,' Whipple said, his voice carrying across the lawn with authority. 'But I'm afraid I must interject. Some additional evidence has come to light that I believe is of utmost importance in relation to the death of Mr Farrier.'

HG's eyebrows shot up, a perfect picture of surprise. If I hadn't known better, I'd have been fooled myself. 'Inspector, what on earth do you mean?' She said.

Whipple retrieved his police notebook with an exaggerated movement of his hand. 'We've uncovered some rather disturbing information regarding Mr Farrier's death. The poison was not, in fact, in the cake as we initially believed.'

A collective gasp rippled through the crowd. I saw Lady Cummings clutch at her pearls, while Sir Herbert's face paled visibly.

'Furthermore,' Whipple continued, 'We believe Mr Farrier's death is connected to the recent attack on Lord Billington, and the tragic accident involving his chauffeur.'

The crowd murmured, the sound growing like a swarm of angry bees. Whipple raised his voice. 'Your Grace, with your permission, I'd like to continue, since we may yet find an answer to several questions from among your esteemed guests.'

HG, still maintaining her pretence of shock, nodded slowly. 'By all means, Inspector. We must get to the bottom of these tragedies.'

As HG descended the stone steps, the guests instinctively formed a circle around her and Whipple. I could see the mixture of confusion and curiosity on their faces.

Inspector Whipple straightened his gait, his eyes scanning the crowd before settling on Sir Herbert Cummings. The tension in the air palpable, and I could hear the collective intake of breath as the inspector spoke.

'Ladies and gentlemen,' Whipple began, his voice steady and clear, 'I must inform you that the death of Mr Farrier was not a mere accident, but a deliberate act of murder.'

A ripple of shock ran through the assembled guests. Lady Cummings allowed a tear to flow.

Whipple continued, 'Our investigation has revealed that the intended target of this heinous act was, in fact, Sir Herbert Cummings himself.'

All eyes turned to Sir Herbert, who stood rigid, his face taut and pale.

'The poison that claimed Mr Farrier's life was not, as we initially believed, in the cake. It was, instead, administered through a most diabolical method.'

I noticed HG's surprise at hearing the news, her eyes never leaving Whipple's face.

'However, I shall leave that detail for a moment,' he continued.

A collective murmur of astonishment swept through the crowd. I saw Sir Herbert's eldest son, Horatio, shift uncomfortably.

The inspector continued his oration. 'The plan was for Sir Herbert to cut the cake, thus becoming the unwitting instrument of his own demise. However, fate intervened. Mr Farrier, in his eagerness to assist his employer, accepted his invitation.'

Sir Herbert bowed his head, avoiding eye contact with the assembly.

'And so,' Whipple concluded, his voice heavy with the weight of his words, 'Mr Farrier unknowingly sacrificed his life for Sir Herbert. A loyal employee to the very end, though in a manner none could have foreseen.'

I watched intently as Whipple's accusation hung in the air; the crowd frozen in stunned silence. The inspector's eyes narrowed as he turned to face Sir Herbert directly.

'But what if,' Whipple continued, his voice low and deliberate, 'What if Sir Herbert knew precisely what would happen when he "requested," Mr Farrier to cut the cake?'

The words had barely left Whipple's lips when a heart-wrenching cry pierced the air. I turned to see Primrose; her face contorted in anguish, and hands clasped over her mouth as if trying to hold back the pain that threatened to overwhelm her.

Sir Herbert's sons stood rooted to the spot, their faces a

mixture of shock and disbelief. Horatio's usual arrogant demeanour crumbled, replaced by a look of utter bewilderment.

Sir Herbert himself seemed to age before our eyes, his face ashen as he stammered out a response. 'What do you mean, Inspector? What reason have I to harm anyone, less still my trusted accountant?'

Whipple's gaze never wavered as he delivered his crushing blow. 'Perhaps, Sir Herbert, Mr Farrier, had uncovered some rather inconvenient truths. Our investigation suggests he may have found discrepancies in the company books stretching back years - discrepancies that benefited you financially. We know that the two of you argued the day before the man died.'

The crowd gasped, and I could see the horror dawning on the faces of Sir Herbert's family. Lady Cummings swayed slightly, steadied by her husband, who looked as though he might be sick.

Whipple placed his hands in his trouser pockets, a subtle signal that his part in this performance was over for the moment. He glanced at HG, who stepped forward with the grace of a seasoned actress taking centre stage.

'The truth of the matter is that my dear friend, Sir Herbert, is entirely innocent of any foul action,' HG declared, her voice ringing with authority. 'The Inspector brought the matter to a head to make public once and for all, Sir Herbert's innocence, so that all may know the truth and stop the vicious rumours that some have spread these last days.'

A collective sigh of relief swept through the gathering. I observed Sir Herbert's face, watching as the tension drain away, now replaced by an expression of immense gratitude.

He gave HG a nod, his eyes brimming with unspoken thanks.

HG continued, her tone now taking on a more contemplative note. 'I have always been aware of the snobbery some in our class have about "new money," as if it were tainted.'

A few guests avoided eye contact with both HG and Sir Herbert.

'Whether such people like it, modernity is upon us, and that is a good thing,' HG asserted, her gaze sweeping across the assembly. 'The world is changing, and we must change with it.'

Whipple now smoothly reclaimed centre stage, maintaining the momentum of events. His presence commanded attention: a skill I much admired in him.

'While Sir Herbert stands exonerated,' Whipple announced, his voice cutting through the murmurs of the crowd, 'The spotlight must now fall on his eldest son.'

All eyes swivelled to Horatio, who stood with his chin tilted upwards, exuding an air of arrogance.

Whipple's tone hardened as he continued. 'Throughout our inquiries, Mr Horatio Cummings has been consistently unhelpful and obstinate. His demeanour has been nothing short of disrespect for the law.'

I noticed several nods from the assembled guests. Clearly, Horatio's reputation preceded him.

'Moreover,' Whipple continued, 'The man makes no secret of his desire to assume control of his father's business empire. His ambitions have already led to tragedy - the death of a young worker at the company's Norwich factory.'

A collective gasp rippled through the crowd.

'The foreman informed Her Grace's Ward, and me, that Horatio showed little remorse and no emotion at the youth's untimely and unnecessary death. Indeed, one must wonder if that same callousness might have driven him to make an attempt on his father's life to secure immediate control of the family's affairs.'

Horatio let out a harsh laugh. 'And just how did I carry out this foul deed?' he sneered, his voice dripping with disdain.

Whipple's response was measured, his earlier words echoing in the tense silence. 'As I said before, Mr Cummings, I shall reveal all soon.'

The assembly watched Horatio with a mixture of suspicion and disbelief. His brashness was evidently familiar to all present, but now it carried a sinister undertone. The once-jovial gathering had transformed into a tableau of shock and suspense, with Horatio at its centre still maintaining his air of defiant arrogance.

At that point, Graham, HG's butler, entered the tense gathering. He carried a small silver tray before him, upon which sat a single white envelope. The crowd parted silently to allow him passage, attentive to the missive he bore.

HG reached for the envelope with practiced grace, her fingers closing around it as Graham retreated from the scene. The guests held their collective breath as she extracted a slip of paper - a telegram.

Her eyes scanned the message, her expression inscrutable. Without a word, she handed the telegram to Inspector Whipple, who examined it while twiddling his ear in concentration.

After what felt like an eternity, Whipple raised his gaze to address HG's guests. 'Forgive me, Mr Cummings,' he said, his voice carrying across the lawn. 'This telegram provides information that means the police may discount you from our investigations.'

A wave of murmurs swept through the gathering. I observed Horatio's face, watching as his arrogant demeanour reasserted itself, his chin lifting defiantly.

Whipple raised his free hand, silencing the crowd. HG seized this moment to step forward, her eyes fixed on Sir Herbert's eldest son.

'Horatio,' she began, her voice stern yet tinged with concern for the man. 'You may have escaped the police's attention this time. However, let me warn you. Unless you change your ways, forget this silliness about taking over your father's company, and above all, to never again put the pursuit of profits above the welfare of those who depend for their livelihood on your family, because you will surely find yourself before the courts on the most serious of charges. Mend your ways, young man. Do I make myself clear?'

For the first time since I'd met him, I saw Horatio's arrogance crumble. His head bowed; shoulders slumped as the weight of HG's words settled upon him. The transformation was startling - gone was the brash young man, replaced by a chastened figure showing the frightened stature of a child, and not of a man.

Whipple next turned his attention to Lord Billington. The crowd's murmurs swelled once more at the mention of his name. Billington, still sporting a bandage on his forehead, bristled visibly.

'What nonsense is this?' he exclaimed, his voice dripping with indignation.

Whipple's demeanour remained calm as he recounted his first encounter with the ill-tempered lord at Hilltop. 'You may recall, Lord Billington, how you berated your chauffeur that day. The same man who died - or should I say, was murdered? - just days ago.'

I noticed a flicker of unease cross Billington's face, quickly masked by a scowl.

Whipple continued, his voice steady and measured. 'We believe your chauffeur was on his way here to ask the Dowager for help. Yet his car - or rather, your car, Lord Billington - was rammed off the road.'

The crowd gasped. I saw HG's gaze never leaving Billington.

'Oh, yes,' Whipple added, his tone almost casual, 'We have found the car, and we know to whom it belongs. What was your employee running from, Lord Billington?'

The fellow's face reddened, his composure cracking. 'This is preposterous!' he spluttered. 'I am the victim here! Why have you failed to find my attacker, Inspector? I accuse you of malfeasance in the line of duty!'

The crowd's reaction was a mixture of shock and curiosity.

Whipple stepped back, giving way to HG. The shift was subtle, but unmistakable. HG's eyes gleamed with fierce intelligence as she took centre stage.

'It pains me to speak so directly to you, Billington, but you raised our suspicion when you insisted Scotland Yard's finest detective attend you. It amounted to a command. Yet you seemed more concerned about the theft of a vase than the death of Mr Farrier, yet only twenty-four hours separated the two events. I thought at the time what a clever ruse it was.'

Billington's face contorted with indignation. 'This is absurd! I demand—'

HG's voice cut through his objections like a knife. 'Be quiet, Billington. I haven't finished.'

I marvelled at the power in her tone. The fellow, usually so full of bluster, fell silent.

HG continued, her gaze never wavering from Billington's angered face. 'We spoke to your head gardener about the theft. He confirmed and could prove, no ladder had been taken from the estate's storeroom. If the vase was ever stolen, it must have been someone within the house. Perhaps even you, to garner sympathy and draw our attention away from your person regarding the events at Hilltop.'

As HG's words sank in, Billington raised his hands in a gesture of despair.

The crowd watched in stunned silence; the tension was palpable as we all waited to see how this dramatic scene would unfold.

'And my injury? Did I fake it by walking into a door, perhaps?'

HG shut him down immediately. 'Cease your impudence this moment. We play not a game. Two men are dead, and many lives are ruined. Have at least some humanity, man.'

HG's words struck Billington like physical blows. The fellow's composure disintegrated before our eyes, his earlier bravado evaporating under the weight of her authority. It was a remarkable transformation, one that left me both impressed and slightly unnerved by the power of HG's verbal assault.

Billington's face, once flushed with indignation, now paled. His eyes darted around, seeking some form of support or escape from the crowd that encircled us. Finding none, he opened his mouth as if to speak, but no words followed. His jaw worked silently for a moment, then snapped shut as if a wasp had entered.

I could hear the collective intake of breath from the onlookers, all waiting to see what would happen next.

Billington's shoulders slumped, the fight draining out of him like air from a punctured balloon.

Then, in a gesture that spoke volumes, Billington tilted his head back, his gaze fixed on the clear blue skies above. It was as if he sought solace in the vast expanse of the heavens, perhaps hoping to find some escape from the harsh realities that now confronted him on the ground.

The contrast was stark - the beauty of the cloudless sky against the ugly truths being laid bare here on earth. I admit to feeling a twinge of pity for the man, despite everything. To see someone so thoroughly undone, their carefully constructed facade shattered in moments, was a sobering sight indeed.

HG's nostrils flared, her face contorting in disgust as she sniffed the air. The gesture was subtle, yet unmistakable. It was as if she could smell the deceit emanating from the man before her.

Whipple stepped forward, his presence commanding attention once more.

'Lord Billington,' he began, his voice carrying a weight of authority, 'You have purposefully misled the police in this investigation. Also, we believe you've committed fraud to secure an insurance pay-out on your supposedly stolen vase.'

A collective gasp rippled through the crowd. I could feel the tension in the air, thick enough to cut with a knife. Billington remained motionless, his face an unreadable mask.

Whipple continued, his tone unwavering. 'I've spoken with the insurance company regarding your claim. They, too, have expressed serious doubts about its veracity.'

I glanced around, noting the mix of shock and curiosity on their faces. Some leaned forward, eager to catch every word, while others recoiled, as if afraid to be tainted by association.

Billington, however, remained eerily still. His lack of reaction was almost more unsettling than any protestation of innocence might have been. It was as if he had retreated into himself, leaving behind only an empty shell.

Whipple paused, his gaze sweeping over the assembled crowd before settling back on Billington. 'For now, I shall leave matters there. We shall see shortly whether you have further questions to answer.'

Again, Billington offered no response. His silence spoke volumes, filling the air with an uncomfortable tension.

Without breaking breath, Whipple looked around for the Boulton-Hicks couple. 'Ah, there you are,' he said.

For a split second, no one knew to whom he was referring, including Ada and Fredrick Boulton-Hicks themselves. I observed their momentary confusion, quickly masked by polite smiles.

Whipple continued, 'May I introduce Ada and Fredrick Boulton-Hicks to those of you who are strangers to them? In fact, they were strangers to Rex and I until Her Grace received an invitation to call upon them within hours of our arrival in Norfolk.'

I smiled to myself; certain the guests must have shared the same thought about their own presence on HG's immaculate lawn. Those standing next to the duo shuffled aside, ensuring the crowd's attention was squarely on them.

Whipple pressed on, his voice carrying across the hushed gathering. 'What was so urgent that afternoon? The event passed without incident, or information relevant to our investigations. Yet Her Grace informs me that you were keen to ask how Lord Billington was. Not Mr Farrier, I emphasise, but your neighbour.'

Ada Boulton-Hicks responded, her voice tinged with forced innocence, 'But isn't that the kind of thing to do? We were simply concerned for his Lordship, that's all.'

I watched the couple, noting the slight tremor in Ada's hands and the tightening of Fredrick's jaw. Their discomfort was palpable, a stark contrast to their earlier composure.

Whipple feigned a look of surprise, his eyebrows arching dramatically. 'Kindness, yes, that is an admirable attribute to possess. Unfortunately, it is not one that extends to the people you employ, is it?'

The Boulton-Hicks' gaze hardened, their earlier facade of politeness now absent.

Whipple pressed on. 'Many of your staff are frightened of you. They say you treat them terribly and only stay because they have nowhere else to go.'

I noticed Ada's hand twitch, as if she longed to silence Whipple. Fredrick's jaw clenched, muscles working feverishly beneath his cheeks.

'Except that two staff have left your employ in recent weeks, but you, of course, know that,' Whipple continued, his tone deceptively casual. 'Indeed, both, a footman and, now…let me see, oh yes, a chauffeur, now dead, of course, joined Lord Billington's household.'

The crowd's attention peaked, hanging on Whipple's every word.

'I put it to you both that this was no coincidence, but a fiendish plan to place them into his household.'

The guests turned to the Boulton-Hicks, their faces a mixture of shock and disgust. The couple, once held in such high esteem, now found themselves the target of harsh glares from their peers.

HG stepped forward again. 'And it is the brutal death of

your former chauffeur that we must now speak about in more detail.'

She turned to Lord Billington. 'We have had no word from the gentleman that his employee was on an errand that night. Yet the poor man's wallet contained three crisp ten-pound notes.'

Billington's face lost colour as HG's words sank in. She then pivoted back to the Boulton-Hicks, her tone accusatory.

'Did you give him the money as payment for gaining employment with Lord Billington? Perhaps to learn his secrets, even have him work in tandem with the footman who recently left your employ, to land a position at Roxby Hall? And then the chauffer finds out something that put his life in danger. In fact, that led to the poor man's death.'

The crowd's collective gasp was audible. I noted the shock on the faces of the assembly. The Boulton-Hicks stood rigid, their expressions a mask of forced composure.

Suddenly, HG's gaze dropped to the floor. The abrupt change in her demeanour sent a ripple of murmurs through the crowd.

After what felt like an eternity, HG raised her head, her eyes blazing with renewed intensity. 'Oh, something I forgot to mention. I refer to the injury that killed the poor fellow. Well, it was a broken neck. A clean severing of the spinal cord. In fact, those condemned to death by hanging suffer the same fatal injury.'

I watched as the implications of HG's words sank in, the crowd visibly recoiling from the brutal truth laid before them. The Boulton-Hicks' innocent demeanour suddenly morphed into a look of panic.

Ada Boulton-Hicks crumbled before our eyes. Her carefully maintained composure shattered, replaced by heart-wrenching sobs that shook her entire frame. She buried her face in her hands, her shoulders heaving with each gasping breath.

Her husband moved swiftly to his wife's side, pulling her into his chest in a protective embrace. The tenderness of his gesture struck me, a stark contrast to the accusations that had been flying moments before.

As Ada wept, Fredrick raised his eyes to meet HG's piercing gaze.

'Enough, Your Grace. Please, enough,' he said, his voice thick with emotion. 'In some respects, you are correct, though not on the more serious charge of killing, or having a hand in the death of our faithful chauffeur.'

He spoke of their plan, of taking advantage of their staff's devotion, but vehemently denied any involvement in the more sinister events at Hillside or the theft of the vase.

As he explained their true motives - revenge against Lord Billington for unpaid debts - I reassessed everything I thought I knew about this case. The revelation that their staff had been sent to uncover the source of Billington's wealth cast a new light on the entire situation.

Fredrick's voice grew more impassioned as he continued, 'Please accept, Your Grace, that I speak honestly.'

Then, as if from nowhere, Graham, HG's ever-efficient butler, and two footmen made their way through the crowd. Their movements were silent and purposeful, drawing curious glances from the assembled guests. As they reached the centre of the clearing, I had to remind myself of the detailed choreography that had gone into the afternoon.

One footman unfolded a small, square collapsible table with practiced ease. He adjusted the feet meticulously, ensuring it stood firm on the uneven ground. The second footman unfurled a crisp white linen cloth and draped it over the tabletop with precision. The frame disappeared entirely beneath the pristine fabric.

Graham, ever the picture of composure, placed a beautifully crafted cake atop the table. Its white icing gleamed in the sunlight, adorned with delicate blue fluting. The solid silver circular tray beneath it added an extra touch of elegance to the scene.

I observed the strange looks passing between the guests. Eyebrows raised, heads tilted in confusion, yet not a word was spoken.

Before departing, the footman who had laid the tablecloth handed HG an oblong leather-covered box. HG held up the enclosure, her movements deliberate and measured. She opened the lid, revealing an exquisite velvet interior that drew gasps from those close enough to see.

With great care, HG lifted out a shimmering silver cake slice, with an ornate, slightly bulbus handle, catching the light as she placed it gently next to the cake.

HG returned to the Boulton-Hicks. Ada remained buried against her husband's chest; her sobs were now reduced to quiet whimpers. Fredrick's face was a mask of anxiety, clearly bracing himself for another verbal assault.

To his surprise, HG's voice softened, taking on an almost compassionate tone. 'I believe your assertion that Billington owes you a considerable sum. This alone strengthens my belief that he "stole" the vase himself to defraud his insurance company. I believe you would have seen not one penny of the sum, if his claim succeeds, which I certainly doubt.'

The tension in Fredrick's shoulders eased, though wariness still lingered in his eyes.

HG continued, 'We shall leave it there, then. You have paid a hefty price for your deceit, although not as high as your erstwhile chauffeur. Guilt is the price you must pay for the rest of your lives.'

I saw Ada flinch at the mention of their former employee, the grip on her husband tightening.

'I have one request of you,' HG said, her tone firm but not unkind. 'Bring back your footman and promise me you will do all in your power to be a just employer. It isn't hard to achieve, you know.'

As HG turned away from the Boulton-Hicks, her gaze swept across the assembled guests. The air crackled with anticipation.

'You know, my friends, some things in life are simple, others forever challenge us. Take, for example, this exquisite cake slice.'

HG raised the implement, its polished surface glinting in the sunlight. I noticed several guests craning their necks for a better view.

'Yes, it has a very particular function, simple, in fact, and yet it is manufactured with artistry and with its function in mind. Except that this cake slice is different. In fact, it has but two reasons to exist. A benevolent use as a simple tool to divide a cake into portions; the second, a malevolent function with one purpose only. To kill.'

The crowd erupted into a cacophony of gasps and exclamations. I observed the shock on their faces, some recoiling in horror.

HG handed the cake slice to Whipple, who stepped forward to address the crowd. His voice carried clear over the tumult.

'When Sir Herbert invited Mr Farrier to pick up the cake slice, neither knew it was an implement of death. No one did, apart from its maker, and the person who commissioned the evil contraption. But who is that person?'

The question hung in the air. I scanned the faces of those around us, searching for any sign of guilt or recognition. Each guest eyed their neighbours with newfound suspicion.

I watched intently as Whipple continued his speech, his voice steady and unwavering.

'And that is why I remarked to Lord Billington that he might have further questions to answer.'

Billington's haughty demeanour once more came to the fore. 'Not again, Inspector?'

Whipple replied without missing a beat, 'Indeed, Lord Billington, of course what you and I know, but our guests do not, is that you collect and commission automatons, don't you? You see, I, along with my co-investigators, saw several when we visited you. Your butler made the mistake of showing us into the morning room. I put it to you that you conceived of a plan to kill Sir Herbert by means of macabre machinery confined within the handle of the cake slice you commissioned for the purpose of murder. Now, what do you have to say for yourself?'

Billington's jaw dropped, his composure cracking for the first time since the interrogation began. He tried to explain the innocence of his collection and vehemently denied commissioning any cake slice. His voice trembled as he addressed Whipple.

'And why exactly should I want to murder Sir Herbert?'

'For the same reason, you stole your own vase. You need money. In fact, your need for money is matched only by Horatio Cummings' ambition for power, and power corrupts Lord Billington. I say the two of you got together.

You agreed to arrange Sir Herbert's death in return for a handsome cash reward.'

The assembled crowd gasped at the revelation. I held my breath, watching the drama unfold.

Lord Billington's face crumpled with a mixture of consternation and desperation. His earlier composure vanished.

'This is preposterous!' Billington exclaimed, his voice rising to a shout. 'I have never commissioned such a thing, and I can prove it!'

The surrounding crowd stirred, murmuring in hushed tones.

'There are only two artisans in the entire country with the engineering skills to manufacture such intricate automata,' Billington continued. 'One is a gentleman in King's Lynn, whom I've never employed. The other is Geovanni Conti, who resides in Suffolk. Yes, I've commissioned work from Conti, but nothing of this sort!'

His eyes, wide with defiance, locked onto Whipple's. 'Go ahead, Inspector. Check my claims. I dare you!'

Whipple's face remained impassive. 'As a matter of fact, Lord Billington, I've already done so.'

The inspector paused, allowing his words to sink in.

'I'm happy to reveal the outcome of my investigations,' Whipple continued. Then, with a tilt of his head, he added, 'That is, if you truly want to know.'

Lord Billington continued to protest his innocence; his face flushed with indignation. The crowd hung on every word, their eyes darting between the accused and Inspector Whipple.

Suddenly, Whipple's voice cut through the tension like a knife. 'Do you think he is innocent, Mr Wilberforce Washington?'

A ripple of confusion swept through the assembly. Murmurs of 'Who?' and 'Wilberforce Washington?' filled the air as guests glanced at one another, searching for any sign of recognition.

My gaze swept across the crowd, finally settling on a figure standing apart at the edge of the gathering. The young man cut a striking figure, dressed as though he'd just stepped away from the Henley Royal Regatta. His white trousers were crisp and immaculate, paired with a boldly striped flannel jacket that defied the sombre mood of the occasion. Atop his head sat a jaunty straw boater, tilted at a rakish angle, just as I remembered him as a jolly chap from Hilltop when he attempted to reclaim his crashed bicycle from the hedge.

What struck me most, however, was his demeanour. While the other guests fidgeted and whispered, this young man stood perfectly still, hands casually tucked into his trouser pockets, eyes fixed on Whipple. His expression was one of mild interest, as though he were observing a cricket match stopped for rain, rather than a dramatic accusation of murder.

As the silence stretched on, Washington did not respond to Whipple's question. He simply continued to stare, a faint smile playing at the corners of his mouth, as though he held some secret knowledge that amused him greatly.

'It is rare indeed for anyone to fool me, Mr Washington, and yet you did. I applaud your acting skills at Hilltop, but then again, you have form,' HG said as she took the floor.

Washington's smile faltered, yet he maintained his composure.

'It took a few days for Inspector Whipple to track your record down, but yesterday, he succeeded. Unfortunately for you, Scotland Yard keeps excellent records.'

The crowd's whispers grew louder.

'It seems you-' HG paused, her lips curling into a sardonic smile. 'I say you, of course, Wilberforce Washington is not your real name, which is altogether less extravagant, isn't it, Bertram Appleyard?'

At the mention of his true name, Appleyard's carefully constructed lie faltered.

HG pressed on, her voice dripping with disdain. 'You are, in fact, a convicted fraudster who plays on the vulnerabilities of, how shall I put it, ladies of a certain age and class? Not for you the daily grind of work. No, you prefer being showered with money by the older women you charm.'

'Now I know where I've seen you before,' Billington shouted, his face flushed with anger. 'You came to my home months ago. I saw you in the grounds and thought nothing of it. My man mentioned you visited a second time when I rode out to horse. He said I'd invited you to view some of my automata, since you were researching the subject and had heard I had a notable collection. Of course, the expert artisan signs all my commissioned work. You must have tracked him down from there. You are a bounder, sir.'

Appleyard stood frozen for a moment, his eyes darting between Billington and Whipple. Then, as if a switch had been flipped, his demeanour changed entirely. The charming smile returned, but this time it held a hint of desperation.

'My dear Lord Billington,' he began, his voice smooth as silk, 'I'm afraid you've misunderstood the situation entirely. You see—'

Before he could continue his explanation, Inspector Whipple stepped forward, cutting him off mid-sentence.

'I think we've heard quite enough from you, Mr Appleyard,' Whipple said firmly. 'Your game is up. The only question remaining is why you attempted to kill Sir Herbert. You know, you almost got away with your monstrous plan. Had you not gone back to Hilltop, it's doubtful we'd have paid any attention to you at all, and Lord Billington would this day begin his incarceration while awaiting trial for murder. When my sergeant told me you'd been found hiding in the kitchen, I asked myself why. It finally occurred to me that you needed to retrieve the cake slice before we tested it. But the article wasn't there, was it? That's when you panicked. Then you made the connection to Lord Billington's chauffeur. He was in the kitchen when you replaced the ordinary cake slice for the Automaton.'

Appleyard's smirk grew wider. 'What fantasy is this, Inspector? I thought you were the best Scotland Yard has? You have no proof such a thing ever happened. The chauffeur can hardly corroborate your claim, can he?'

The crowd grew restless as their disdain for the fellow increased.

'Not an unreasonable assessment, young man,' interjected HG. 'Yet you forget two important issues. First, I checked with a certain gentleman in King's Lynn if there were others possessing his skills. He gave me the name and address of the only other artisan that met his own high standards, but of course you know who this other person is, because you glimpsed his signature at Lord Billington's residence.

'Second, you imagined all traces of your vile weapon vanished with the death of the poor man you caused to crash the Bentley. That's where your luck ran out. You see, the police later found the innocent-looking cake slice you'd had made, in the rear footwell of the Bentley. It seems the man you killed was, in fact, on his way to see me, perhaps to admit his part in your evil plot so the police might go easy on him for being unaware of the implement's true purpose.'

The pace of events sped up as HG exposed the fragility of Appleyard's defence. Now the inspector took a further step towards him and pointed an outstretched finger, his disgust clear for all to see.

'I had that instrument of death taken apart, piece by piece. And what do you know? A cunning mechanism came to light. At first sight, the cake slice looked identical to the innocent item in the kitchen at Hilltop. However, apply pressure to the handle and a tiny spike bites the palm of one's hand like a viper. That's why Mr Farrier cried out but collapsed before he knew what was happening to him. Then, as the cake slice fell from his hand, the spike retracted into the handle as if it had never been there.'

Whipple's voice fell from an angry shout to a controlled, calm, monotone.

'You are a murderer, Mr Appleyard. What have you to say for yourself?'

The fellow's calm facade finally broke. His face contorted with rage, eyes blazing with a fury that seemed to consume him entirely.

'You want to know why I intended to kill old man Cummings? To make him pay for what his eldest son did to me,' he spat, his voice rising to a near-scream. 'Horatio Cummings cheated me. Three years ago, I took my invention to him at their Norwich factory, and he stole the idea after telling me it wouldn't work. He stole it! I intended to destroy that family, and I almost did.'

Appleyard's fists clenched, his skin white, as he continued his tirade. 'Two years later, I found out he'd patented my invention himself and has since profited from it.'

The crowd gasped again, yet Appleyard paid them no mind, lost in his own world of anger and resentment.

'I wanted revenge on the company; to ruin it. Just imagine how much damage I might've inflicted had I killed the head of that cursed family,' he snarled. 'I knew his eldest son's blinding ambition and lack of talent would finish the company off. As for the chauffeur, well, that was just bad luck. He found out about my plan when we met in the kitchen on the day Hilltop opened.'

Appleyard's voice took on a mocking tone as he continued. 'I moaned about having no money and my bike being ruined. The chauffeur was angry about how that Billington bloke treated him. We grabbed two bottles of wine lying about when the place was empty as the commotion started upstairs. We found a quiet spot and got drunk. I told him more than I should have.'

He paused, a bitter laugh escaping his lips. 'The next day, he contacted me demanding £1,000, or he'd welch on me. I couldn't let that happen, so I followed him in my car. That night, outside this place, I thought he was going to do it, so I did him in instead.'

Appleyard's eyes darted around the crowd. 'I figured you'd never trace the car. The bump would look as if it was on the driver's side, and I knew you wouldn't expect to see a left-hand drive vehicle around here. When I took it to be repaired, I used a Scottish accent and changed my appearance, knowing you'd check all the local garages. I assumed it would confuse you.' He deflated slightly, shoulders slumping. 'I guess it didn't.'

A stunned silence fell. The only movement came from the four police officers who'd been waiting for Whipple's signal. They sprang into action with practiced efficiency, descending upon Appleyard with practised efficiency.

Within seconds, the murderer's wrists were secured behind his back, the metallic click of handcuffs echoing in the still air. Appleyard's face, which had been contorted with rage just moments before, now wore an expression of resigned defeat.

Whipple twisted the end of his moustache as the officers began to move the criminal.

'Before you take your leave of us, so to speak; A question for you. How did you get up here so quickly to carry out your dreadful plan?'

Appleyard smiled. 'You can blame that on Muddleford. When he bailed me at the front desk of the police station, I overheard him ask his sergeant if he'd "Sent off that telegram to Inspector Whipple." He obviously didn't connect me with you, or he wouldn't have raised the subject in my hearing. I knew then I had to get a move on to deal with Billington's chauffer in double-quick time, so I drove through the night. The rest, you know.

'Get him out of my sight,' Whipple instructed, his tone flat. 'I'll see to him later.' Then he added, 'Also arrest Mr Horatio Cummings for fraud. While you're at it, alert the Factory Inspectors in Norwich, and have them briefed on a breach of the Factory and Worksop Acts at the Cummings' Norwich factory. Horatio Cummings must pay for the death of his father's young employee.

Horatio's arrogance and cruel nature had grated on me since our first encounter. It seemed fitting that his theft of Appleyard's idea would lead to his downfall.

As the murderer was led away, Whipple turned to address HG's guests.

'Thank you for the part you've all played in catching a killer and exposing a second young man who turned the tables on a fraudster to become one himself. Although

Horatio Cummings may yet profit from stealing Appleyard's idea, he could have no idea what vicious events he'd set in train.' Whipple paused, his gaze sweeping across the faces before him. 'A true lesson in life, Your Grace, my lords, ladies, and gentlemen.'

Epilogue

I STOOD in the meticulously manicured garden of Thorpe Manor, basking in the warm glow of success that seemed to radiate from every pristine flower bed and neatly trimmed hedge. The last of the guests had departed not long since, their carriages and motorcars kicking up dust along the winding driveway as they exited Thorpe Manor. Now, only HG, Inspector Whipple, and I remained; left to reflect on the extraordinary events that had unfolded over the past few days. As I gazed across the sprawling grounds, a sense of pride settled on me. We'd unravelled a devilishly complex mystery.

HG's eyes sparkled with satisfaction as she summarised our triumph.

'Well, gentlemen, I believe we can chalk this up as a resounding success. A murderer caught, a fraudster exposed, and justice served.'

Her voice carried a hint of pride, and rightly so. I nodded, feeling a mixture of relief and excitement racing through my veins. The last few days had been a whirlwind, filled with twists and turns that would have left lesser minds reeling. But HG, as always, had navigated the labyrinth of clues and red herrings with remarkable precision with the adept help of Inspector Whipple.

She turned to the detective, a mischievous smile playing on her lips. 'Arthur, to show my appreciation for your exemplary work, I've arranged a little treat.' Her eyes twinkled, and I moved closer, eager to hear what she had in store for our steadfast inspector. Whipple, for his part, maintained his usual stoic demeanour. However, I detected a hint of curiosity at the slight tilt of his head.

From her silver chain purse, HG produced a ticket, which she presented to Whipple with a flourish. My curiosity piqued at the ornate design on the oblong card.

'A seat in the members' enclosure at Lord's Cricket Ground, my dear Arthur,' HG announced with obvious satisfaction. 'I've spoken with your superior, and you've been granted paid leave to enjoy the next Test Match.'

The detective's expression softened, a rare glimmer of genuine pleasure dancing in his eyes. It was clear that HG had hit upon something truly special for him. The thought of the fellow, starched collar and all, sitting amongst the crème de la crème of cricket enthusiasts at the hallowed ground was almost comical. Yet, I felt a warmth spreading through my body at HG's thoughtfulness.

Whipple's eyes widened in disbelief. 'HG, I...I don't know what to say.'

'A simple "thank you" will suffice,' HG chuckled.

As Whipple stammered his gratitude and held the small card as if it were a bar of gold, HG turned her attention to me.

'And as for you, Rex...'

I noticed a peculiar glimmer in HG's eyes. A mixture of

mischief and anticipation. A look I recognised as a harbinger of something unexpected.

'My dear boy. Your dedication and quick thinking have been invaluable in this case, and, indeed, several other investigations of late. I wanted to show my appreciation of your growing prowess.'

HG's praise was not given lightly, and I treasured each instance. As she spoke, I noticed something being positioned at my rear. Curiosity gnawed at me, but I resisted the urge to turn around.

'Do you remember that bicycle you mentioned in passing at Hilltop? The one you admired but couldn't quite afford?'

My heart skipped a beat. Surely, she couldn't mean...

'Well, Rex,' HG said, her smile widening, 'Why don't you turn around?'

I spun on my heels, and there it was, a Raleigh Road Racer – the exact model I'd dreamed of owning, its polished frame gleaming in the soft evening sun. I was speechless, overcome with emotion.

'HG, I...may I...' I stammered, gesturing towards her cheek.

She smiled warmly and nodded. 'You may.'

I leaned in and placed a grateful kiss, my eyes brimming with tears of joy.

HG clasped her hands together, looking thoroughly pleased with herself.

'Well, gentlemen,' she announced, 'I think it's time for more tea and iced fancies, don't you?'

Next in the Rex and Dowager Series

vinci-books.com/dappermurder

When a model falls mid-stride in a 1920s fashion show, the trail leads straight to Norwich's most guarded circles.

Turn the page for a free preview…

A Dapper Murder: Chapter One

NORTHWARDS TO NORWICH

I PUT on my leather driving gauntlets and slipped into the driver's seat of the Rolls Royce.

The Dowager Duchess of Drakeford (or HG as I may address Her Grace in private) and I bade farewell to the Home Counties. Our destination? The verdant landscape of Norfolk.

'I hope you've packed enough iced fancies and lemonade, Rex,' came a crisp voice from the rear seat.

A smile tugged at my lips. I assured HG I'd prepared well for our lengthy journey.

The conversation flowed with an ease between us, a testament to the time we'd spent together as she tutored me in the art and science of the amateur sleuth. HG had a remarkable talent for attracting trouble, or better yet, for trouble to seek her out.

I helped her investigate, and did other things too, while Detective Inspector Whipple made sure we followed protocol.

'It feels like only yesterday we were on our last adventure in Norfolk. Poor Mr Farrier, what a sad case that was.'

As I pondered the case, a rush of satisfaction flooded over me. Despite the misdirection and utter evil at play, HG, Whipple, and I brought the perpetrator to justice.

I nodded to show empathy for Farrier.

'Yes, dear Rex, sad indeed, and so many lives ruined.'

I navigated the Rolls through narrow lanes, past village greens where older children played cricket. The younger ones favoured tag and skipping, as their laughter carried on the light breeze. As the occasional motor car and horse-drawn cart passed by, the drivers tipped their caps in friendly greeting.

We soon found ourselves in the bustling market town of Bury St Edmunds. The streets brimmed with activity. Shopkeepers arranged their wares and townsfolk tested produce for freshness between finger and thumb. The smell of fresh bread wafted from a nearby bakery, mingling with the earthy scent of livestock from the market square.

HG tapped on the glass partition. 'Rex, do slow down a tad. I think we are about to pass by the Angel Hotel.'

I wondered why the building piqued HG's interest.

'Ah, now that's an interesting question,' she began. 'In 1861, one of our literary giants stayed at the hotel. You see, Charles Dickens read *the Pickwick Papers* and *A Personal History of David Copperfield* to a paying audience at the Athenaeum - Look yonder. There it stands. My parents took me to a performance, although, of course, I was quite young. To my inexperienced eyes, he was an old gentleman with unkempt hair, when in truth he'd have been but forty-nine years old and in his prime.'

A car hooter sounded from the vehicle behind for the second time as I listened to HG. I looked into the rearview mirror to see a fellow gesticulating for me to get a move on. Reluctantly, I engage first gear, rotated my outreached right arm, and pulled away from the kerb. The angry chap stalled his motor car, which I thought just deserts for his inconsiderate actions.

As we left Bury St Edmunds, the terrain opened before us. A patchwork of green fields and golden wheat hugged the gentle undulations of the Suffolk landscape. The occasional windmill stood sentinel on the horizon, its sails turning in the mid-morning sun.

Crossing into Norfolk, the terrain flattened and gave way to the vast expanse of the Fens. Field drainage ditches lined the narrow roads, their still waters reflecting the sky above. In the distance, I made out the silhouette of a wind pump, a reminder of the constant battle against the encroaching waters.

I nodded, feeling a sense of anticipation building within me. After several months of feverish investigation, I looked forward to a peaceful interlude. Also, the hope I might meet up with a certain lady mechanic I'd met during our previous visit to Norfolk.

As I brought the vehicle to a halt, I stole a glance at HG. She had her eyes fixed on Thorpe Manor; Pride, certainly – this was her Norfolk seat after all, but also something else. A hint of nostalgia, perhaps, or touch of melancholy.

I mentioned to HG that the Manor looked splendid.

She didn't respond at first, lost in her own thoughts. I took the moment to survey the grounds. The lawns were immaculate, stretching out in a sea of green towards the distant tree line. The rose beds near the house offered a riot of colour, the result of the head gardener's continuing meticulous care.

'Indeed, Rex,' said HG as she finally spoke, her voice soft. 'Thorpe Manor always knows how to put on a show,

I stepped out of the car, happy at the chance to stretch my legs after the long drive. The air felt crisp and clean, carrying the scent of cut grass and fragrant flowers.

HG's gaze lingered on the upper windows of the Manor; so much so that I enquired if all was well.

She emerged from the car with her usual grace, patting my arm as she did so. 'Just remembering, dear boy. This old house holds so many memories for me. The emotional connection I have with the place catches me out each time I visit.'

I understood her reflective mood. For all her strength and sharp wit, even HG wasn't immune to the occasional interlude of sentimentality. We stood for a moment as we took in the Manor's splendour.

As we climbed the wide stone steps to the front door, Graham, the butler, negated my need to clasp an ornate wrought-iron bell pull by opening both leaves of the sumptuously carved Jacobean doors.

'Your Grace,' he said in a respectful tone as he offered a bow from the neck. 'So nice to see you again. All is ready for you, and the cook has just taken a fresh batch of your favourite fruit scones from the range. Refreshments in the saloon, perhaps?'

HG thanked the butler for his foresight. 'You've outdone yourself once again, Graham. And do convey our gratitude to cook for those delightful scones. Nothing quite compares to her baking.'

Graham's chest swelled with pride at the compliment. 'Thank you, Your Grace. I shall pass on your kind words to Mrs Palmer.'

HG then inquired about the programme for the

upcoming fashion show in Norwich. Graham assured her he'd received the document and would bring it to the saloon with our refreshments.

HG removed her gloves and placed them on an ornate side table. Her fingers traced the intricate carving of Tudor roses that adorned its surface.

'The craftmanship never fails to take my breath away,' she murmured. 'Eight generations of my family have touched this very spot.'

My gaze followed hers to the gallery above, where gilt-framed portraits of her ancestors gazed down upon us. Their stern faces seemed to soften in the warm light that filled the space.

A grand staircase curved upward; its oak balustrade polished to a mirror finish by countless hands over the centuries. The wood gleamed like honey where the sun caught it.

The gentle tick of a long-case clock marked time in the corner, its brass face catching glints of the afternoon sun. Through leaded windows, glimpses of the rose garden beyond added splashes of colour to the mellow tones of ancient wood and stone.

HG gestured toward the saloon doors, her silver hair catching the light as she moved forward. 'Rex, dear boy, would you care to accompany me to the fashion show tomorrow?

I hesitated, my mind racing to find a polite way to decline. The thought of spending hours observing the latest women's fashions held little appeal. I'd much rather delve into the Manor's archives to discover its rich history, which I found fascinating.

HG's eyes twinkled with mischief as she observed my reticence. 'I assume your reluctance has nothing to do with a certain lady mechanic you encountered during our last visit?'

I felt heat rising to my cheeks. Trust HG to catch me off guard. I didn't even know her name. However, her clever hands and forward ways, had indeed crossed my mind more than once since I discovered we were to return to Thorpe Manor.

My face flushed as I stammered out a denial. 'No, no, HG, it's not that at all. I simply thought I might use the time to delve into the Manor's archives. There's so much history here, and I—'

'Oh?' HG's eyebrow arched, her amusement clear. 'And this sudden passion for local history has nothing to do with avoiding my company on the morro?'

I protested, my words tumbling out faster than I could control them. 'I'm merely interested in the architectural evolution of Thorpe Manor. The Tudor foundations, the Jacobean additions—it's all quite fascinating, really.'

'There's time enough for that,' she said, waving away my feeble excuses. 'So, we've reached an agreement. You shall accompany me to Norwich, where I shall teach you all there is to know about haute couture.'

I resigned myself to the inevitable, mumbling under my breath about the cruelty of fate.

HG eyed me with a hint of a smile. 'Did you say something?'

The game was up. 'Not at all, HG. I was just thinking to myself how much I'm looking forward to our refreshments.'

'Yes, I thought that was it.' She gave me a motherly smile, seeing right through my poor attempt at deflection.

I returned a tortured smile of defeat as we reached the rich oak doors of the saloon. The scent of warm scones distracted me from thoughts of tomorrow's ordeal by catwalk. I marvelled at the seamless blend of Tudor and Jacobean styles. The room exuded an air of timeless elegance, a testament to the centuries of history that had unfolded within the walls.

The grand fireplace, with its high mantle shelf adorned with intricate carvings, caught my eye. Above it, the great coat of arms of Elizabeth I commanded attention, a reminder of the Manor's illustrious past.

In contrast to the Tudor and Jacobean elements, the furniture was Edwardian. Luxurious chairs and sofas, upholstered in rich fabrics that matched the heavy curtain swags, and invited one to sink into their plush embrace.

On a side table, our refreshments awaited. A silver teapot sat atop a methylated spirit burner, keeping the brew at the perfect temperature. The aroma of the scones mingled with the subtle scent of Earl Grey, making my mouth water.

HG and I helped ourselves to the spread, balancing delicate plates laden with scones, clotted cream, and strawberry preserves. We took our seats in the comfortable armchairs, the weight of the journey melting away as we sank into the cushions.

On a side table next to HG's chair, a programme for Saturday's fashion show rested. The sight of it brought a small sigh to my lips, a reminder of the ordeal that awaited me.

I savoured the rich, buttery taste of the scone, letting the flavour linger on my tongue. HG and I sat in companionable silence, the only sound, the rhythmic beat of a grandfather clock. It struck me how comfortable we'd become in each other's presence over the years. The silence between us was never awkward, but a shared moment of contentment.

HG placed her cup on the small table with a soft clink.

She picked up the programme for the fashion show, her eyes skimming over the pages. After a few moments, she set it back down and turned her gaze to me.

'Rex, what do you remember about the children's home where you stayed before you became my Ward?'

The question caught me off guard, stirring memories I hadn't revisited in quite some time. I paused, gathering my thoughts before responding.

The home had been a haven, a stark contrast to the uncertainty that had plagued my young life after father's sudden absence. The staff had been kind and attentive. I recalled Miss Thompson, the matron, with her stern demeanour that concealed a heart of gold. The other children, a disparate group, found solace in each other. I had much to be grateful to HG for in easing my past struggles.

I mourned father during those days, his absence an ache that never subsided. Yet, looking back, I recognised how fortunate I'd been. Things could have turned out much worse. The streets of London were unforgiving, especially to a young boy alone in the world. The home had provided not just shelter, but a chance at a future.

As I shared these recollections with HG, I noticed a softening in her eyes, a hint of something I couldn't quite name. Compassion, or perhaps pride in her role in reshaping my destiny, may have motivated her.

Changing the subject back to the charity event, I asked HG if she was expecting a good turnout for the show.

She raised an eyebrow, her lips curving into a knowing smile. 'The upper class never miss an opportunity to be seen by their peers in the latest fashions, dear Rex'

The fashion show wasn't just about clothes; rather, a social battleground.

HG continued, her voice taking on a sardonic tone.

'Above all, they'll fight like cats to get a seat in the front row. Heaven forbid they're not prominently displayed in the press photographs. And seated with the fashion designers too.'

I chuckled at the image of Norfolk's elite clawing their way to the front seats and commented that it sounded more like a spectator sport than a fashion show.'

'Oh, it is,' HG agreed, her eyes twinkling with amusement. Forget the clothes; the real entertainment is the social climbing and jockeying for position among the wealthy.

I shook my head, marvelling at the intricacies of high society. 'And here I thought it was just about admiring new frocks and suits.'

'That, Rex, is precisely why you need to accompany me,' HG said, patting my hand. 'There's so much more to these events than meets the eye. It's a masterclass in social dynamics, political manoeuvring, and the art of subtle one-upmanship.'

I couldn't argue with that logic. At least now I understood why HG was so insistent on my presence. The issue transcended mere fashion.

Just then, Graham, the butler, entered the saloon and approached HG. I couldn't hear what he said, but watched HG's expression change. The mirth from our earlier conversation vanished. Now a firm look ruled.

'Thank you, Graham,' HG said, her voice calm but laced with an undercurrent of irritation. 'Did Lord Wentworth provide any further details?'

Graham shook his head. 'I'm afraid not, Your Grace. He seemed quite flustered and said he'd explain more when he sees you tomorrow.'

HG dismissed Graham with a nod, then turned to me. 'Well, Rex, it seems arrangements for my little fashion show have taken an unexpected turn. It appears young Milly Davenport is up to her old tricks. This time she has her claws into the Fairbridge twins.

I sought clarification if she was the young lady who regularly appeared in *The Tatler* magazine.

'The very same,' HG confirmed, her lips pursing. 'A young lady with more influence than sense, I'm afraid. She's developed quite a talent for stirring up trouble, then making sure it makes the headlines.'

I felt a twinge of curiosity and asked what the Fairbridge twins might have done to upset the young lady.

HG's eyes narrowed. 'The answer to that will invariably be, nothing. However, that won't stop the minx if its sensational publicity she's after. The twins are lovely girls, kind-hearted souls and we must nip Miss Davenport's intended attack in the bud.'

My confused expression encouraged HG to elaborate.

'Perhaps it results from her father's lineage,' replied HG. 'He, too, could be cruel for no apparent reason. In the end, he suffered what he'd done unto others.'

I asked what HG meant.

'Croaked it on the toboggan run in St Moritz several winters ago. He'd heard a rumour that the track was about to be closed because of a sudden rise in the air temperature, so he thought he'd beat the odds with one last run. Turned out the rumour was false; he pushed too hard and ended up shooting over the ice wall of the track and losing his head... literally.'

I recoiled in shock.

'Of course, he wasn't the first member of his family to end up in a coffin a little on the short side. Two of his forbears ended up kneeling at the block on Tower Hill. It goes to show that you can't go around spreading malicious rumours and walk away unscathed—at least not in the Middle Ages, when it came to kings and queens you couldn't.'

HG observed my reaction, breaking out into a broad smile as I considered if she'd just told me a tall tale, or spoke the truth.

'I can see you don't believe me. However, I can assure you it to be true. Speaking of which, we can't dismiss Milly Davenport entirely. If she follows through on her threat, it could cast a pall over the entire event. And more importantly, it could harm the twins' reputation.'

I watched as HG rose from her chair, pacing the room with measured steps. Her mind processed the problem, considering angles and possibilities I could only guess at.

'We'll need to speak with the twins,' she said at last, turning back to me. 'And perhaps have a word with Miss Davenport as well. There's more to this than meets the eye, I'm certain of it.'

A Dapper Murder: Chapter Two

SHOWTIME

AS I EXPECTED, HG had a full day of activities planned before the fashion show began at 7.30 pm. Not even the prospect of Mrs Palmer's delicious full English breakfast tempted my mentor to delay our departure. Instead, we made do with hot toast, Fortnum's strawberry jam and English breakfast tea served in our respective rooms.

I wolfed down my breakfast, the rich strawberry jam a fleeting pleasure on my tongue as I rushed through my morning ablutions. The clock ticked, each second bringing me closer to the Dowager's appointed departure time. I fumbled with my tie, cursing under my breath as I struggled to achieve the perfect Windsor knot.

With not a moment to spare, I dashed down to the garage, my polished shoes clicking against the gravel drive. The Rolls Royce purred to life, its engine a reassuring rumble in the crisp early October air. I manoeuvred the magnificent vehicle around to the front entrance.

As I stepped out to open the rear passenger door, I

caught sight of my reflection in the gleaming paintwork. A quick adjustment of my cap, and I was ready.

The grand doors of Thorpe Manor swung open at nine o'clock on the dot. HG emerged, a vision of elegance in a tailored travelling suit, her hat adorned with a jaunty feather that danced in the breeze.

I stood to attention, hand on the open door. 'Good morning, HG.'

The Dowager descended the steps with a regal poise, her eyes twinkling with anticipation for the day ahead. As she reached the car, she met me with a warm smile.

'To work, dear Rex, to work,' she declared, settling into the plush leather seat.

I closed the door with a soft click. What adventures awaited I wondered.

We had just set off when HG opened the glass partition that separated us. 'We go first to Lord Wentworth to discover what else he might tell us about Milly Davenport's little game. Head for Aylsham, Rex, I shall give further instruction anon.'

I guided the Rolls Royce through the winding Norfolk lanes; the countryside unfurling before us like a living tapestry. The morning mist hung low over the landscape, a mysterious blanket that cloaked fields and hedgerows in ethereal white. As our journey continued, the strengthening sun worked its magic, burning away the fog and revealing the lush green world beneath.

The transformation was mesmerising. Wisps of mist rose from the earth, twisting and dissipating into nothingness as the sun's rays pierced through. As if the land was exhaling, breathing new life into the day.

Ancient parish churches dotted the landscape, their weathered stone spires reaching skyward. These buildings stood as silent witnesses to East Anglia's prosperous wool trade era. Each church seemed to anchor its village to history, a tangible link between past and present.

As we drove, I marvelled at the timeless beauty of Norfolk. The patchwork of fields bordered by centuries-old hedgerows, the occasional windmill silhouetted against the brightening sky - a scene that had changed little in hundreds of years.

The Dowager remained silent in the rear, no doubt lost in her own thoughts about the day ahead. I focused on the road, enjoying the peaceful drive and the gradual awakening of the surrounding countryside.

Before long, I caught sight of a signpost ahead. As we drew closer, I made out the words: 'Aylsham - 3 miles'. Our destination was near.

'Rex, keep a sharp eye out for a left turn,' HG's voice floated from the back seat. 'There should be a sign for Cockleford Manor.'

I nodded, tightening my grip on the steering wheel. 'Yes, HG. I'll—'

The words died in my throat as the very turn she'd mentioned materialised before us. I stomped on the brake; the tyres screeching in protest as I wrenched the wheel to the left. The Rolls lurched, and I winced at the thought of HG being jostled about in the back.

As we swung onto the narrow lane, I caught sight of a farm-hand in a horse-drawn wagon. The poor chap had been about to turn right and now found himself face to face with our imposing vehicle. His weather-beaten face twisted into a scowl, and I braced myself for a barrage of colourful language.

Guilt gnawed at me. I glanced in the rear-view mirror, expecting to see HG's disapproving frown. To my astonishment, she grinned, her gloved hand raised in a cheerful wave to the farmhand.

Curiosity piqued; I looked back at the wagon. The farm-hand's scowl had vanished, replaced by an expression of surprise. As I watched, he lifted his ragged cap from his head and gave a curt, respectful nod in our direction.

I blinked,stunned by this exchange. It seemed that even here, in the depths of rural Norfolk, HG's influence held sway.

'Do watch out for the roe deer,' HG intoned as we made progress down the narrow lane. 'They are frightfully common in these parts and jump out of the hedges without a care for what might hurt them.'

I admit to being more concerned about the damage the beasts might inflict on the Rolls. I chose not to express this view to my mentor, who held all wildlife dear to her ample heart.

As we rounded the last bend, Cockleford Manor came into view. I couldn't help but raise an eyebrow at the sight. After the grandeur of Thorpe Manor, this place seemed almost quaint in comparison. The timber-framed structure, while charming, was a far cry from the sprawling estate we'd left behind.

I voiced my surprise to HG, remarking on the modest size of Lord Wentworth's abode.

'Ah, Rex,' she replied, a hint of amusement in her voice. 'This is an early medieval timber-framed house, built for a Gentleman Farmer who likely owned no more than a couple of hundred acres. Lord Wentworth acquired the house and grounds in the 1890s, at the pinnacle of his distinguished naval career.'

I stopped the Rolls before the historic building, its age clear in the worn wood and glass.

Once alighted from the car, I made my way around to assist HG. As she emerged, her eyes swept over the Manor with keen interest, no doubt piecing together its history from the architectural details.

We approached the oak front door, and I noticed an ornate brass door knocker fashioned in the shape of a wolf's head. Its eyes seemed to follow me as I reached out and grasped the cool metal. The sound of the knock echoed through the house, announcing our arrival to Lord Wentworth.

I watched in surprise as the door swung open, revealing not a butler or maid, but Lord Wentworth himself. His jovial face beamed at us, eyes twinkling with warmth. I felt a pang of shame, realising I'd judged the man's worth based on who answered his door. How foolish of me! A person's character isn't determined by the number of staff they employ; I chided myself.

'HG, my dear!' Lord Wentworth exclaimed, his voice rich with genuine pleasure. He stepped forward, planting a respectful peck on the Dowager's cheek.

I blinked, taken aback by the casual use of my mentor's initials. That level of familiarity was unusual outside our immediate circle.

Lord Wentworth turned his attention to me, his grin widening. 'And you must be Rex!' he boomed, letting out a hearty belly laugh that seemed to shake the timbers of the house. 'HG tells me about you every time we meet, and often in her correspondence. I daresay I know you as well as she does!'

I felt my cheeks flush, both flattered and embarrassed by the notion that I featured so much in HG's conversations and letters. The stark reminder highlighted my limited knowledge of my mentor's life outside our investigations.

'It's a pleasure to meet you, Lord Wentworth,' I managed, offering a polite bow from the neck.

His lordship ushered us into his home with a sweeping gesture. 'Come in, come in! Let's not stand on ceremony.'

I followed HG and our host through a narrow hallway, its walls adorned with faded portraits and nautical memorabilia. The floorboards creaked beneath our feet, each step a whisper of the house's long history.

We entered what I presumed to be the morning room, a cosy space that seemed to embody the very essence of a bachelor's existence. Mismatched furniture, chosen for comfort rather than style, filled the room. A well-worn leather armchair stood sentinel by the fireplace, its arms bearing the scars of countless evenings spent in quiet contemplation.

Books and newspapers were strewn across every available surface, creating a sort of organised chaos that spoke of a mind constantly at work. A half-empty teacup teetered on a stack of leather-bound volumes, a ring of tannin staining the saucer beneath.

As I took in the scene, a peculiar scent tickled my nostrils. It was earthy and slightly musty, not unpleasant, but certainly noticeable. I couldn't quite place it until a giant form lumbered into the room.

An English Mastiff, its jowls drooping and glistening with saliva, padded across the worn carpet. The beast's presence filled the room, dwarfing the furniture around it. It paused by my side, regarding me with doleful eyes, before continuing its leisurely journey to the fireplace.

With a heavy sigh, the dog lowered itself onto the hearth rug, sprawling out before the crackling flames. Lord Wentworth chuckled at the sight.

'That's Henry,' he explained, gesturing towards the

canine behemoth. 'He's supposed to keep his master safe. As you can see, he much prefers his own company and a roaring fire. The ungrateful hound only ever pays attention to me when it's time for food.'

Henry cocked his head, giving his master a "So?" look." The dog's expression was so human-like, I had to stifle a laugh.

Lord Wentworth gestured towards a pair of armchairs and a worn leather settee. 'Please, make yourselves comfortable.'

Each piece of furniture served as an impromptu storage space. I lifted a stack of nautical charts from one armchair, while HG moved a collection of newspapers from the settee. Our host made space on the chair by moving some books and a part-built model ship.

'I don't stand on ceremony here, young fellow, so let's dispense with formal titles, eh? Just call me Alfred,' he said, settling into his newly cleared seat.

The invitation caught me off guard, though I maintained what I hoped was a neutral expression. Such informality from a peer of the realm was unprecedented in my experience.

'What am I thinking of? I forgot the tea,' Alfred announced, rising from his chair. 'Just a tick. I'll arrange that now.'

I expected him to leave the room, wondering if he had any household staff at all. Instead, he made his way to the fireplace, having to step over Henry, who remained sprawled across the hearthrug.

Confused, I watched Alfred remove a brass stopper from a wall-mounted trumpet instead of pressing a service button.

'Ahoy there,' he bellowed into the device. 'Tea for three in the library.'

I exchanged an amused glance with HG as Alfred cupped his right ear in the brass cone he'd just shouted down to hear the response.

'Well, that's that sorted out. Now, I presume you both want to hear what young Milly has been up to?'

'She is certainly proving to be a nuisance on what is already a very busy day, so let's have it. Why is she picking on the twins?'

Alfred settled back into his chair, scratching behind Henry's ears as the massive dog had somehow dragged himself closer without any of us noticing.

'I was at Sir Charles Mountford's place - the Lord Lieutenant, you know - just two evenings past. Small gathering, nothing too formal. That Davenport girl was there, commanding attention as she does. Quite the show she put on.'

HG's eyebrows lifted a fraction. 'Do go on.'

'Well, the interesting bit came later. I'd stepped out to use the facilities when I overhead two maids chattering in the hallway. Normally I wouldn't pay attention to such things, but something caught my ear. One of them mentioned overhearing Miss Davenport in quite a state.'

'What exactly did they say?' HG asked, leaning forward.

'The maid claimed she heard the girl ranting about not receiving an invitation to some event, saying she'd show up regardless and create a scene. Something about the Fairbridge twins spreading tales about her.'

HG's eyes narrowed. 'Most peculiar. I know for certain she received an invitation to the fashion show.'

'That's not all,' Alfred continued, pausing as a knock at the door announced tea. An elderly maid entered with a laden tray, setting it down without ceremony before departing just as swiftly.

'I had a word with Charles afterwards,' he resumed, pouring tea into mismatched cups. 'He seemed troubled by the entire business. Said it felt orchestrated somehow - as if she meant to cause a distraction for some other purpose entirely. Though he couldn't fathom what that might be.'

'Did the Lord Lieutenant elaborate further?' HG asked, accepting a cup with a tiny chip on the rim.

'No, that was all he'd say on the matter. Though he appeared rather concerned about things.'

A shrill ring pierced our conversation. An ancient telephone mounted on the wall behind Alfred's desk demanded attention with its insistent jangling.

Alfred heaved himself up from his chair, navigating around Henry, who had sprawled across even more of the floor space. 'Pardon me,' he said, reaching for the earpiece. 'Cockleford Manor, Wentworth speaking.'

His expression shifted. 'Ah yes, one moment.' He extended the earpiece towards HG. 'It's for you, my dear. Your man Graham.'

HG rose with her usual grace and took the receiver. 'Yes, Graham?'

I watched as she listened; her face betraying nothing beyond mild interest. 'I see... Of course... Yes, I understand... I see... Very well, Graham.'

She replaced the receiver with deliberate care. 'It appears I'm needed in Norwich. The venue manager for tonight's fashion show is rather distressed about some sort of disagreement that's brewing.'

'Trouble?' I asked, already expecting our imminent departure.

'The tone, though lacking specifics, suggested urgency.'

HG smoothed her skirts. 'Alfred, I do apologise, but we must cut our visit short.'

'Not at all, not at all.' Alfred waved away her apology. 'Duty calls, what? Though I must say, this business with young Miss Davenport becomes more intriguing by the minute.'

I helped HG gather her things while Henry watched us, showing no inclination to move despite our flurry of activity.

THE ROLLS-ROYCE PURRED along the country lanes as I pressed the accelerator. The Norfolk countryside sped by. In no time, we were in Norwich's medieval city centre.

The transition caught me off-guard - one moment in the open countryside, the next a warren of crooked streets barely wide enough for our motor. Ancient buildings leaned together, their upper floors seeming to whisper across the streets below.

I chuntered about the narrow, twisting medieval streets as I swerved to avoid a cart pulled by a disinterested nag.

We emerged into a wider space, and I caught sight of a street sign that made me pause.

'Tombland? A macabre name for what appears to be the heart of the city. Something to do with the cathedral, perhaps?'

HG's laugh held genuine amusement. 'Not at all, Rex. The name comes from the Old English for "open ground" or "open place". This was Norwich's market square in Anglo-Saxon times. That is until the Normans invaded and decided they needed the space for something grander.'

She gestured ahead through the windscreen. 'See, the castle still stands, though not in its original form.'

I followed her pointing finger to where the massive square keep dominated the skyline, its pale stone walls a testament to Norman might.

'They moved the market to build that?'

'Indeed. The Normans didn't ask permission when they wanted something. The market's current location was their choice - and 900 years later, it's still there.'

In under a minute, I drove the Rolls Royce to the Assembly Hall's old carriage turnaround. A magnificent Georgian building with three wings surrounding a gravel courtyard and central lawn. A single majestic oak rose from its centre, casting its shadow across all three wings of the splendid establishment.

I stepped out and circled the Rolls, noting a fellow with polished black shoes kicking up clouds of gravel dust as he sprinted towards us. His morning suit coat flapped behind him like a distressed bird's wings.

The poor fellow's face blazed red as a summer strawberry, and perspiration dampened the edges of his waxed moustache. His hands wrung together in a constant motion that spoke of acute anxiety.

HG extended her hand with practiced grace as she emerged from the car. The manager seized it as though grasping a lifeline, pumping it up and down with such vigour I feared he might wrench Her Grace's arm clean off.

'Your Grace, such an honour, such a pleasure.' He fumbled in his trouser pocket, producing a handkerchief that had seen better days, and mopped his gleaming forehead.

HG's voice carried that blend of authority and kindness

she reserved for those in obvious distress. 'Do compose yourself, Mr...?'

'Pendlebury, Your Grace. Edward Pendlebury.' More dabbing at his forehead. The handkerchief looked utterly defeated by now.

'Mr Pendlebury, there's no need for such agitation. I'm certain everything is proceeding exactly as planned.'

His eyes widened to saucers. 'This way, Your Grace. Please, this way.' The words tumbled out in a breathless rush before he spun on his heel and dashed towards the building's entrance.

HG shot me a raised eyebrow before setting off after him, her heels clicking against the gravel. I lengthened my stride to keep pace, wondering what could have reduced a grown man to such a state of nervous excitement.

I followed HG and the flustered Mr Pendlebury into the main hall, where chaos reigned. The beautiful Georgian room had become a place of conflict and competing egos.

Two lighting technicians, high on ladders, directed the lighting above the runway. One shouted, 'It goes there!' While the other responded, 'Not unless you want them girls looking like ghosts!'

In the corner, a cluster of young women in various states of dress dabbed at mascara-streaked faces with delicate handkerchiefs. The show director, a severe-looking woman in a charcoal suit, sat slumped at a small table, her face buried in her hands.

Near the entrance, two men - one in shirtsleeves, the other in a rumpled jacket - stood nose to nose, fists clenched. Their angry mutterings carried promises of imminent violence.

HG surveyed this scene of pandemonium, her spine straightening like a steel rod. With deliberate steps, she strode to the centre of the hall, her silver-tipped walking stick striking the polished oak floor three times. The sharp crack echoed through the space.

'Enough. Stop this nonsense at once, do you hear?'

The effect was immediate. Silence fell like a heavy curtain. The quarrelling men stepped apart. The sobbing models froze mid-sniffle. Even the lighting technicians ceased their bickering to stare down at her commanding presence.

'Who,' HG's voice cut through the newly minted quiet, 'is in charge of this catastrophe?'

For a long moment, no one moved. Then, from behind a black curtain that shrouded the runway's wooden scaffolding, a slight figure emerged. He wore horn-rimmed glasses and a suit that looked as if he'd slept in it. His thin shoulders hunched forward as if bearing an invisible weight.

HG's eyes narrowed as she peered at the diminutive man. 'What, prey, causes this childish behaviour?'

The small man tried to speak, but no words followed. In the end, he gave up trying and shrugged his shoulders.

'I see,' said HG in an irritated tone. Dismissing the man, who appeared keen to vanish back behind the curtain, my mentor once more survey the scene.

'The show begins in six hours and it will begin on time. Do you all hear me?'

No one dared answer back. Instead, heads bobbled up and down.

'Then to work everyone; Models, please retreat to your dressing stations. You two up there. I want those lights fixed in the next ten minutes. You two by the door. If you don't behave yourselves, I'll biff you both about the head and have no doubt about it-do you understand?'

The two men gave HG a look of disobedient school

boys about to be caned by the headmaster. Their submission was complete.

Finally, HG approached the woman, who still held her head in her hands.

'And what's to do here?' she whispered. 'Tell me how I may help?'

From the distraught woman's demeanour, it seemed HG's enquiry was the first kind word she'd received all day.

Eventually the woman, who, once she'd shown her face, emerged much younger than her office attire, had me believe. In fact, she wore a kind countenance that I knew from experience, HG would warm to.

The lady appeared recovered at the end of the low-toned exchange.

'That's better,' began HG. 'Now, take yourself off somewhere quiet and have a nice cup of tea. I'm sure the wonderful Mr Pendlebury will arrange things, isn't that so?'

Pendlebury puffed out his chest, now returned to rude health. 'Of course I shall, Your Grace. If you will, young lady, please follow me and I'll find us a place of refuge among all this…'

Pendlebury didn't finish his sentence. Instead, he seemed to give a slight shiver at proceedings, before leading the young woman out of the vast hall.

AT 7.30 PM, the fashion show began as the lights dimmed, to be replaced by two spotlights illuminating the show runway. A large contingent of the "Norfolk Set" was in attendance. HG had been correct to say few high society would dare miss the gathering. Their fear of missing out on the latest gossip, or the opportunity to seek influence from those above them in the rankings, won out.

I could see that HG had her wits about her, keeping an eye out for Milly Davenport, or indeed anything else that might impact on her ability to raise funds for her charity.

'Do you see here, Rex? I do wish I'd had a chance to nab her before the show started to stop her nonsense once and for all. Alas, we shall now just have to see what occurs. With luck, she's decided to abandon her silliness.'

Before I could answer, music signalled the beginning of the show. Soon, a procession of models paraded up and down the narrow runway. The crowd applauded each new appearance, though I must admit that to me, the frocks all looked the same.

Then came a sound that confused all present. A loud, crisp, bang. The crowd looked around, as did HG and I, to see if a piece of scenery had fallen, or some other object had hit the wooden floor with force. There followed a momentary silence, broken by a blood-curdling scream from backstage.

A loud commotion filled the hall as people struggled to see what had happened.

HG acted without a second's hesitation. 'Follow me, Rex. I think we both recognise that sound.'

As the house lights brightened, I followed HG at pace as we made our way down the side of the enormous room to the stage steps. Moving deeper into the bowels of the inner workings of the stage area, we found the models changing and preparation area. Fifteen feet to the right, we progressed into a small room without windows or doors, other than the one we'd just entered through. There we found a small gaggle of young women stood over a prone body.

'Her name is…I mean, was, Lucy Daws, said a blond-haired model still crouching down, cradling the victim's head in her lap.

HG stood to one side, observing all before her. 'Did anyone see what happened?'

The crouching girl cried. 'I was just speaking to her in the dressing room. Then she left. I heard a bang and came out to see what was going on. I came in here, and…'

The girl couldn't finish the sentence. Instead, she buried her head against the dead girl's shoulder.

HG gestured for me to join her a few feet away from the commotion.

'Get Pendlebury to ring the police. Tell him to keep things quiet.'

As I made to make off, HG caught hold of my arm. 'Whoever did this is may still be on the premises. Look, there's no way out of this room apart from that one door. We must do nothing that may provoke the murderer to kill again.

Grab your copy…
vinci-books.com/dappermurder

About the Author

Keith's fascinating novels skillfully combine the heart of a retired assistant principal with the imagination of a gifted author, taking readers on a captivating journey through Norfolk's scenic landscapes and rich history.

Acknowledgments

A special thank you to Peter R, without whom *A Spiffing Murder* would not have made it to publication.

www.ingramcontent.com/pod-product-compliance
Ingram Content Group UK Ltd.
Pitfield, Milton Keynes, MK11 3LW, UK
UKHW042134080226
467833UK00002B/18